STO

Sammi's rea ... been spontaneous, ar ... nove. "If this is Unsel ... she thought and co

But if she di ... it now she might never, as Gate energy, particularly the temporary kind that emerged in the humans' world, didn't always stick around long. She would locate it, and deal with it later, if indeed there was a something to deal "with." If something had come through that she could not handle alone, well . . . she had better not encounter it, that was all.

Right away she noticed the electricity in the area was out. Streets and neighborhoods slept in darkness. Ahead near an intersection was a cluster of black and white cars with blue and red flashing light bars. An accident? No, they were not on the street, they were in a parking lot, shining their spots on something tall and dark. She pulled up and stopped. If the cops noticed her they didn't seem to care; they appeared to be too stunned by what they were observing.

Sammi got out, and stood a few feet from the idling Caprice. Thin fog boiled from the pavement, and the asphalt's black warmth seeped up through her sneakers. In her room she had heard the wound tear, but here it was, festering before her. Huge stone monoliths from nowhere, standing in a mall parking lot.

"This isn't from Underhill," she said to the warm, wet night. Whatever magics were responsible for bringing this massive stone circle to this land were likely well beyond any the Unseleighe might summon. "This is Stonehenge," she thought, "brought from England, via Gate or some other construction."

"Time to speak with the King," she thought. "I'll likely need Avalon's help after all."

ALSO IN THIS SERIES

Born to Run
by Mercedes Lackey & Larry Dixon

Wheels of Fire
by Mercedes Lackey & Mark Shepherd

When the Bough Breaks
by Mercedes Lackey & Holly Lisle

Chrome Circle
by Mercedes Lackey & Larry Dixon

Elvendude
by Mark Shepherd

Spiritride
by Mark Shepherd

Bedlam Boyz
by Ellen Guon

Bedlam's Bard
by Mercedes Lackey and Ellen Guon

MARK SHEPHERD

LAZERWARZ

BAEN

LAZERWARZ

This is a work of fiction. All the characters and events portrayed in this book are fictional, and any resemblance to real people or incidents is purely coincidental.

A Baen Books Original

Baen Publishing Enterprises
P.O. Box 1403
Riverdale, NY 10471

ISBN: 0-671-57806-5

Cover art by C.W. Kelly

First printing, May 1999

Distributed by Simon & Schuster
1230 Avenue of the Americas
New York, NY 10020

Printed in the United States of America

Prologue

Only five seconds into the game, and Joystik had reached his favorite position, a large barred window on the second level. From here he covered the arena's main alley, a vulnerable zigzag of partitions where the inexperienced usually wandered through. The position gave his vest targets good cover, while allowing him to watch the activity below. Sniping was always good here.

From this position he also covered the ramps leading to this level, and for a time he could enjoy a monopoly on the blue-yellow-red targets moving aimlessly below. As usual the prey didn't seem to notice the game had started, and from his window Joystik quickly picked off four players, favoring the ten-point chest and back targets over the easier five-point ones on the shoulders. The packs now temporarily down, he pulled back, counted to five, and resumed his position. As expected, they hadn't moved; in fact, they didn't even seem to notice they had been tagged.

I know I was never that stupid, Joystik thought, tagging the same four again. He had cupped his hand over the small metal speaker on top of the weapon to protect his position, a legit move as long as he didn't cover his lighted targets. The loud sci-fi sounds these guns made could betray one's location as surely as the flashing lights. He repeated the process, methodically taking their packs down and adding to his score three more times before one of them bothered to look up.

"There he is! Up there," the kid shouted, shooting in his general direction. The beams danced harmlessly on the walls and ceiling behind him. The four were moving towards him, and didn't seem to be firing at each other. They were obviously teaming up, an infraction in a solo game where everyone was against everyone, or was supposed to be. He could notify a judge and turn them in, but that took too long, and every second counted. And unless the judge caught them red-handed he probably wouldn't take them out of the game. Instead he kept one eye on the ramps while scanning the arena for more targets.

On the opposite side of the arena was the other upper level, slightly lower than his own. A lively exchange was taking place over there, orchestrated by Irishman, another member and this month's top player. Joystik sent one of his ten rapid fire rounds into the middle of the melee, heard the unmistakable groan of a pack or two going down. Directly below, another target walked into view, but he left that one alone. If he gave away his position to that player he would be an easy target through the metal grate he stood on, and this was too good a place to forfeit just yet. The other level was returning fire now, but just moving an inch or two to the left completely concealed him. Soon they tired of shooting at nothing and returned to their more immediate threat, Irishman.

Joystik glanced at the tiny computer screen on the back of his gun, where his rank in the game appeared. He was number one, but with Irishman in the game it was probably close. Better start looking for more points.

Irishman is still blasting away over there . . .

The points came looking for him. The four clueless ones from down below had found the ramp and were tromping loudly up it, announcing their presence before he saw them. A few paces away was another window, giving him a clear shot of their back targets.

"He's tagged me again! There's the bastard up there!" one yelled, sounding rather indignant at being tagged in a game of laser tag. While their packs were down they continued up the ramp, but Joystik was inwardly chanting the five second mantra, and resumed his previous position when their packs came back up . . . and took them all down, again. He was ranked number one, with 780 points. Not bad.

But the game was quickly becoming a matter of principle, not points. These four morons were teaming up against him, disregarding the rules and the code of ethics which Joystik embraced and honored. They even had the build of football players, a particular subspecies of high school critter that Joystik found repulsive. Maintaining a 4.0 didn't endear one to one's classmates, and when one blew the test curve in chemistry one could become downright unpopular, especially when the star quarterback ended up flunking the class, resulting in an automatic suspension from the team . . . a week before the Big Game. Life is not good for overachievers, and the fallout can reach into the next school year. Meanwhile, it was summer vacation, and in the arena Joystik could forget reality and be exceptional at something other than academics.

No physical contact was allowed in the game, but when he finally saw the four players he wondered briefly if they would disregard this rule and beat the crap out of him anyway. They certainly weren't pleased. One of them was the star quarterback. It didn't look like they'd recognized him. Yet.

In the upper level was a smaller maze, and Joystik could traverse every inch of it with his eyes closed. Another player came up the ramp, then another, distracting the original four, giving Joystik time to disappear in a hidden hallway along the back.

But he didn't leave the upper level, just waited a few seconds, then reappeared. The four had taken *his* sniper position, and were firing at targets below. With his speaker covered, he took out their back targets, and ducked back quietly. The plan worked; they thought they were getting tagged from below, not behind. They were too stupid to look at their screens, which showed *which* targets got tagged. All the better for Joystik, who continued the ruse for another few cycles, relishing their anguished moans of defeat.

This easy scoring might have continued for the remainder of the game, but one of them realized the fire was coming from behind, not below. In seconds they had him surrounded, and were firing mercilessly at him.

When Joystik had first started playing, being surrounded unfairly like this had enraged him to no end, sometimes to the brink of tears. It was completely unfair and prevented any kind of retribution . . . until he discovered the secret of dodging, a crude form of tai chi learned on the fly in situations like these. Being small and underweight gave him the advantage. He twisted and wriggled away from the crisscrossing beams until he got his pack back, and started returning fire. In their confusion he stepped away from the trap, and proceeded to thump them, one by one. Thumping was a particularly useful form of revenge which rendered the opponent defenseless, and required intensive recitation of the five-second mantra, times four. As he backed away he re-tagged each one of them a half second before their guns came up. One could effectively thump a group like this only when their pack cycles were spaced enough apart . . . and they were. It was precisely the tactic they had tried using against him, only now it was one against four.

Just when he thought they were going to give up on the game and come after him with fists, lights came on in the arena. On the back of the guns flashed the message, "Game Over."

Hoo rah. Let's hear it for the team.

He ducked out at the other end of the upper level, and chose a long circuitous route towards the exit. The other players would stumble about for several minutes looking for the exit anyway, and this gave him a chance to refresh his mental map of parts of the maze he usually didn't use. Under the upper level, south side, Joystik found himself in a tight maze of narrow hallways and no wall openings, a strategically unimportant part of the arena, but good for some one-on-one with another experienced member.

Leading off to the right, however, was a tunnel he'd never seen before. It went directly into what he had thought was the solid south wall of the arena. Puzzling. *A service hall of some kind?*

He went into it.

Long and dark, the tunnel narrowed, with tubular black lights illuminating it. *Probably not a service hall, but a part of the maze, maybe a new wing not opened yet?* It probably wouldn't get him to the exit, but he had a few minutes to explore. Besides, he didn't look forward to confronting the football players in full daylight. His treatment would be bad enough when he returned to school the following semester.

The tunnel curved into pitch blackness. With a penlight he kept handy for special lights-out games, he shone it ahead of him, revealing only more tunnel.

This didn't feel right, Joystik decided, and turned to go back. Just then, his vest winked back to life, as if another game was starting. Was the computer malfunctioning? If so he was looking forward to a free game.

On the gun's screen flashed the message, "You have been selected."

For what? This was the kind of message you saw during special team games and role-playing stuff they did on members' nights. Intrigued, he waited for the screen to tell him more.

A thick mist began to fill the tunnel, similar to the water based fog they filled the arena with, but that had a metallic, unpleasant smell to it. *Time to get out. Something's going wrong here,* he thought, now afraid the stuff might poison him. But his feet wouldn't move, or his body . . . The floor rushed up to catch him as he fell over.

He figured intoxication must feel like this, but having never done alcohol or drugs, he had nothing to measure the experience by. Whatever it was had immobilized him, and a scream rose from his throat.

Someone grabbed his arm, then the other, and two someones, dark and unidentifiable in the fog, were carrying him deeper into the tunnel, away from the exit he now wished he had gone straight to, football players be damned.

Chapter One

The graveyard shift at the mostly vacant shopping mall was the least eventful gig the security company had to offer. And it was why Rick had asked for it; he had been a professional student for years, and he needed a way to earn money without actually working. Most nights were eight-hour stretches of peace and quiet, with no distractions, or interruptions besides his hourly rounds; a perfect environment for study.

According to the weather reports he'd heard in the car, however, tonight promised to be different. Two storm fronts were about to collide over Tulsa, and perhaps kick out a few twisters. At the 11 P.M. shift change he scoped out the basement, then checked the batteries in his Maglite, an aluminum club that happened to cast light. So long as the basement didn't flood, he figured he would make it through the night intact.

At midnight his rounds led him to ten different clocks around the darkened mall, where he checked in by inserting his key. The key left the letter *T* on a tape, which his boss would read later to verify his attention to the job. Only a few lights were on, just enough so he could see where he was going, but not enough that he could really *see*. Lightning flashing through skylights briefly lit the darkened recesses, showing him things in the corners and doorways he had never seen before, and couldn't quite make out. A quick sweep with the Maglite's beam didn't help much. *Creepy*. Moving on, he laughed at his jumpiness. This was a first for this place, which until tonight had all the animation of a morgue.

The place is actually giving me the heebie-jeebies, he thought, mildly annoyed. He had a test the next day, and if he didn't get in a good night's study his grade would be doomed. By the time he had finished his rounds the storm was raging full steam, shaking the skylights and rumbling through the mall with a deep, bassy boom. His station was at the information booth at the main entrance. Most nights this gave him a good view of a crumbling parking lot; tonight it was a parking lot drenched with rain.

He turned on the fluorescent lamp under the counter and reached for a heavy tome, *Early Oklahoma Law*. He was looking forward to learning what mandated a hanging in this territory a hundred years ago, which he found disturbingly more interesting than torts and misdemeanors.

When he had gotten to the part about stealing horses, a blast of lightning ripped through the sky, followed immediately by a shroud of darkness. The fluorescent lamp went out, as did all the scant lighting in the mall. The emergency lights did not come on, which didn't surprise him. *Hell, they probably weren't even connected,* he thought, standing up.

Wind howled against the quadruple pairs of glass doors, shaking the half inch-thick plate glass as if it was Saran Wrap. The Maglite cast a single white finger on the floor as he stepped from behind the information booth. He regretted not having his weather radio, which he'd left in the car.

He considered wading through the soaking rain to retrieve it. If he had to go to the basement, it had better be for a good reason. Surely, a tornado warning in his vicinity would justify being late for a round, or missing it altogether. He had never had cause to test his boss's tolerance for lateness or absence from his post, and he didn't really want to now. Maglite in one hand, building and car keys in the other, he went to the glass entrance.

At the inner wall of doors, where a thin pool of water was seeping in, he peered into the storm, mildly alarmed at the swaying light poles. If one snapped and fell on his Subaru, it would destroy it, a monumental disaster in any college student's world. Sloshing through the foyer, he put his hand on the outer doors, and hesitated.

The storm had stopped, totally. No rain, no lightning, no thunder. Nada. To a nonnative, Rick mused, this might mean the end of a storm. Yet to a native of Oklahoma like himself such an abrupt cessation in hostilities meant a tornado might be about to land on your head.

To hell with it, he thought, *I'm going to the basement.*

As he turned to retreat, a deep blast of lightning struck somewhere out there, nearby. The blast thundered through his diaphragm and shook him down to his toes.

Still, the rain hadn't resumed. He suppressed an urge to run to the mall's comforting depths, and turned around. Gradually, his eyes readjusted, then widened as he perceived something tall and menacing, a narrow object, or a group of objects, in the parking lot. Something that hadn't been there before.

My eyes are playing tricks on me, he figured. It was the only explanation.

Tall, immobile, the large objects were blocking the view across the street to a newer mall, where a few parking lot lamps struggled to stay on. The silhouette reminded him of broken teeth, with random spaces between.

Then fear gripped him.

My car.

All possibility of a tornado forgotten, he went outside to inspect this new phenomenon.

Not only had the rain vanished, the pavement was starting to dry. Thunder rolled in the distance, sounding like it was coming from the next county. His light passed over the objects, but they were too far away to see well. The sight of the towering structures was eerie enough to encourage him to turn back, but the threat to his car kept him moving. *This is stupid. Nothing happened to the car,* he reasoned, but reason didn't seem to have a place in his world right now.

His foot met soft, grassy ground where he had expected pavement. Then a knoll that took a bit of effort to walk over. His flashlight passed over grass, with bare patches of light soil.

Did a bolt of lightning blast a crater here? No, that was stupid. *Did the grass spontaneously grow?*

Over an extensive stretch of grass he walked, the flashlight confirming what his feet felt: soft, but dry, ground. He reached down, patted the grass, a blanket of velvet unlike the native prairie grass of Oklahoma, or even of the ubiquitous Bermuda.

He stopped before a large stone arch, easily three times his height. Other arches, and single, standing blocks of stone, joined it in a circle. *I know what this is. Where have I seen this before?* he thought. Beyond the first few megaliths, the light's beam diminished. More shadows.

The car . . .

Back towards the building he found his car. At least he found *half* of it. His spirits sank as he studied the remains of his Justy, parked where he had remembered parking it. The front half of it lay precisely at the grass's edge, neatly severed behind the driver's seat. Bare cross sections of steel body glinted back, shiny and polished under his flashlight. He touched it; still warm.

Still warm from what?

An enormous circle of turf had landed on the parking lot, complete with stones, taking out half his car in the process. Also, a light pole was missing, from about where the stones stood. He suspected it was wherever the hindquarters of his car had ended up.

Wherever the hell that is. He reached down and touched the distinct division between turf and pavement. Perfectly level. He dug his fingers between the grass and asphalt, found the pavement cross section smooth, as if cut by a laser. Just like the steel body of his car.

Now I know where I've seen this, Rick realized, staring at the megaliths. His high school band had traveled to Europe one summer, and one of the stops was the Salisbury Plain in England. He recalled the balmy afternoon he had stood at the famous archeological site. Then, it was perplexing to his seventeen-year-old mind how a civilization from the stone age could move the slabs of rock from a quarry twenty miles away.

If that was perplexing, he thought. *This is downright un-fucking-real. What the hell is Stonehenge doing in a parking lot in Tulsa, Oklahoma?*

Sammi McDaris breathed a sigh of relief as the Boeing 727 rolled to a stop at Tulsa International's gate 22. Through her tiny window the thunderstorm continued to rage, buffeting the plane with stiff gusts.

Now we're down. Thank the gods! she thought as she pulled her carry-on out of the overhead compartment. Passengers had stood the moment the unfasten seat belt light came on, clearly grateful the flight was over. She was too tired to fight the rush for the door, and instead let it carry her along at its own speed. She didn't much care for using human technology to travel, but when concealing her origins from her new employer the FBI, she didn't have many options.

It would not have done to simply gate here, in part because the Bureau had already mailed the tickets, but mostly because they were sending her new partner to pick her up. From what she could tell over the phone Special Agent Owen was a crusty, twenty-year veteran nearing retirement. In their brief phone conversation he had said point-blank that he didn't like working with women, and had made it clear who would be in charge of the investigation. She smirked, imagining his expression if he saw her true form, or even an enhanced one, with fangs, or long, sharp claws to complement her pointed ears. It was a tempting notion, but one she dismissed. Preserving her cover was critical, for without it she wouldn't be able to do her work among humans. And strolling out of a circle of light would not have convinced many of the sleep-deprived travelers, or her new partner, that she was of this world.

Once in the main concourse she looked around for Owen, found only one other human in a suit, and he was young and kind of cute. Late twenties, with short dark hair, possibly with some Native American blood . . . no, definitely Native, with high cheekbones and dark, smooth skin. He had a boyish face and a build that was clearly athletic even under the suit. Certainly not Owen. But he was walking toward her, and when their eyes met he definitely recognized her. Concealed beneath his coat she sensed the lump of cold iron that could only have been a handgun.

"Samantha McDaris?" he asked, face brightening. He was holding up his badge. "I'm Special Agent Hawk." He extended his hand. "Welcome to the Tulsa field office."

"Thank you," she replied, shaking his hand, giving it a firm pump to let him know she meant business. "What happened to Special Agent Owen?"

Hawk's face darkened, and he looked down as he walked beside her. "Owen had a heart attack last night."

"Oh dear," she said as they started down the concourse, keeping up with his quick stride. "Is he . . . ?"

She didn't want to ask if he had dropped dead, and considered a more diplomatic way of posing the question. Hawk saved her the trouble.

"He's going to make it, but he's still in the hospital. It also looks like he will be taking an early retirement."

"I see," she said. In a way, she was relieved. Working with Owen hadn't sounded very promising. But it also meant they were less one agent; to work this case they would need all the warm bodies they could get.

Hawk didn't seem to want to talk further in the airport. He waved at the security guard at the metal detectors, and led her to the baggage conveyor, where luggage was already parading past. "The rain has stopped," he noted. It was dark and just past nine P.M., but the flight was booked solid. People streamed by, some giving them furtive looks, apparently aware of their G-man aura. She claimed her bag, a single large Samsonite. The handle snapped up and she rolled it and the overhead bag behind them as they started for the parking lot.

His car was, of course, a Crown Victoria, unmarked except for the federal plates. Once they loaded the suitcases in the trunk, Hawk continued, "I've been reading the files you sent on the Lazer Abductions. The more I read, the more interested I got. I want a chance to work on it." He started the car and guided it through the parking lot.

"Good," she said, and ventured, "Meaning no disrespect, of course, I don't think Owen was all that enthusiastic about it."

"He wasn't," Hawk replied. He paid the parking attendant and drove towards an on ramp, and once on the expressway he continued, "In fact, he rather disliked the notion of diverting FBI resources to missing children. I disagreed and still do, but never said as much to him directly."

This is looking promising after all, Sammi thought, her estimation of the Tulsa field office rising a notch. As they drove south on I-169, the rain started up again, and lightning streaked the sky. "If you want my opinion, I don't think the FBI has done nearly enough about the missing children problem. Sure, the National Center for Missing and Exploited Children sends us information regularly, but it seems the Bureau is reacting to the problem instead of leading the way." He clicked the wipers up to a faster speed. "I mean, when so much of it goes across state lines. And kidnapping is our game, or it's supposed to be. Even after the shakeup after Hoover's death, it doesn't appear that we're doing what we're supposed to."

He's new, she thought, *New, and brash, and independent. I think I can get to like this guy. No, I know I can. In fact, I already do.*

"How long have you been with the Bureau?" Sammi asked.

He cast a sly smile towards her. "You can tell I'm new. That's okay, I am. It's been about a year now. Owen took me under his wing, so to speak, when I came here, but right away I knew he was old school. You know, statistics, public image, go after the big cases but fill out the schedule with lots of minor, easy ones to make the numbers come out right. And I'll tell you right now, I don't agree with that."

"I see that you don't," she said, mildly amused, but mostly impressed. "And I like that. I've been on for almost two years. Before that, I was a homicide detective in Dallas."

Hawk perked up at the mention of Dallas. "You were? I'm from Dallas." Without being too obvious, he glanced over at her, apparently studying her more closely. "I thought you looked familiar. You were working that crack cocaine case. The one that killed all those kids in the rich neighborhood. I remember that."

"You have a good memory," Sammi noted. She also wondered how much he knew, too. . . . That was when many things came to the surface, or nearly so, including her elven identity.

"I went to school there," Hawk said. "I remember hearing about it. Your name was mentioned in a newspaper story, along with your picture."

Hawk has an eye for details, she observed. *Wonder if he has an eye for magic. Or glamories.* She briefly checked her own magical shields, making certain her human seeming was still in place. It was.

"Anyway, regarding the Lazer abductions. I counted one hundred fifty entries in the NCIC. That can't be all of them."

Reminded of a glaring problem with the law enforcement system, Sammi sighed. The National Crime Information Center was useful only when it was used. Convincing local law enforcement to enter cases was sometimes difficult, particularly when dealing with what appeared, at first, to be runaways. Then what turned out to *not* be a runaway became a "domestic dispute," something local, something *they* should handle, if anyone did. The net result was that only a portion of the actual Lazer Abduction cases made it into the computer, making it even more difficult to make important connections between them. It wasn't until she had practically stumbled across the phenomenon in Baltimore, on her first assignment, that she discovered the most important connection of all: Elven magics, tied directly to Underhill. The only magical device that would leave such a strong sign was a Gate, and she held no doubts that one had existed right there in the Baltimore arena in the not so distant past.

"No, I'm sure there are more," Sammi said. "But how many more, I can't say."

Hawk seemed confused. "How can kids disappear in a game arcade?"

"Well, Lazerwarz is not really an arcade," Sammi explained. She was patient, she knew he had never seen one; the Tulsa arena wasn't due to open until next week. What irked her were the agents who had seen one and still didn't understand what it was all about. "It's a laser tag game. The arena is very large and dark, with a labyrinth of mazes. The object is to hide in the maze and 'tag' the others with a low intensity laser. The one with the most points wins."

"So it's like the infrared rigs the army uses to train in," Hawk said.

"That's it," she said, glad that she wouldn't have to explain it in increasingly simpler terms. "That's also why it's gone over so well. Kids are getting tired of Nintendo and arcade stuff."

"The files mentioned you thought the arenas themselves were involved in the disappearances."

She felt him pull back on the speed as traffic slowed in front of them. "I *suspect*," Sammi replied, being careful. "There are too many coincidences. But I don't have any evidence. That's why I'm here in Tulsa, before this new one opens. I can study it from the very beginning."

Out of the corner of her eye she saw him grinning, just a little. She asked, "Sounds like something you'd enjoy?"

"Yeah, I think *so*," Hawk replied enthusiastically.

"Good. Because as soon as it opens, we're going to be playing it quite a bit. Are you in good shape?"

Hawk cast her a puzzled look. "I like to think so. Why?"

"Because if you're not, you will be."

The puzzled look turned to confusion.

Do I have to spell it out? She thought, then replied,

"Have you ever been chased around by a horde of crazed teenagers with ray guns?"

Dobie started at the window's sudden, fierce rattle, and sat up awkwardly on the bed, blinking the dream away. Deep thunder rolled off the house, shaking the aging timbers down to the ground. Lightning strobed against pale, paisley wallpaper, reminding him of an old black and white movie. He was alone here, as he had been since his mother passed on the previous summer. The two story house was no mansion, but it felt big and empty without her. She had died here, but had left no ghost behind; sometimes he thought he heard the wheeze of the oxygen machine, but this was a vague, probably imagined sound. He often saw her in his dreams, but he never awakened afraid from those.

This dream had been a repeating, special dream, and he didn't feel so alone now; he'd just left a world populated by people who were bigger than life and were far more interesting than the ones he saw every day at the burger stand.

One of the deep dreams, with color and words and strange names, in a foreign tongue. Was the language real, something that once existed? Dobie scratched his head. It had to have been real, at least at one time. He lacked the imagination to make it up. Everyone knew that.

He went to his particle board-and-formica desk and turned on a lamp, a bedside fixture with stallions on a torn cardboard shade. Beneath the glaring light he held out his hands, palms up. It was a ritual he'd performed as long as he could remember, a calming, stilling exercise that never failed to put his mind and body at ease. He spread all of his fingers, seven on each hand, until the tips formed a half-circle. His hands shook. Then, after deep breaths, they relaxed. *The circle has something to do with it,* he thought, as his heart thumped a little less loudly in his chest.

But don't get too damned calm . . . I have to get down what I just dreamed! On the desk was a ragged spiral notebook, a remnant from his junior year at high school, that was his dream journal. *I have to start now. Before it goes away.*

With a Bic pen, he started writing:

Fear, he wrote, *is far more intense during sleep. You are completely helpless, and a tiny part of your brain knows that when you're under . . .*

He paused, feeling vulnerable, and considered striking out what he had written. Then left it as is. *No one will read this anyway.*

The Bic scratched away. *I saw the straw tents tonight, but what I thought were teepees are actually houses, some pretty big. Rocks made up the walls in places, and in others it looked sort of like a basket, with stuff woven in between timbers. It seemed like each family had their own hut. I was part of the big family, where the chief was, but I didn't live in his house. The chief was my uncle or something.*

Also, some of the strange sounding words. Here are some of them: Ma ha, hoo lin, iffy, anoooin, tarn, danann . . . and Ayver.

He stared at that last one, knowing it meant something, a rather important something. The word brought erotic images to mind. The ache in his loins drove home how important this word was.

A word . . . or a name? he thought. Moving on, before the dream was completely gone, he wrote down what he could, in the language he possessed.

The people are like Indians, but they are white. Very white. With long hair, beards, and they are big. I am big, too, but I'm still a child? I guess I was. Their shields are metal, not buffalo hide or wood (well, some of them were, with long pointy things like bullhorns running lengthwise) but they don't have many bows and arrows, mostly spears. And the metal is strange, kind of yellowish but light, so it can't be gold. They don't even have toilets. They must be poor. The metal makes a strange sound when things hit it . . . like spears and clubs and stuff. Then—

It stopped there. All he could remember was now on the paper, the rest dissolving in his brain like sugar in hot coffee.

His eyes tracked back to the one word. *Ayver. Is it a word, or a name?*

Dobie was staring at the page as lightning ripped through the sky. Then the lamp went out.

"Aw shit," he said to the darkness. He was used to losing power during a storm. Dobie's neighborhood was a confusing landscape of old frame houses, machine shops, small factories, and an abundance of DO NOT BLOCK DRIVEWAY signs. Lining the main artery of Charles Page Boulevard were beer bars, cheap motels, and large angry dogs of no particular breed barking through flimsy, sheet metal fences. Whatever primeval network of wires brought electricity to this forgotten area north of downtown was probably so old it couldn't stand up to a stiff breeze, and on most occasions it didn't.

In the silence he listened to the echoes of his dream.

Is something outside? Thunder pounded the sky again, this time a long, piercing rip, the kind that makes you hold your breath until the inevitable sledge-hammer pounding, announcing lightning contact with some unlucky point on the ground.

Drums, chanting, drums, more chanting . . . It was coming up the stairs.

Then it was gone.

The lights came back on as he stood, and he found himself so light-headed dizzy he thought he was going to be sick. Then the nausea passed.

What the hell was that? he thought as he reset the

flashing clock for 4 A.M., the time on his watch, and set the alarm for 8:45. At 9:00 he had to be at work at the Mega Burger just down the street.

I'm imagining shit again.

Dobie crawled back into bed, wondering what it all meant. Certainly, if the strange dreams had something to do with a past life, a possibility he hadn't discounted, his previous occupation must have been more interesting than his present one of flipping burgers at minimum wage.

He stared at the ceiling, remembering the sound, and considered going downstairs with his shotgun to check things out.

I'm imagining shit again.

Or maybe I'm not.

Hawk dropped Sammi off at the Professional Suites, an extended-stay establishment the Bureau was generous enough to pre-pay a week. Sammi also received an extra bonus, Owen's white Caprice, which was parked in front of her room. "He told me to check it out to you until he was back on his feet. This is his cell phone, too," Hawk commented as he handed her the keys and the small Nokia. "I'll see you at eight sharp tomorrow morning."

"I'll be there," she said as she clipped the cell phone to her carry-on. "And thanks. I'm glad I'm working with you."

Hawk flashed her that boyish grin as he pulled away. Sammi thought whimsically as she hauled her suitcase into the suite. *He must have filled in the unspoken words: "Working with you, instead of Owen."*

Once she was inside, the storm let loose a new torrent of rain, which hammered the ceiling with a ferocity that surprised her. "Welcome to Oklahoma," she said to herself. The state had a reputation for violent weather, and tonight it was living up to it.

She turned on the lights, and was impressed with

what she saw. This was no mere hotel room. It was truly an efficiency apartment, with a kitchenette, and a little work area separate from the "bedroom." She had a week to find an apartment here, provided it looked like she would be here for a while. There was always the chance the Lazerwarz angle could be a dead end; there might not be any connection at all, and the Gate she sensed in Baltimore might have been there in spite of the arena, not because of it.

Yeah, right. I think I'll start looking for apartments as soon as I can.

She opened her carry-on bag, which held her IBM ThinkPad, and set the computer up on the desk. With the laptop was a thick paper file, a copy of which Hawk had received a week earlier. It was an annoying holdout on the old technology that the Bureau seemed determined to cling to; some of the older agents were downright technophobic. In the file were missing persons reports, photos of kids, and the scribbled comments some of the agents in the Baltimore office. There was also a thick envelope containing several free passes to Lazerwarz; at six dollars a game, it wasn't cheap. She knew the passes would be gone soon because she would be playing often, to get a feel for the arena and for the person running it. With few tweaks to her glamorie she would make herself seem a little younger, so as not to seem so out of place.

Her eyes fell on one of the pictures, a school photo of Alan Barker, the boy who disappeared from the Baltimore arena. He was a young blond kid of about sixteen, an honors student with an invitation to attend Princeton, with an IQ of about 150. He was also a laser tag enthusiast, the local terror of the arena, and played under the code name "Joystik." One afternoon after playing ten rounds of Lazerwarz he vanished without a trace. His RX-7 was still parked in front of the arena. And no one, as usual, saw anything.

Alan had an excellent relationship with his parents, didn't do drugs, started a Students Against Drunk Driving program at his school, and volunteered for AIDS hospice work. And the local police had wanted to say he had run away from home, at first. When they learned that his father was Congressman Barker of Illinois, they reassessed their theory and sought help with the FBI. It was the first time the Bureau had found out about the Lazer Abductions, even though fifty cases had been entered, or were waiting to be entered, at the NCIC.

The FBI had already set up the MCLP, the Missing Children Location Program, at the academy in Quantico, Virginia. Volunteer requests for MCLP went out to all the field offices, yet the response was, to say the least, underwhelming. That was when Sammi, then a new graduate, stepped in. She volunteered to coordinate the flow of information between the NCIC and the FBI, pointing out "domestic" cases that should be included in the missing persons files. Three other agents around the country worked on MCLP, but Sammi was the only one devoting her undivided attention to it.

Her gaze returned to the photo. *This kid is bright, with a future, and great rapport with his parents.*

He didn't run away.

She considered turning on the ThinkPad, but closed her eyes against the thought, realizing how tired she really was. It might have been different had she been in her native realm of Underhill, where the energies were a tad more tamed than those here, particularly during this thunderstorm. Lightning wreaked havoc with the magical workings of even the most experienced elven Mage, and keeping a glamorie in place during the bumpy plane ride had sapped her strength.

"To hell with it," she said to the suite. Feeling slightly naughty, she let the glamorie fall aside and stood, regarding her purely elven form in the mirror.

My ears have lengthened with acquired wisdom, she thought with a chuckle as she playfully admired the image she went to so much trouble to conceal. Her slitted cat's eyes, green and large and inhuman, were a frightening sight to all but the elvenfolk. Seeing her own image, unfettered by the earthly trappings of the human race, reminded her how long it had been since she had enjoyed the company of her brethren.

She lay back on the bed, frowned at its hardness, and fought the inevitable ache of loneliness that intruded at times like these. She missed home, even though she worked and lived among the humans as a matter of choice. Rare invasions from hostile elven clans notwithstanding, life Underhill had taken on a predictable quality, a monotony that some of the elves found unbearably dull. The solution, heretical in some elven courts but welcomed in hers and others, was to cross the barrier separating them from the human race. They would assume human forms, learn human trades, play their games, and live their lives in disguise, always ready to Gate back to Underhill if their true identities were discovered by humans too difficult or violent to control. Some elves lived as humans for a brief time, some longer. Some, like herself, for a good span of a human's adulthood. Sammi had spent her time in law enforcement, and her elven abilities had enabled her to spot dark magic from her homeland, and deal with it; something a human cop simply could not do. While investigating Alan's disappearance at the Baltimore arena, she'd discovered the traces of a Gate, along with the more insidious remnants of Unseleighe magic. All the more reason to get involved: if the Unseleighe were abducting children, it was her duty to her clan and to the human race to deal with it.

Sammi stood and prepared for a long, hot shower. Her experience with travel told her she would never sleep until she had bathed, no matter how fatigued she was. But outside lightning continued to rake the sky, and she had second thoughts about getting into the water. Tempted to disregard common sense, she started unpacking her bathroom items, longing for the Shower Massage that beckoned in the stall.

Then *it* hit.

The dark scream was a wound, the ripping of barriers between realms. She closed her eyes and looked for its source, finding a hot, bright mass in her mind's eye, in a place not too far away.

Great Danaa, she muttered as she turned off the shower. What she felt was no lightning hit, but something far more telling, and sinister. *Only the gods could pull together such strength,* she thought as she fumbled through her bags for jeans, sandals and a T-shirt. Half numb, she put these things on, and picked up the keys to the Caprice.

She saw clearly where the power source was, but had no idea who would have a need for such a construction. What she sensed was a Gate, but one of such magnitude one could move an army through it. It was coming from inside the city limits of Tulsa, and was close enough she could drive there in a few minutes, she guessed. The Caprice was parked just outside her room; a wave of stale cigarette smoke greeted her as she slid behind the wheel. The ashtray was open and overflowing with butts. No wonder Owen had had a heart attack.

The rain had ceased, though the storm was still raging in the distance, spiking the horizon with lightning. She pulled out of the parking lot and entered the expressway for downtown Tulsa. The source was getting closer, somewhere on her right. *Here, let's take this exit*, she thought, getting off on 41st Street.

Her reaction to investigate the matter had been spontaneous, and she took a moment to reassess her move. *If this is Unseleighe magic, shouldn't I have backup?* she thought, and considered aborting her recon. But if she didn't locate it now she might never; Gate energy, particularly the temporary kind that emerged in the human's world, didn't always stick around long. She would locate it, and deal with it later, if indeed there was something to deal *with*. If something had come through that she could not handle alone, well . . . she had better not encounter it, that was all.

Right away she noticed the electricity in the area was out. Streets and neighborhoods slept in darkness. Ahead near an intersection was a cluster of black and white cars with blue and red flashing light bars. An accident? No, they were not on the street, they were in a parking lot, shining their spots on something tall and dark. She pulled up and stopped. If the other cops noticed her they didn't seem to care; they appeared to be too stunned by what they were observing.

Sammi got out, and stood a few feet from the idling Caprice. Thin fog boiled from the pavement, and the asphalt's black warmth seeped up through her sneakers. In her room she had heard the wound tear, and here it was, festering before her.

"This isn't from Underhill," she said to the warm, wet night.

Whatever magics were responsible for bringing this massive stone circle to this land were likely well beyond any the Unseleighe might summon.

This is Stonehenge, she thought, recognizing the monoliths. *Brought from England, via Gate or some other construction.*

None too eager to introduce herself to the officers on the scene, she got back into the Caprice and drove slowly away from the situation. After all, she didn't have any ID with her; she had left it at the room. Just as well, it now looked like she had a cover to protect.

Time to speak with the King. I'll likely need Avalon's help after all.

Chapter Two

And there it was, again; a Gate signature flickered dimly at the periphery of his magical sight, taxing his already strained attention. Llanmorgan of Avalon tried to ignore the sign and focus on the King's magecraft lesson, the halving of a Mage light with a bronze sword. The tedious task was now complicated by the Gate sign *and* King Aedham's scrutinizing his every move from a few paces away. A chilling wind had descended on the practice arena occupying the palace's flat cobblestone roof, worsening matters.

A Gate, a teacher hovering over me like a vulture, and a cold north wind. What ideal *conditions for working magic!*

The bright, apple-sized sphere hovered a few paces before him, fueled by a whisper of node power. His task was to maintain the light while contemplating its neat bisection; contradictory desires which both demanded his full consideration. He had heard this was typical of what the King asked of his students, as they would protect the elfhame one day with their skills. Despite an earlier enthusiasm for the apprenticeship he wondered if he was up to the task.

And again, there's that distracting Gate sign! Does the King sense it too?

"Your focus is wavering," the King observed dryly.

"What have you on your mind besides your assignment? Nubile maidens at a bale fire?"

Biting back a sharp reply, he turned to face the King, but found he could not. Instead his eyes fell on the King's odd footwear, an indulgence His Majesty had brought with him from the world of the humans. Whatever beast had been slain for the brightly colored pelts certainly didn't live in Underhill. Magic held the boot's seams together, and the soles made a mousy squeak. Aedham referred to them as either "ny kees" or "sneekers," and insisted they never be polished. The King fancied strange human creations, and of these the shoes were the least peculiar. At least there was a discernible use attached to them.

"No, sire," Llan replied humbly, and returned to his task. The light flickered, threatened to go out; he paused to let it reach a certain brightness, and struck. The blade missed, nudging it a hand's breadth to the right.

The King sighed in exasperation, and Llan's ears burned with embarrassment. *This is not that difficult!* the youth berated himself. *And here I fail, before the King, of all elves . . .*

Llan considered mentioning the Gate sign but thought this might be construed as an excuse. Instead, he remained silent, and raised his sword once again.

His strike, sharpened with some of his own anger, fell true and neatly bisected the sphere. The light halves sparked, then formed two smaller spheres half the size of the original.

"Splendid!" the King complimented, slapping Llan on the back. But his tone darkened somewhat as he said, "Now, line them up, one above the other. And slice them into *four*."

To Llan's incredulous look he said, "It can be done. Accomplish this feat, and we will be done for the day."

"Aie," Llan said, not feeling altogether confident.

Using the sword as a wand, Llan moved one sphere over the other and, shrugging, focused on the two, raised the blade, and took aim.

A few paces away, the door to the palace roof creaked open, stealing Llan's concentration from him anew. The spheres began to drift apart.

"Forgive me, King," said the newcomer. "I did not know you were conducting lessons, I didn't."

Niamh, the King's Engineer, lurked uncomfortably by the door. Smaller than most elves, he looked like an intelligent beaver, with a nose the size of a potato, and large buck teeth.

"Continue," the King said to Llan before walking over to Niamh.

Llanmorgan realigned the two spheres and composed himself for another attempt, but his attention was drawn by the animated discussion the King was having with Niamh. The Engineer confirmed that yes, indeed, someone was about to Gate, and clearly the King had not noted this in his own mage sight. Feeling somewhat redeemed, the apprentice sliced the two spheres as if they were apples, and with satisfaction watched the halves turn into four small spheres.

When he glanced back at the King, he and his Engineer were gaping at his accomplishment.

"Did he just cut two mage lights into four?" the Engineer muttered, clearly amazed.

"Indeed he did," the King replied. "And they began as *one*."

"No!" Niamh said, walking over to examine his work.

"If someone is about to Gate here, then we should greet them," the King said, moving towards the door. Niamh turned to join him.

Llan followed, saying, "I don't understand, Sire. You said it could be done. What is so astounding about quartering the mage light?"

"I said it could be done," the King said, with a

smirk. "I didn't say it could be done by *me*. Or, until now, anyone else in the Elfhame. At least," Aedham amended, "on the *first* try." He opened the door and began descending the stairwell into the palace.

Llanmorgan sheathed his sword and followed them into the palace, beaming over his accomplishment but trying hard not to show it. Smugness usually led to more assignments. Yet he couldn't resist a *little* showmanship. Llan sent the mage lights ahead of them, lighting their way down the dark stairwell.

"I didn't notice how dirty these stairs had become," Aedham commented. "Perhaps our young apprentice here would like to find a broom . . ."

As one, the spheres dimmed to a dull glow. Aedham visibly suppressed a laugh, while Niamh made no such attempt, chortling without reserve all the way down the stairs.

I didn't accept the apprenticeship to sweep floors! Llan seethed in mock resentment, though such a chore was not beneath him, even after rubbing shoulders with Aedham and his royal court for the past year. He was from a proud middle class family who had volunteered to help Avalon rebuild. His fortune had turned the day the King spied him making a mage light, a task the young elf had thought simple and intuitive. But the making of mage light was a skill normally mastered after years of training, though no one had bothered to tell Llan that while he was growing up. Llan's father, and of course Llan himself, eagerly agreed to an apprenticeship when offered, and within the passing of a day the young elf found himself elevated to a social status he had never thought possible.

But this court was a strange mixture of youthfulness, gaiety and irreverence, qualities that would have been out of place in Outremer. Most elvenfolk were fiercely traditional, and observed the old ways with a passion. Though elfhame Avalon was ancient, indeed had been named after the original elven land of a time so distant hardly anyone remembered it now, its new leadership was young and had lived for a considerable time as humans in the humans' world. Mingling with the lesser beings was not unheard of, though it was usually done on an individual basis, not by an entire elven court. Llan knew that a ruthless Unseleighe tribe had conquered Avalon, and Avalon had fled to the humans' world for temporary refuge. Yet who would have thought that so much human culture would rub off on them? At times Llan thought they were human after all, masquerading as elves. This would explain not just their fondness of human technology, but their *mastering* of it, using it in ways neither human *nor* elf had ever imagined.

"Any idea who it is?" the King asked.

"It must be Lady Samantha," Niamh replied as they reached the foot of the steps. "She has the only sigil combination. Unless she gave it to a human, which she would *never* do."

Llan had heard of the King's mysterious sister who lived among the humans by choice, but had never had the opportunity to meet her. She worked in secret as a constable of sorts. Llan found it amusing that an elf would make for herself a position of power there, even for the benefit of both races. And she did so completely undetected. Whatever life that would be, it would not be dull . . . which was precisely why some elves chose it.

Now she was coming here. From the urgency in the king's voice Llan surmised this was unusual, and perhaps a sign of trouble.

"I would like you to meet her, Llan," Aedham said as they reached the base of the stairs, which stood at the head of the Great Hall. "She's been pestering me about taking on an apprentice, and now she can see that I have." Banners festooned the granite walls—portraits of Aedham's mother and father, Queen Faldi and King Traigthren, respectively. At the end of the Hall was an enormous black oak throne, though Llan had never seen the King sit in it. From the kitchen adjoining the Hall wafted the smells of a delicious meal in the making, and from the doorway servants peered in to see what the King was up to, evidently aware that *something* of interest was about to take place.

"Ah. Here it is," Niamh commented as a ring of yellow light, dim and translucent at first, took shape in the center of the spacious Hall, hovering a hand's breadth above the flagstone floor. Llan found it a bit disturbing that it was manifesting with no obvious help from a mage, even though the magics responsible had been laid out in advance, and were now being activated by the appropriate sigils.

Suddenly a silhouette appeared in the ring, and out stepped a rather attractive elven Lady in strange human attire, with shortened hair that at first gave her the semblance of a male. Then the rest of her appeared; this was *no* male. Her dress was oddly tailored, of a fabric not unlike silk, and was far too short for an elven high court, but which suited Llan's tastes perfectly. The shoes were delicate, with little stilts on the heels that gave her a considerable advantage in height. She stepped from the Gate, graceful as a deer, and instantly looked as if she *belonged* here, despite the human trappings. The Gate vanished, and Lady Samantha reached to embrace her brother.

"You've arrived just in time for supper," Aedham said as he hugged his sister. "Have you brought me my CDs?"

Samantha looked only momentarily pained. "I'm afraid I forgot those, kiddo," she said, then noticing Llan, amended, "Sire." Even the apprentice noticed the smirk. "I've come with some interesting news from the Overworld."

"Whatever the news is," Aedham said expansively,

"you can share it with us all. This is Llanmorgan of Outremer, and he is my new student."

Her eyebrows raised appreciatively at the mention of Outremer. *Of course. She is from Outremer, as well.* As instructed by the court, Llan bowed slightly at the waist and took her hand gently, *not* kissing it, as that would indicate he was somewhere on the same social order as she . . . which he definitely was not. It would be all too easy to let this new familiarity get the best of him; being privy to this conversation was overwhelming enough.

"Let's adjourn to the drawing room," the King said. "The *modern* one," he added with a wink.

Llan felt the hairs on his neck stand at attention, and his ear tips felt slightly "dizzy." The King kept two drawing rooms, a traditional one and the modern one, full of human devices that defied all logic and explanation. Llan had seldom gone into that one, out of respect and perhaps a bit of fear that he might disturb something, or turn something on and not know how to deal with it or turn it off. It was said that no magic was used in the creation of these devices. Llan wasn't so certain.

"Turn on CNN," Samantha said as the King led them into the comfortable if slightly puzzling environment. As they situated themselves in two oversized couches which somewhat resembled traditional furniture, Niamh activated the "big scream" at a large cluster of crystals. Each faceted stone, every one as big around as his arm, were mounted on a stand beside the device; he knew this was connected to the crystal port in the King's study. From there, Niamh had once explained cryptically, they "pirated a variety of services from the human realm."

The scream came to life, and Llan winced. The "big scream" hadn't actually screamed yet, but he feared one of these times it would. Instead the colorful images appeared on an amazingly flat surface, unlike the faceted crystal surfaces of most elven communications devices. Llan sat opposite the two, with the "big scream" on the opposite wall, between them, giving him a good view of everything.

"So tell me, sister, what has brought you home for this visit?"

She seemed uncomfortable or uncertain of where to start. "I wish I could come for no other reason than to see you again," she said, at length, "instead of with what is likely bad news."

Aedham turned grim. "What would that be?"

That is where Llan's comprehension of matters ended. Samantha began a long description of a type of sport the humans indulged in, but it was not played with a ball or mallet but those most mysterious of all human inventions, *lasers*. Niamh had demonstrated one in his workshop, and the apprentice was astonished to learn that it employed no node power to generate a hot, tight beam, intense enough to burn wood and even iron. The game sounded dangerous, until she explained to Llan directly, evidently sensing his misunderstanding, that the lasers were not high-powered, and were used as a means of direction. Another magical beam of "you vee" did the actual scoring . . . or something. It was a game that humans paid coin to play, and there were no spectators. The game took place in an arena of mazes, where it *was* honorable to hide, but *not* honorable to strike or touch other players. Once he got past this confusing point he began to understand. It was a game of stealth and skill, not brute force, like the kind Llan was familiar with.

It sounded like great fun, even after she mentioned the Unseleighe Court.

"I would not come to you with this unless I was certain," she explained, and Aedham listened intently, visibly disturbed at the mention of the court that had conquered his kingdom and murdered his family. "And the children. They are disappearing with increasing regularity, but besides the kids' parents, the humans don't seem to be bothered much. It's why I took this particular job on, you see. I thought it was a matter of human indifference, which I wanted to do something about."

"What evidence of the Unseleighe court have you found?" Aedham asked.

"Well, a few things. At one of these arenas was a darkness, an undeniable force that felt much like Japhet's work. Something that draws on fear and hate."

"That just about describes all Unseleighe workings," the King replied.

"True, but this instance, it had a particular flavor to it. Like one we had encountered before. The house, for instance, where Daryl Bendis nearly died. It was very much like that."

"You are certain," the King asked, but it did not really come across as a question. *Yes, she is certain,* Llan thought.

Niamh stood and approached the scream, as if to get a better view. A stone circle had appeared on the device, which the Engineer took an extreme interest in. Llan knew that the humans used many of these stone circles in an attempt to reach Underhill, but most ended up being simply concentrated pockets of human-raised magical energy.

Aedham continued, "Granted, if Unseleighe forces are prowling the Earth once again, and even though we eliminated Japhet Dhu and his father, I don't doubt this could happen." Aedham shifted in his chair, and Llan sensed a vulnerability in the King he'd never seen before. Then again, he'd never heard him discuss the Unseleighe in such straightforward terms. "But my duty, as always, is to the elfhame."

"And as you have said before," Samantha pointed out, "the Unseleighe, at least this particular clan, would never have penetrated the human realm if they hadn't been searching for you."

Aedham sighed, an indication that his sister might be winning the argument after all. "I agree, we have some responsibility to protect the humans from this disease, but let me point out that we are not responsible for the evil in their world. Most is of their own doing."

"Most, but not all," Sammi replied, undeterred. "Humans do not have the capability to transport an archeological site from one continent to another overnight, through mundane means." She glanced at the big scream. "Much less through the largest Gate I have ever seen or, in this case, felt."

"What?" Aedham followed her gaze to the images on the scream. "Niamh, turn that up, would you?"

With a small surge of magic, Niamh urged the scream to be louder. The human's voice boomed from small black boxes on the walls and floor.

". . . was discovered early this morning by commuters after an evening of violent thunderstorms. Local officials have no explanation for the sudden appearance of several dozen stone megaliths, each weighing up to thirty tons . . ."

"Bloody hell!" the King exclaimed. "That's Stonehenge!"

"Indeed, it is," she said, smugly. "And what's more, it has appeared, of all places, in the parking lot of the next Lazerwarz arena." She explained her voyage in a rocking airship, the contact with a human she would be working with, and her settling in at an inn. She described the blast of energy that ripped through the world and deposited something nearby. She went to investigate, and found this stone circle where it simply should not have been.

"And you sensed Unseleighe forces here," Aedham said reluctantly.

"Thick enough to scoop up in cauldrons, bucko," Sammi said. "But I wonder if the Unseleighe can even manage this degree of power."

"They have surprised us before," Aedham said.

"But not quite like *this*. It's obviously Stonehenge. But look how they're carefully avoiding using the name."

"Perhaps they don't know yet," Aedham said. "I mean, this just happened. It's not even the same time of day in Britain.

Niamh, change the channels to BBC, would you?"

The Engineer reached over to the cluster of crystals. "Changing channels" appeared to be more involved than just nudging the device with magic. The scream flickered, then settled on another image.

The scene British television presented was similar to the local one, only instead of the circle of trilithons there stood a circle of black asphalt, in stark contrast with the green countryside. A small crowd had developed, and a human voice spoke, ". . . not certain if this is related to the crop circle phenomenon or not, but this certainly calls into question the possibility of forces beyond our comprehension . . ."

"It looks like they swapped both features spontaneously," the King observed, still sounding mystified. "I wonder if . . . have they made the connection yet?"

"It doesn't look that way. But they will." Sammi sounded resigned. Llan knew little about the work elves did with humans, but even he could see this was more than Lady Samantha had bargained for. "It makes no sense that they would intentionally attract attention to this place, if they are kidnapping children through these arenas."

"The Unseleighe motives have never been reasonable. Perhaps they are simply trying to hide in plain sight."

"Perhaps." Sammi paused, then added, "You were saying about evidence of Unseleighe activity?"

In a niche carved out of Underhill's land of the Unformed, in the palace he had created for himself and his new kingdom, in the audience chamber where he sat on a massive bronze throne, Mort fumed.

Stonehenge?

Mort viewed the fragmented image in the crystal with disbelief, convinced now that the gods themselves were capable of unlimited stupidity.

Stone . . . henge?

It had to be a joke. Morrigan would find such a prank amusing, particularly if she saw him now, he was certain. She had transported across the globe one of the most famous human archeological sites and dropped it at his very doorstep, where he least wanted to attract attention. *Just wonderful.* His amazement centered not on the fact she could pull such a stunt off, but that she would do it, right here, a week before his arena was about to open.

It was no joke. With a wave, he dismissed the image, and the crystal blinked into darkness.

He wanted to kill her, and would do so if she could be killed, or at *least* berate her for the sheer stupidity of the situation. Yet, he could not.

Why? Because he had asked her to do it.

Not in so many words, of course, but his challenge was vague enough that any fool might have made anything of it they wanted. Evidently, Morrigan *was* any fool, and had done the one thing that would cause the most irritation, with the least possibility for retribution.

"She will be calling on me any moment now," he muttered to the empty audience chamber, aware of the gentle susurrations his words made on the stone surfaces around him. He'd built the chamber with acoustics in mind so as to make his physical voice loud, booming and frightening, to impress upon his human captives his omnipotence. It didn't matter that he could extinguish their life with a thought, they wouldn't know that yet, and if he demonstrated his ability he would be out a potentially useful human slave. His few attempts at torture were fruitless; he couldn't find the happy medium between not enough pain and too much, and ended up with a handful of psychotic, blathering youths with mush for brains. So he made do with the *voice*, a trick he'd learned while working for Zeldan, back when they were trying to find the cowardly Avalon High Court.

But that was so much history now. The search for King Aedham had been a learning period, a series of exploratory forays into the world of the Unseleighe and Seleighe courts, their intrigues and hatreds and foibles, not to mention some valuable experience with the humans and their confusing, contradictory land. The experience was paying off. Mort had an army now, and he was the commander in chief, with several *thousands* of years of experience to guide him.

With his long, spindly arms, he reached for the servant's tray on the column next to him, where he had left his mug of used motor oil. He had acquired a taste for the thick, black sludge while working in the human world above, savoring the spice of minute particles of cold iron suspended in it. The elves would have found it deadly, but Mort found it tasty and a bit intoxicating. Mildly appalled, his human slaves had watched him drink the stuff, their expressions muted through his spell of control.

They must think I'm a God, Mort had thought. *Well. I am, or will be very soon. So long a road to travel, and I am the only one on it, the only one left to reap the rewards.*

My people will inherit the Earth, above and below, once again. We will rule it and milk it and rape it until it screams for forgiveness, and once it does, we will do the same for the inhabitants, just to remind them who is in charge.

This is going to be fun.

His education was over. Mort's time in the Unseleighe Court merely fed an insidious, festering desire to conquer all. Zeldan Dhu, and then later his son, Japhet Dhu, had thought him an obedient minion, and to a certain degree he was, but while in their employ he had been . . . *learning.* Perhaps he should give Zeldan more credit than that, as he was the elf who had found him in Dreaming, an inert and dormant, utterly *mindless* Mort, and had then breathed new life into him. If Zeldan had granted him life only to be his servant, then so be it; his long Dreaming was over.

The more Zeldan had reminded him of his place as his minion, the more Mort fixated on rising above it. In private, of course. His inability to express his desires only intensified them.

For Mort was a Foevorian, one of an ancient race, the first race and therefore the first *rulers*, of Underhill, of the human's world, and of everything in between. The distinctions between the two realms did not really exist then; the polarity of spirit and matter developed later. Mort's earliest memories were of the sea, and of the civilization that dwelled there. The humans had vague historical references to a realm called Atlantis, but it was far too complex to be considered a single domain.

Other races might have called this heaven or utopia, and would have been satisfied with it, never to evolve to some higher level. Not Mort—then called Morca—or his people, who were leaders with no followers. They rose from the sea to find a race of subjects. Yet they were quickly disappointed.

They found instead a massive sheet of ice, reaching across half the globe, with nothing to speak of living there. They returned to the sea, awaiting a better time.

When the better time came they found a mighty island that would later be known as Eire, linked to the greater continent by a mass of ice retreating over a narrow bridge of land. The land was populated with four-legged creatures and, in small numbers, two-legged ones, who hunted with stones and fed on the four-legged creatures. It was a simple matter to rule the two-leggeds; the Foevors became their gods.

As the two-leggeds ruled the four-leggeds, it seemed a natural progression that a *one-legged* creature rule the two; thus the Foevors assumed their first physical state, that of the Clapperlegs, to rule in proximity to their minions. Yet they were a graceful race, despite their lack of symmetry. The form of one leg, one arm, one eye suited their purposes, as it frightened the two-leggeds into submission. They made themselves twice the size of the two-leggeds, with twice the strength and, of course, already had twice the wisdom.

As time passed, the ice melted and the land bridge vanished, and the Foevors lost track of what was going on in the larger continent. Then more two-leggeds arrived on ships, and they were better warriors, with weapons of metal. Their large numbers made them formidable, but the Foevors still had the advantage of physical size, and had sharpened their magical abilities. They drew power from the ground and the sea, whipping up great storms to sink the invaders' ships. The balance of power usually favored the Foevors, and following the few times it didn't the Foevors reconquered their land, and slew the enemy into extinction. During one such invasion the enemy had killed their King, Conan, and in retaliation Morca had successfully led a great armada of warships; as a victorious leader he had his first taste of glory. And Morca decided he wanted more of it.

He might have become the Foevorian King. His popularity was enormous, his leadership abilities were unquestionable; what other Foevor could conquer the two-leggeds with their own devices? Amid his newfound fame he changed his name to Morta, and began seeking ways to consolidate his power, to fill the void left by King Conan.

Morta would have become ruler, if not for the elves.

The Tuatha De Danaan, the people of the goddess of Danaa, weren't so much formidable as they were *annoying*. They came at the worst possible time, in the middle of the night, when most of the Foevorian horde had nodded off from too much drink and revelry. The Tuatha took up residence on another part of Eire without so much as a raised voice. Right away, Morta was blamed for the "invasion," and new leaders, the loudest voices of dissent, took his place.

The Tuatha were no ordinary two-leggeds. They were magical, and it was rumored they came from the spirit world, or were descended from gods, or both. Were the Foevors too quick to proclaim their sole right to these magical origins?

It seemed so. When the Foevors declared war on the trespassers, the war turned to magic, and the Tuatha were superior in these skills. The ensuing war rent the universe into two distinct realms, one physical and one of the spirit. During the long, tortuous battles many Foevors began to seek refuge in the spirit world. In the shadow of a victorious Tuatha, Mort sought safety in this as yet unnamed spirit realm, and made himself as invisible as possible, fearing an unjust retribution from his own people. The Foevors were a defeated and divided race, and took up residence in isolated, far-reaching pockets in the new realm.

It was with no small pleasure that Mort later watched the Tuatha's defeat, by yet another tribe of two-leggeds called the Milesians. They banished the Tuatha to the nether world regions through a door under a hill, thus the name, *Underhill*. But with no power base Mort saw no way to take advantage of the circumstance. As above, so below, the factions lived in uneasy peace. In time, dissent split the Tuatha into smaller groups; the polarity reached a breaking point, and they divided into the Seleighe and their nemesis, the Unseleighe courts. The former remained benevolent to the humans, accepting their defeat with honor, while the latter blamed the humans for their fall from grace and took great pleasure in tormenting them regularly.

Mort studied the Seleighe and Unseleighe, pretending to be interested in Zeldan's and then later, Japhet's objective: the elimination of Avalon from Underhill. Meanwhile he gained power and knowledge, while planning for the day he and his people would again rise up and take the victory that was their right. With Mort at the helm, of course.

He drained off the last of the oil and set the mug down with a loud *clang*. The sound summoned one of his servants, a mousy little boy named Alan, who had been harvested from the Baltimore arena. Alan wore a tunic of dirty canvas, and moved about numbly, in a daze. The red carranite crystal embedded in his temple made sure of that; through the crystal Mort controlled Alan and the rest of the multitude of slaves he'd acquired through his Lazerwarz arenas.

As Alan poured the sludge from a pitcher, Mort's viewing crystal came to life with the fragmented image of a sour Unseleighe warrior. "Master, you have a visitor," said Yuaroh Dhu, a wizened elf with a severe, chiseled face. Mort had hired Yuaroh and his Unseleighe clan as mercenaries for his ambitious endeavor. So far there had been no battle to speak of, and Yuaroh had turned out to be a capable receptionist. And a perceptive one; he knew the Morrigan was not one to be turned away.

"Of course I do," Mort sighed, and began rubbing away the beginnings of a massive headache. "Send the bitch in." The crystal winked out, and a moment later a shrill peal of laughter further confirmed her presence.

"Mort Mort Mort, my dear *Mort*!" Morrigan shrieked cheerfully, entering the chambers with a flourish. This was not the Morrigan Mort remembered. What had once been a round, dumpy woman figure with a hooked nose was now a slim, svelte attractive goddess in a sassy red evening dress. Her red hair was all that remained the same, though now it was in a *big* style, flowing around her like blazing aura. She was dressed, and morphed, to kill. *Who* would be killed remained to be seen.

Mort pretended not to notice, and reminded himself this elegant creature had just dropped Stonehenge on his parking lot. *I don't have to be nice.*

"You don't seem happy, Mort," Morrigan prodded, daring to come within arm's reach of his throne. She was in constant motion, posing for a second here, holding her well rounded hips there, as if she were modeling on a catwalk. If it was meant to distract him, it was working. Her new appearance was arousing, but he wasn't about to let her know that.

"I am *not* happy, Morrigan," Mort replied, waving the crystal back on, with the fragmented picture of Stonehenge standing amid asphalt. "What, may I ask, is the meaning of this?"

"Oh, Mort," she replied flippantly, with a loud, rude expulsion of air from her lips. *At least some things, don't change,* Mort noted. "You *know*. The *challenge*. Don't tell me you've already forgotten."

Mort waved his hand again, and a chair appeared for Morrigan to sit on. It would not do to have her flouncing her assets about while having a serious discussion, derailing his train of thought, which she seemed intent on doing.

"I know about the challenge," he said evenly. She sat and crossed her legs, her red dress riding up on her thigh like a silk drape. *Not the effect I was after,* he thought, but pressed on anyway. "The challenge was to move a stone circle from the old land to the new. It was not to move the most famous of archeological sites—"

"Stonehenge is but a rest stop in the realm of spirits—"

"Not in the human's world, it isn't!" Mort screamed.

He did not regret raising his voice. His guest recoiled noticeably. "This was a *covert* operation you wanted in on, Morrigan! That means keeping it secret, keeping a low profile, away from the prying eyes of humans and their law enforcement!"

Morrigan sighed, and crossed her legs the other way. The effect . . . well, Mort had to transfer some of his newly aroused lust to other places in his appearance. The two horn buds which were more or less a permanent feature on his forehead lengthened somewhat. "And then there is that little matter of your betrayal of the Foevorians to the Tuatha. You were on our side, we had thought."

Morrigan rolled her eyes. "History, Mort. And ancient history, at that. Let me also remind you that I didn't betray you to Zeldan. When I found you in bed with the Unseleighe, I played along, just to see what might come of it. Did you really think I didn't recognize you as a displaced Foevorian?"

This took Mort by surprise, since until now he had thought his disguise had been perfect. *Still, she may be bluffing.*

"I would say that would make us even," Morrigan continued. "And tell me, what is more important to you: the past, or our glorious future together? I can teach you many things about the humans, I know their weaknesses better than you do."

"You know nothing of the humans, Morrigan," Mort replied hotly.

"I know more than you think," Morrigan hissed back. "While you were Dreaming lo those many centuries, I have studied the humans and interacted with them. You could not have possibly known that it was I who helped the druid Merlin move the stones there in the first place!"

Mort didn't know who Merlin was. It was one of the pitfalls of Dreaming. One couldn't keep abreast of current events.

Morrigan continued, "Remember, I am a *god*, you miserable fool. They *worship* me."

Her thighs kept shifting; her ankle, sheathed in an elegant red stiletto pump, rocked up and down restlessly. Mort's horns grew more, their sharpened, curved tips almost touching. *Hate it when this happens.* He surreptitiously turned his horns upwards, to allow them room to grow, a certainty if this conversation continued along this vein.

"While you, Mort," she continued, "are the remnants of a race conquered an eternity ago by the Tuatha. If it weren't for Zeldan you'd still be in a coma. And yet you had the *audacity* to deny me my rightful place at your side?"

There it was. *She's shaming me into accepting her, in the most humiliating way possible . . . bad publicity! This was no accident.*

"You are denied no more," Mort said, his anger surrendering to a resigned calm. *She's won this round. Time to move on to the next.* "Now, this is what I have in mind . . ."

Alfred Mackie reached over and answered the telephone on the night table beside his bed, resisting an urge to rip the cord out of the wall.

"Yes?" he answered tentatively.

"It's William, Doctor," said the youth on the other end. "You're not going to believe this, but . . . Stonehenge has disappeared."

"Do tell," Alfred replied with a distinct lack of concern.

"It's *gone*, I tell you," William bemoaned, and the doctor of prehistoric archeology slowly sat up in his hotel bed. A hell of a thing to be told in the middle of the night if he were alert and sober, and Alfred Mackie was neither.

"I . . . see. Who is with you?"

"Just the others. We came from the pub. . . ."

Alfred might have dismissed this as a prank. Perhaps the other students had convinced William, who was barely old enough to shave, that mystic forces or UFOs or a squad of Yiddish grandmothers had spirited away the stone circle. Easy enough to consider, as Alfred had seen the four of them in the pub, and Alfred had had the impression this was William's first drinking experience.

"Can I speak with, let's see, Stuart?" Alfred asked. Stuart was not immediately available. William was on his cell phone, and the others were out inspecting the site, which had mysteriously turned into a circular asphalt parking lot. "Perhaps I should come on down," Alfred said, though his first impulse was to go back to sleep. There had been a wedding party on his floor and sleep had come only very late. And the beginnings of a hangover did not encourage him either.

"Please do," William said. "And could you bring the camera? I think we should record this, don't you?"

"Of course." Alfred sat up and put his feet on a cold, linoleum floor. "I'll be down soon. Stay there."

Alfred hung the phone up and took a deep breath. The wall thumped, twice, three times, from his neighbors, the newlyweds. *Bloody hell.*

After a quick shower he threw on an old cardigan, picking up a digital videocam on his way down. Stokes College spared little for accommodations in the field, but they had managed to purchase good equipment for the VR project, he had to give them that. His old Mercedes gave him hell when he tried to start it up, but finally it turned over. When he turned north, on Castle Road, on his way out of Salisbury he saw a hint of dawn on the horizon.

There were many reasons why he shouldn't believe William, and disregard the whole incident as a joke. That's what most professors, supervising fieldwork for their archeology students, would do. The night belonged to youth, and Alfred was nearing sixty.

But there were many more, potent reasons why he should believe him. Alfred had always known when someone was telling the truth . . . at least the boy *believed* the stones had vanished. Also, while lying awake and staring at the ceiling, Alfred had felt the universe ripping. He had observed this disturbance only a few times before, and though he had not actually seen them, the *sidhe* undeniably had been involved.

Last month the college had acquired several donated file servers, and Alfred had suggested a virtual reality walkthrough of Stonehenge. In an effort to compete with the other archeology schools the administration had approved a tidy sum for additional hardware and studentships. No one had yet done a thorough, *scientific* VR of Stonehenge, and Stokes wanted to be the first. Finding archeology students with computer expertise was surprisingly easy.

Alfred turned left onto the A303, passing a sign for Stonehenge. The English countryside appeared to be asleep, and the traffic was light. He passed the junction of A360 and A303. By now dawn had cast a pallid glow on the landscape, enough to see that something important was missing from the horizon.

"*Dear gods*," Alfred muttered to himself. "Someone has mislaid the Henge."

A lone car was parked at the entrance, and three figures were milling about the site, one waving at him. A black circle had replaced the sarsens and bluestones, and what appeared to be the wreck of an automobile, or part of one, lay at the circle's edge. A single light pole stood off-center on the circle, unlit. But there had never been lights installed here; there was no electricity. He pulled up beside the Golf GTI, noted that one of his students, Stuart, had passed out in the back seat.

William came running up to the Mercedes.

"Did you bring the camera?"

Alfred nodded, and numbly handed the boy the videocam.

"Come on, let me show you," William said, bubbling with energy. Alfred let him lead, riding the trails of his excitement like a hitchhiker, drifting past the fence surrounding the site. Another student joined them, reeking of ale, but was otherwise coherent.

"We are in the right place, aren't we?" Peter, the project's junior technician, asked in all sincerity.

Alfred stared at him for a long moment, taking in his look of utter bewilderment, and in a flash found it all quite funny. Alfred started to laugh.

Peter scowled. "It's *not*?"

Alfred grew serious. "It is. What possessed you boys to come out here in the middle of the night, anyway?"

"The ale," William provided.

"We w-wanted to see how the sun aligned with the heelstone," Peter quickly amended.

"It was the ale," William insisted, and giggled. Peter gave him a harsh look.

"Of course," Alfred said. "Well then. Let's have a look."

Alfred took one look at the site and saw that not all of Stonehenge was missing. The barrows surrounding the stone circle and the enormous heelstone appeared to be untouched. Only the enormous sarsens and the bluestones, the inner circle, were gone.

"What's Lars doing?" Alfred said, noticing the other student kneeling next to the remains of the automobile in the distance.

"He's found part of a car," William said.

They came to the edge of the asphalt circle, which was, or had been, a parking lot of some kind. Right away Alfred noticed the spaces were a bit larger than those provided in most English parking lots, and were configured strangely. He examined the asphalt's edge and noted a smooth surface running deep into the turf. Joining the asphalt was the native chalky soil.

"Incredible," Alfred finally said. "There must be— Check the area for tire tracks. Something must have moved the bloody things!"

"We've already looked," Peter said. "There are none. And nothing short of an armada of Sikorskys would have lifted them out of here, and even then I don't think they could. Then there's this *pavement*. It's old and worn. If it were transported here intact, there would be cracks, but there are none! It's like it's been here for the last thirty years."

Alfred sent Peter and William off to start taping the site, reminding them to take in the barrows, ditches and heelstone for reference, then caught up with Lars at the wreck.

"What have we here?" Alfred said as he approached the car.

"Be careful. There's petrol all over the place."

The wreck appeared to be a small Subaru, sliced in half as if from a giant guillotine, its cut edge aligned with the end of the asphalt.

"The license plate says Oklahoma," Peter said. "That's in the United States."

"Indeed it is," Alfred said. Looking into the back seat, he found a few books on law, all American, a *Playboy* magazine, a spiral notebook. And an address book.

"This belongs to a man by the name of Rick Ordover," Alfred said, examining the front page. "Maybe we should give him a call. Would you kindly retrieve the cell phone from William?"

Peter fetched the cell phone, and Alfred deftly punched in the number, completing the call with assistance from an operator.

A strange sounding ring, then a muffled voice.

"Hello?"

"Good day," Alfred said. "Could I please speak with Rick Ordover?"

"Speaking."

"Mr. Ordover, my name is Dr. Alfred Mackie, with the College of Stokes in Wiltshire. That's Great Britain. Say, are you by any chance missing half of a Subaru Justy?"

There was a long pause before Rick finally replied, "Yes, I am. Where did . . . what did . . . Are you near Salisbury?"

"As a matter of fact, I am."

Another long pause. "You're looking for Stonehenge, aren't you?"

"Indeed we are. Do you know where it might be?"

"I know exactly where it is. At the corner of 41st and Yale. In Tulsa, Oklahoma."

"In a parking lot?"

"In a parking lot."

"Good heavens," Alfred exclaimed. "You don't know why it might happen to be there?"

"I haven't a clue. It happened during a lightning storm."

Alfred stared at the cell phone, at the asphalt circle, the severed car. *What* had happened during a lighting storm?

"I may be coming to the United States. Could I call on you?"

"Yeah, sure," said the American, slightly perplexed. "Say, are there law books in the back seat?"

"There are. Would you like me to bring them?"

"Yeah. They're not cheap. I'm a law student."

"I understand."

Once the surreal conversation was over, Alfred debated over who to call next. The boys were still milling about, now somewhat aimlessly, as if the strangeness of the situation was starting to numb them. If he called the authorities, or anyone else for that matter, they would surely not believe him. He took a brief excursion over the circular barrows, the oldest parts of the site, and found them as undisturbed as before, as were the fifty-six Aubrey holes along the inner perimeter, and the two small inner mounds. The heelstone and the "slaughter stone" were as they were before. He proceeded to a medium-sized burial mound to the southeast, explored the shallow ditch around it, finding nothing amiss. Everything about the site was absolutely normal—except for the missing trilithons.

He stood for a time at the burial mound, a smooth dome covered with a thin layer of grass. This was not a dark place, reeking of death and petrified bones, but a fount of information, the sum far greater than the individual souls composing it. His ancestors, some druids, some chiefs, some common folk, were laid to rest here for the purpose it was serving now: as a link to the otherworld. Here was the network of magical sites, the holy wells, the sacred trees, the multitude of other stone circles, all connected by hidden, prehistoric roads that had not quite been erased from the Earth. Some called them ley lines, but to Alfred and the Order, they were a communications network to the great spirits.

He reached along this network and in a flash saw what had happened to Stonehenge.

This is not the work of the sidhe, *but the work of the gods.*

The mound told him more: the moving of Stonehenge was not an anomaly, even in this modern world, but part of a larger plan started long ago. Before the Celts, before the Romans, even before the first mammoth-hunting humans wandered this portion of Europe. Alfred felt his insignificance stronger now than ever.

An eagle circled the sky, an unusual sight for the Salisbury plain. It kited momentarily, then swooped down for a gentle landing on the mound's peak. The bird regarded him in an unnerving way, as if Alfred were to soon become his meal; but Alfred knew this was no eagle, or any physical creature, of this realm.

I am Lugh, said the eagle, and a golden aura blazed

to life around it, emphasizing the fact. *There are too few of your kind left, druid. I thank you for attending.*

In the presence of the god of light, Alfred thought he should feel more awed than he did. Lugh had appeared to the Order in many forms, including the eagle, but this was the first time Alfred had encountered him alone.

The Foevors are intent on setting fire to the realms, Lugh said, shifting from one talon to the next, a decidedly eagle-like motion. *The Foevor Morca is their leader.*

Alfred replied, *I thought the Tuatha De Danaan defeated them aeons ago. Do they even exist?* He found himself easing into the mental dialog with little effort.

They exist. They are intent on conquering the underworld, and this realm. It has always been their desire. To rule, without question, without responsibility. Their arrogance was the weakness the Tuatha exploited before. Now, when most of the gods are sleeping, their arrogance has become one of their strengths.

Alfred hazarded a glance behind him. William was taping the site again, and the other two were going back to the car, perhaps to check on Stuart. They didn't appear to notice the eagle perched on the burial mound.

Their numbers are growing. And they have the advantage. The sleeping gods would never see them for what they are.

Alfred considered a more immediate issue. *Why did they take the stones?*

Lugh pondered this a moment. *It was part of a challenge. An alliance has been forged. By taking the stones they have disrupted the energies here, making many things difficult. They have the advantage now, but I seek to change that.*

Alfred asked, *It goes beyond the stones?*

Far beyond the stones. My son is in danger. You know my son, druid. You are part of his past, you are part of him. You helped make him what he is, you are what he is. He needs your help. I need your assistance, Cathad.

At the mention of his druid name, Alfred sensed a shift in the realms. A door opened, and he looked into a long forgotten room.

My son, The Hound, is an incarnated human. Go to the stones, and you will find him. Aid him. Fulfill your duties as a druid. Help him remember who he is.

Lugh uttered this last request with disturbing intensity.

Go to the continent in the west, and aid my son, Cu Chulainn.

Lugh leaped gracefully into the air, circled once, and flew to the north. In moments he was a tiny spot in the sky, then nothing at all. Alfred watched the bird vanish into the morning sky, and with its passing came a surge of *strength* not felt since youth.

It's good to be back in the game again.

Chapter Three

It just figures that the night something interesting happens, I have to close the store, Dobie thought as he poured water on the grill, let it boil, then scraped the scorched hamburger from its dulled steel surface. The radio next to the register blared the news of the mysterious appearance of "megaliths in Tulsa," and it sounded like everyone in the world was there to see it. Everyone, of course, except himself, who was stuck here closing the Mega Burger for the thousandth time.

At least I'm not straining the grease tonight.

The Mega Burger was one of the oldest fast-food joints in Tulsa, so dated it didn't even have a drive-thru window. It was one of those ancient derelicts with cluttered windows and tacky white and blue tile, with all of the hassle of a '50s style drive-in and none of the charm. But the Mega Burger was a minute's walk from his front door, which made up for quite a bit. Since graduating from high school two months earlier, he didn't feel compelled to go to college, which he couldn't afford anyway. He didn't feel like doing much of anything different; he had some money and a place to live, and right now that was all he really wanted. With his seven-finger deformity he should probably stay put, his thinking went. Until he was eighteen, anyway. He might not be able to find a job anywhere else.

He went through the motions of closing the store: mopping the floor, washing the milkshake machine, taking the trash out. The two other employees, a Hispanic kid who didn't speak much English, and his boss, a large round woman with greasy blond hair, drifted through their tasks, saying nothing, hardly looking at each other. This was how Dobie preferred it. He didn't like being looked at.

After work he would normally go home and catch some HBO or Cinemax on cable, but tonight was different. As soon as he heard about the mysterious megaliths at a closed down shopping mall he knew he had to go check it out. If he had stopped to think about how out of the ordinary the plan was, he might have changed his mind and gone home, to perhaps re-read *The Hobbit* for the hundredth time, or watch *Men in Black* for the eleventh. The idea of aliens living undetected among humans was one he thought about every day.

With barely a nod to his boss he clocked out and walked the short distance to his ramshackle house. On the front porch, which presided over a postage stamp-sized yard, was an old River Trails bike he'd picked up at a pawn shop for fifty bucks. It didn't occur to him to change out of the orange polyester Mega Burger shirt and ball cap. He was just going out to see something unusual, not to be around people.

The storm of the previous evening had cleaned the air, and brought down some coolness from the north. Peddling at a casual rate, Dobie first took the 23rd Street bridge, then crisscrossed over medians to the Riverparks bike trails. The river was high from the recent rains, he saw through the trees on his right. A full moon lit his way.

Chugging up, then coasting down an incline, Dobie found himself at the intersection of 41st and Yale, where cops directed slow-moving traffic with luminous orange cones. Cars lined up in all directions, bumper to bumper. *They must have come to see the megaliths.* At a Texaco, news crews with vans and satellite uplinks had set up shop. Two newsmen, one local, one from Oklahoma City, were talking into cameras under bright light. Dobie walked the bike across the four-laned intersection with a tight knot of pedestrians.

A huge crowd had gathered on this expansive, until now abandoned parking lot. Dobie remembered the day his mother had brought him here to buy school clothes for the seventh grade. It was one of the few times his mother had taken him out in public, which they usually avoided because of his hands.

The atmosphere here was carnival-like, though the crowd of people was strangely quiet. Four or five deep, they stood around the towering blocks of stone. A reporter was wandering through the crowd, asking questions. Dobie avoided her, and got back on the bike, peddling slowly through the sparse outer fringe of the crowd.

On a long expanse of sidewalk in front of the mall entrance, Dobie got off the bike. He took in the megaliths from this new vantage, and a chill of recognition took his breath away.

No one's saying it, but they might as well. This is Stonehenge.

He chained the bike to a gas meter against the wall; here he noticed the J.C. Penney had become something else, in fact looked like it was about open. The letters on the new sign were funky and gnarly, spelling out *Lazerwarz.* He'd heard about this place. It was a laser tag arena. Something Tulsa, or Dobie, had never seen before. Hanging across the glass foyer was a banner that read GRAND OPENING, JULY 19TH. That was tomorrow.

He cupped his hands around his eyes and looked in. A vending machine cast a dim light, revealing little of the interior. He made out a counter, a sign that said "Stage One Pay Here," and the faint glow of a computer screen somewhere off in the back.

Someone was in there. Dobie watched the silent, ghostly figure move out of sight, past the counter and vending machine. It paused to look back at him. It had no face.

Shaken, he stepped away from the glass, noticed the crowd's reflection cast in it. *That's what it was. Someone walking around out here.* Still, he moved further away from the store front. He might set off an alarm or something. Someone, or something, might see him, if it hadn't already.

Time to get a closer look at these stones. Now he worked his way through the crowd, an amoeba of humanity struck dumb, except for the few furtive whispers of "Stonehenge," or "UFOs" or "It's gotta be a fake." Standing among this many people would normally intimidate the hell out of him, but tonight something was different. It reminded him of the final scenes of *Close Encounters,* when the giant UFO came down and landed, and everyone was standing around it in amazement.

Closer to the stones a handful of police milled about like security at a rock concert. Three separate strands of yellow police tape fenced in the site where the black asphalt became white, chalky soil. People were moving right up against it, to get a better view. The cops' expressions were grim, like pallbearers at a funeral.

Dobie could not understand why. Standing amid the stones under the full moon was supposed to be a joyous event. He just knew it. The moon lined up with one of the stones, and if he moved a little to the right, it lined up with two. It was the purpose of the stones, to bring people together and show them the heavens. He didn't know how he knew that, he just did.

Headlights shone briefly from behind; Dobie turned to see a red Corvette convertible ease casually into view, its lone occupant regarding the gathering of people with mild interest. She was a beautiful redhead, with a glittering crimson evening dress, looking for all the world like a movie star.

And she was staring straight at him.

Trying to be nonchalant, Dobie attempted to avert his gaze, but found he could not. Their eyes had locked, and he was certain this was no accident, that she was trying, and succeeding in getting his attention. *Me? Why? There must be a mistake.*

But apparently there was no mistake; with a single crooked finger, she was gesturing him over to the car.

Gleefully, Morrigan admired her handiwork on the bank of monitors in the Lazerwarz control center. Video cameras covered every square inch of the premises and a good part of the parking lot in front, giving her a complete view of the situation.

Why did Mort object so violently to this? No one was even looking at the arena, and the media had made no mention of Lazerwarz. *All they care about are the rocks!*

From the main control center, amid the security monitors and Compaq file servers, she was indeed a goddess, ruler of all she surveyed. Mort had left her alone to gloat over Stonehenge, to go do whatever Mort did in his Underhill palace. She hoped he would fix those silly horns of his; they had begun to spiral from his forehead like a bizarre headdress.

The human race still behaves like ignorant cattle, she noted in the monitors. Something that could not be explained by their finite science had attracted this vast audience. *Mort really needn't concern himself with secrecy so.*

As a young human walked in front of one of the cameras, she did a double take. He looked familiar, but how could he be? Was the Seleighe Court looking into their project already? She zoomed the camera in and framed the youth, who was chaining a bike to a fixture just outside the arena. *No elf could handle cold iron like that.* She relaxed, but only a little. Mort had tweaked these cameras to detect any magical beings; a blazing white aura appeared around the youth.

If not of a god, then of a god's offspring. But . . . among humans? That had happened long ago, when the Tuatha were themselves above ground and fighting for their right to stay there. Since the *sidhe* went Underhill, and the realms had split between matter and spirit, the gods had not bothered much with the humans.

Perhaps a reincarnation. Yes, that just might be it.

Whatever the spiritual heritage of this human meatball, she needed to investigate it. His presence here, at this time, would not, *could* not be a coincidence. And the more she learned about him before Mort did, the better.

Morrigan took the exit down to the stairwell, paused to cast some temporary concealment for herself, and entered the main front lobby. He was standing just outside, now looking at the arena.

I know who he is! she exclaimed to herself. *That signature in his aura, it is not just any god's, it belongs to Lugh, the god of light. Yet this is not Lugh . . . this is one of his sons. Which one?*

Taken by surprise, the concealing magics slipped, and the youth saw her, if only briefly. Cursing herself for her carelessness she retreated into the service hallway, hoping she hadn't frightened him off.

In her chariot called a Corvette, Morrigan drove around to the front of the mall. She had first seen the Corvette as a hindrance, a human trapping that she could just as easily have done without. Now it was an asset: the men of this world seemed drawn to it, almost as much as they were to her. All the better to entice the youth, who had only gone to inspect the stones closer. His aura was no less brilliant now than on the monitors, and here, sharing the same space with him, his presence was more tangible.

This can only be Cu Chulainn, The Hound of Ulster!

The humans didn't notice the divine presence among them, but then the humans saw little to begin with. And something else, too: the youth, in this human incarnation, *was a virgin*!

She would have never believed it if someone had told her. As she spied him from a discreet distance, she became more convinced that the lad had no idea of his real identity. During various incarnations it sometimes happened that gods and their by-blows lost touch with their souls, and forgot their glorious pasts. Memories did not always follow their owners, and when they did they might be hidden, to be discovered later as the human organism grew and developed. And this human organism, this mere *youth*, had much growing to do.

These immediate findings did not discourage her.

Dormant powers can be awakened.

In Cu Chulainn, The Hound of Ulster, there was much power to awake.

Before the beginning of time, when matter and spirit were one, Morrigan consorted with Cu Chulainn's grandfather, Dagda, the god of goodness. From their union sparked a line of gods and goddesses who later, inevitably, turned upon each other. The Foevorians were one of these races, though explaining this to Mort would be pointless; the little Foevor would never admit that anything existed before his race did. She remembered Lugh Long Hand, Dagda's son, as being boisterous and generous, but lacking in ambition to rule and control. Lugh had wanted a human son, and seduced a human maiden, Dechtire. Their union produced Cu Chulainn.

Morrigan first heard of the youth while spying on the druids' ceremonies. Establishing a link into such festivities from Underhill took little power, as the druids raised most of it themselves. And they loved to hear themselves talk. They spoke of an amazing youth, barely old enough to father children, who had become the Champion of Ulster. The boy had fought an entire army with barely a scratch to himself.

The art of war had for some time enjoyed Morrigan's patronage, and war was a frequent occurrence in these primitive human lands. They were great sport to watch, particularly when she intervened on the behalf of one side or another, depending on whatever obeisance, or lack of, the armies paid her. Their worship gave her power, and she reinvested it in the army of her choice. Thus the cycle repeated, sometimes precariously; her influence was not a guarantee of victory.

If what the druids said were true, The Hound's appearance threatened this delicate balance, and she decided that such a warlike lad should have some personal, intimate knowledge of the patron god of war. She studied the landscape of Ulster from afar, and when she finally laid eyes on him, the notion of gods frolicking with humans, or half-humans, was not so disgusting anymore.

On the day she had chosen to meet the young Cu Chulainn, she found herself glowing with the first flush of youth. Until now she had favored war, death and slaughter, without much attention to the life-renewing pleasures of love. Cu Chulainn had changed that; she intended to give him what every warrior desired, a woman by his side . . . if only for an evening.

She wore a long red dress, and a red cloak which billowed behind her as she rode her chariot. Satisfied that she looked her very best, she called to Cu Chulainn with her loudest voice, as she knew he was sleeping soundly after a series of battles. Cu Chulainn appeared armed for battle on chariot, led by his charioteer; confronted with a maiden, he seemed at a complete loss for what to do next.

He called out, "Who is this maiden in red who has come calling on the Champion of Ulster?"

He does not know I am a goddess, she thought. *All the better.*

"I am the daughter of King Aranrod, of a far-off land," she said, making up the fiction as she went. It would not do to frighten the lad with her true identity. *Let him think I am a princess instead.* "I have come to meet the warrior who has made such a name for himself," Morrigan called. She knew of no warrior who would resist such flattery.

But the youth was not moved. "I know of no King Aranrod, and if it is a far-off land what is its name?"

"It doesn't matter the name of the land," Morrigan continued. "It is *I* who seek you, not my people . . . and I wish to become acquainted with the mighty Cu Chulainn."

His expression was unreadable. Morrigan's patience grew short. *Time to drop a few hints as to my identity.* "It is a land with no sun, far below. The druids know of this land, but they speak little of it."

"You speak in riddles!" Cu Chulainn shouted. "Who are you and state your business!"

My, but the lad is dense, Morrigan thought, sending a touch of magic his way, in an attempt to stir up his lust and get directly to the point. "I have come from the land of the spirits to find the Champion of Ulster, for I have fallen in love with him!"

She sent this last plea with a push directly to the root of his loins, but the son of Lugh seemed to deflect her intentions with ease.

He certainly isn't aroused. He's . . . angered?

"I do not have the time to make idle talk with every maiden who finds me desirable!" replied the Champion.

"You really don't know who I am, do you?" spat

Morrigan. "Who is it who watches over you in battle, who protects you and aids you?"

"It is no woman who aids me!" shouted Cu Chulainn. He seemed ready to charge. "And I don't need your protection, or whatever favors you seem willing to trade."

That did it.

"You young fool! How dare you insult the goddess of war! If you will not accept my love and assistance, then you will have my wrath!"

Just as Cu Chulainn was about to charge, Morrigan made her chariot vanish, then turned into a large black crow, one of her favorite otherworld forms. The bird circled about the Champion twice while he waved his sword ineffectually at it, then flew off with an indignant squawk.

Beyond a vast ocean, a continent away and many centuries later, Morrigan looked upon the youthful yet wimpy incarnation of Cu Chulainn in the orange polyester Mega Burger shirt, feeling like an eagle ready to pounce on a field mouse. Since he hadn't gotten a good look at her yet she was free to make herself into whatever she wished. *Let's see, what erotic fantasies has the young man indulged in lately . . .* His mind was utterly unshielded. As she reached surreptitiously into his soul, she entered a gallery of his recent memories, none of them betraying his divine origins. But Lugh's fire was there, deep down and undisturbed. For the time being she would leave *that* part of him alone.

She found what she sought. An actress, seen in a recent movie. *How quaint, and sad. Not even someone he would have the slightest chance of bedding. The youth must be desperate for love. I shall oblige him, certainly. Then, after I have wrung every last bit of physical pleasure I can from him, he will know a goddess' wrath!*

As her eyes met his, she motioned for him to come over to the car.

✧ ✧ ✧

Dobie approached the convertible cautiously, suddenly aware of a pleasant fluttering in his stomach. The woman was an absolute knockout, small and slender, with a striking likeness of Sandra Bullock; he'd seen *Speed* and *Speed 2* the week before, and had fantasized about her more than once. The Corvette didn't much interest him, but it was attracting attention from the men in the crowd, and here he was, being summoned to it right in front of them. He felt an unfamiliar rush of male pride.

But what could she possibly want with me? His mind raced. By the time he reached the car, he'd decided she was looking for directions for someplace far more interesting than here, to be with someone far more worthy than himself.

"Hi," Dobie said, his male ego withering now that he had to actually talk to her and not sound like a chump. It seemed an impossible task. When his hands didn't get him into trouble, his mouth always did.

She didn't say anything, first regarding him with an appraising expression, her eyes tracked from his face down, hesitating midway before proceeding to his feet. When the inspection was over, she smiled, and Dobie did a double take.

Is this Sandra Bullock after all?

No, it could not be, not in a million years. They stood gazing at each other awkwardly. Conversation, about anything, would be a welcomed miracle.

Then the miracle occurred. "Saw you checking out the arena over there," she said, nodding towards the Lazerwarz glass doors. "Do you . . . play?"

"Um. It's not open . . . yet," he said, feeling foolish.

"There are other arenas," she said, as if it was something he should have known anyway. "It's really a wonderful invention. It came from . . . Under . . . *England,* some time back."

"Cool." Having blurted the first few words in a tentative conversation, Dobie started to relax.

"Would you like to see it?" To his confused look, she added, "The *arena*. I'm the district manager. Come *on*. Hop in. I'll give you a tour."

The passenger door opened, by itself. *She must have a latch somewhere. New cars and all . . .*

As he climbed in, whistles and whoops of appreciation rose from the guys in the crowd. Dobie felt his ears burning. She didn't seem to notice.

"As you can see from the banners, we open tomorrow," she said conversationally as she sped the Corvette expertly around to the back of the mall, to a large garage door which opened automatically. In an enormous loading bay, fluorescent lights flickered on, and she pulled the car to a stop.

"My name is Morgan," she said as her hand closed around his on the seat. "Don't be shy. You really are quite cute."

Dobie didn't know what he liked most, the part about being cute, or the fact that she didn't even comment on his seven fingers, which she could not have missed when she clasped it. His hands had felt like enormous, awkward clubs, but caressed by her delicate one, they felt normal for the first time in his life. Her hand lingered there, then traced a curve over his palm. She held it up, as if reading it.

"You will be glorious in this life," she said, then giggled at his heightened confusion. In explanation, she added, "I studied palmistry in college."

He sat there, staring at her, wondering for the first time if she was playing him for a fool.

"What does palmistry have to say about seven fingers?" he asked, and he regretted how cross it must have sounded coming out.

She shrugged vaguely, and brought his fingers to her face, holding them against her cheek, and his big, clunky seven fingered hand felt like a silken, feather pillow. Then, taking his index finger into her mouth, she sucked on it, expertly lapping her tongue around his knuckles.

Dobie's gulp echoed in the loading bay.

She released the finger, winking as she said, "Well, you know what they say about men with seven fingers." Morgan opened her door and got out. "Let me show you the arena. Then we'll go for a drive."

He was more interested in going for that drive now, before considering what a tour of the arena might involve. As he followed her lithe, curvy, incredibly *sexy* body into a dimly lit hallway, he also wondered *who* said *what* about men with seven fingers. It sounded like something he should know.

At the hallway's end he found himself in the front lobby he had been spying on only a few minutes before. The lighting rose subtly as they entered, and Dobie figured everything, from the Corvette's passenger door to the lights, was on a big omniscient computer that could see everything they did. On the walls were airbrushed murals of scenes from a fantasy land. The smell of new paint was overpowering, and the place had that brand-new, never before inhabited feel.

"The arena is in here," she said, entering another door, which had been decorated with bits of junk and metal, circuit boards and a big valve handle, giving the impression of an entrance to a spaceship. In the darkness, black lights cast a purple glow on orange fluorescent. Lined up on racks along the walls were numerous futuristic vests, each with a holstered ray gun.

"We can run up to ninety players in a game," she explained.

She held up a small black object, that was either a VCR remote or a cell phone. "With this I can run the computer and set up a round."

"How do you play?" he asked, intrigued.

"I'll show you," she said, lifting one of the vests off the rack. He felt her warmth, and her breath against his face, as she lowered the vest over him. "I'll activate a game."

She did something to the VCR remote thing and a panel against the wall flashed to life. Red, blue and yellow lights on the vests blinked and flashed in unison. Morgan put a vest on, pulled the gun out and checked something over the grip where the hammer on a revolver would be. Dobie glanced at his and found a tiny computer screen with a full color graphic that said *Lazerwarz.*

"My pack is in test mode," she said, firing the gun at him. A ruby-red line of light discharged from the barrel's end, with a loud ray gun report straight out of *Terminator*. "You can fire as many times as you like. When I hit a target on your vest, I score points."

"Do you ever die in the game?"

The severe look she gave him turned his blood to ice. "*You* never die."

Dobie pulled the somewhat bulky gun from the holster, finding it rather light. It had a good feel to it; his hand fit the contours of the grip perfectly, as if it were made specifically for him. The game hadn't started yet, but already he was feeling a change come over him, a rather exuberant, aggressive feel. He wanted to kick ass. While attempting football in school, he had seen the same change in others, but never in himself; he was lousy at sports. *Is this a sport I can actually be good at?*

Morgan was eying him in that exhilarating if disconcerting way, as if she knew what he was experiencing.

"You just gained about three inches in height," she said, and he realized he was standing up, straight up, proudly. "Now let me show you the arena."

Dobie looked around him. "This isn't it?"

"Don't be silly," she said, and another smaller garage door rolled up on his left. "*This* is the arena."

His first impression was that of great space, though he couldn't see very far through a thick, soupy mist. Dissonant techno music *thump thump thump*ed through the gloom, and he found himself on the outskirts of a vast maze. Hallways and tunnels branched off in every direction at wild, chaotic angles, and deeper in the maze was an upper level looking down on the first. It would have been impossible to see without the array of black lights spaced randomly throughout the interior; patterns and whirls painted in orange and pink fluorescent paint blinked back, giving some sense of distance.

Wordlessly Morgan walked into the mist and vanished.

A moment later, a beam of laser shot from the mist, tagging his main chest target; his pack made a horrible dying sound, then went dark. A moment later, it came back up.

"What are you waiting for?" he heard her say from the mist.

Somewhat humiliated, he fired back, but she had already moved. Now he was getting the idea. Feeling a bit like a commando he ventured into the maze, gun forward, then caught a glimpse of red-blue-yellow target lights ducking behind a wall. Over the weird electronic music he heard her stiletto pumps clicking through the maze.

Then, through a hole in one of the walls, he saw her targets, and fired. Her pack squawked and went down.

"Touché!" she shouted. He moved back, but too late, the second she was back up she tagged his shoulder targets. The game of hide and seek went on like that, tagging back and forth as they moved throughout the lower level. Dobie began to see how big the arena was, and they hadn't even found the way to the upper level yet. At least half the mall had been transformed into this strange and darkened netherworld. Then Dobie's confidence soared. After all, she was in heels. He had the advantage.

And she thinks I'm cute.

Then suddenly, the game was over. The pack went down, and stayed dark, while a cluster of white strobe lights flashed high on the wall over the entrance.

"Not bad for a first game," she said, suddenly beside him. Her abrupt appearance startled him. *How can she move like that in those shoes? Or in anything. I didn't even see her.* "Now. How about that drive?"

Morgan looked absolutely glorious with her hair in the wind, Dobie observed when he could pry his eyes away from the oncoming road, which was rushing under them at a terrifying rate of speed. He regretted not buckling in, and if he did now he would only look like a wimp. She seemed completely unalarmed at their speed, which reached 100 mph and more, or by the relatively slow-moving traffic, which had become a slalom course. Conversation was impossible; he could hardly hear himself think over the wind and the roar of the Corvette's V8.

The wind was making his eyes water. Through the lens of his tears Morgan's outline morphed into an old warty hag, something that would ride a broom on a cheap Halloween door decoration. He wiped his eyes, and saw the Morgan he wanted to see, and now wanted. His erection, trapped in an uncomfortable knot of cotton underwear and pubic hair, strained for release.

The strangeness of the situation weighed heavily on him as the Corvette's nose pierced the hot, humid night. Indignant honks, Disppering behind them, saluted their passage. The other motorists were all lesser beings now, bugs to be squashed underfoot . . . Morgan's foot. Dobie had never felt this way before, a ruler in the kingdom of darkness, in a glorious red chariot with a lovely maiden at the helm. Life was suddenly much better than it had been just a few short hours before.

Who is this creature, who came charging into my life without warning? A tiny voice in the back of his mind told him that to ask too many questions might be a mistake, might break the delicate spell a benevolent witch had cast on his existence. Speeding through the evening seemed like fun for the sake of itself, and until they pulled up in front of the expensive Doubletree Hotel he hadn't seriously thought they had a destination. A valet appeared from nowhere and whisked the Corvette away. Dobie's jaw dropped when he saw her tip him a hundred dollar bill.

He thought they might have attracted more attention. A cheesy teenaged kid in a fast-food uniform and a gorgeous woman, dressed to kill. *Hell, they probably figure me for her little brother.* But no one seemed to see them. The walls and columns were either gold, chrome, or mirrored, and a vast landscape of carefully nurtured philodendrons and lilies, mulched with cedar, cascaded around them. They moved though the cold, air-conditioned lobby as if they owned it. A glass elevator injected them into a world Dobie had never seen before, a land where only the wealthy and privileged dared to enter. She opened two enormous, solid wood doors on a suite.

"Make yourself comfortable," she said, as she flipped on a light.

An expensively decorated living room invited them in, and the heavy wooden doors closed behind them like a palace gate. A balcony overlooked downtown Tulsa, the night skyline looking like that of Los Angeles or New York to Dobie's unworldly eye. For the first time in his life, Dobie felt kind of glamorous.

"Would you like a drink?" Morgan said, and poured two glasses of whiskey from a lead crystal decanter at a bar in one corner.

"Yeah, sure," he said nervously, now suddenly aware that he reeked of onions and pine cleaner and sweat. Morgan handed him two fingers of Jack Daniels in a tumbler. The whiskey had a bite he was more or less expecting; he managed to get it down without asphyxiating.

"We're going to have sex, you know," she said over the edge of the glass. "Would you like that?"

Dobie nearly dropped the tumbler. He nodded, and stammered out, "Yeah, uh, can I like, uh, take a shower?"

"Suit yourself," she said, with a smile. "Don't bother getting dressed when you're through."

Their eyes locked, and Dobie saw that indeed, this was not a dream, he was actually going to get laid by a wealthy, gorgeous woman driving a sports car. Any doubt to the contrary evaporated in the pungent fumes of Jack Daniels. He turned towards the bathroom as a smile threatened to rip his face apart. About five seconds later he emerged, scrubbed pink with Neutrogena bar soap. As per instructions, he left his Mega Burger uniform on the floor, but had to at least wear a towel around his waist. All the while he was astounded at his sudden fortune. Having seven fingers on each hand had never worked out for him like this before.

Morgan was nowhere to be seen in the suite, but from an open door near the bar flowed soothing harp music . . . and the scent of an exotic incense.

"In here," he heard Morgan call from the bedroom.

The incense was much stronger now as he stood in the bedroom doorway. A completely naked Morgan sat up in a bed the size of Texas, her red hair cascading around her shoulders but not *quite* concealing her marvelous, rounded breasts. She patted the empty space on the bed next to her. "I saved you a spot," she said.

The towel fell from Dobie's waist, but did not fall to the floor.

Chapter Four

The ride in the oversized Chevy Caprice brought back memories of Dallas, where King Aedham had grown up disguised as a human. *Was it really that long ago?* he wondered, watching Tulsa's late afternoon traffic go by as Sammi drove. *I was only eighteen summers when fate dropped the responsibility of Avalon on my shoulders.* When Avalon fell he knew precisely who the enemy was (Zeldan Dhu) and what the enemy wanted (his head on a stick). Once he had identified the problem it had become a matter of gathering the resources, and the courage, to defeat the Unseleighe.

Avalon's rebuilding had been much more difficult. Still, with the help of neighboring elfhames he reconstructed the palace in the fork of two mighty rivers, kenning the hardest granite possible for its construction. Aedham's teacher, Marbann, had embarked on a diplomatic campaign to reestablish ties with the other elfhames near and far. If they had to face an Unseleighe threat again, they would do so in an impenetrable fortress and a united Seleighe front.

Now the situation was not so well defined. He and Sammi were against an unidentified *something* which was probably more powerful than all the Unseleighe combined, and the threat to Underhill, if any, was unknown.

If we only knew what this was before walking into it!

The elven King remembered how to be a human . . . and a part of him would remain human. For this mission they had reassumed their human names, and had worn their casual clothing, jeans and T-shirts, so as not to attract attention. The glamories they wore to conceal their elven features would easily fool humans, but might not pass inspection by an expert, such as an Unseleighe Mage.

Sammi would never have asked for help unless she was certain she was in over her head. When Adam saw the stones towering in the shopping mall parking lot, he wondered if they were *both* in over their heads.

"The crowds have thinned somewhat," Sammi observed, and began looking for a parking space. "But the interest is still there."

Cops had cordoned off a large portion of the lot to isolate the stones, but since the mall was mostly unoccupied there was plenty of parking. A crowd of bystanders lingered around the Henge while official academic types took pictures, measurements, and soil samples.

It was the same scene Adam witnessed earlier on cable TV from Sammi's room, where he'd gone to recover from the gating, which had for reasons unknown been harsher to the senses than usual. On CNN the British government had confirmed that Stonehenge had indeed been inexplicably stolen, but had stopped short of accusing the United States of the theft. News agencies had speculated openly that the stones which had appeared here were one and the same. The Mayor of Tulsa, Susan Savage, had issued a statement that the incident was still under investigation. The owners of the property insisted they had nothing to do with it, and pointed out the publicity, not to mention the stones themselves, would get in the way of planned-for development. The Lazerwarz manager denied any involvement as well, in spite of heated accusations that the timing was suspicious. The Henge had appeared two days before the arena was about to open.

Meanwhile caravans of New Age groups, UFOlogists, psychics, fundamentalist preachers, anyone with an axe to grind, a statement to make, or a view to air in the international media were en route to what was once a quiet, mid-sized, Midwest city.

It's going to get really weird around here, Adam thought as he took in the scene. *Or weirder.* It made less sense now than it did before—the stones were directly in front of the arena. *Why attract so much attention, and a horde of bizarre human tribes, to their base of operations?*

"Let's swing by the stones," Adam said as he shut the Caprice's door. "Everyone else is. Let's blend in."

On their way to the site Sammi regarded the arena with calm detachment. Then her face registered recognition; she turned to Adam. "Just like the rest of the Lazerwarz arenas. Security cameras everywhere."

Adam saw at least five cameras mounted on the eaves and walls of the large concrete structure. Pseudo-Greek columns adorned the front walk, where hedges had been recently chopped into shape. Multicolored tile formed a rough approximation of a landscape across the facade. The only indication that this was no longer a '70s vintage department store was the large purple and yellow neon sign which spelled out *Lazerwarz*.

"I wonder how many kids are going to disappear in that place," she said sadly. Her pessimistic outlook surprised Adam. *She's already counting the victims, and the place has been open for only a few hours.*

"None, if we can help it," he said resolutely. They had come to inspect the arena first hand, to probe for and, if detected, stop whatever was stealing the children. Also, it was part of their duty as the *sidhe* to maintain Underhill's secrecy, and the King was painfully aware that his activities among the humans had blown Avalon's cover more than once. Perhaps they could accomplish both goals today; the notion seemed reasonable in Underhill, but now Adam wondered if they were being too optimistic of their abilities, or of their luck.

They drew closer to the crowd at the stones, where a shrill middle-aged woman was talking to a police officer. "So is this Stonehenge or isn't it?" she demanded. In the intense summer heat the officer was sweating profusely, and had a look of extreme irritation. He simply shrugged.

"They're going to be hearing a lot of that," Sammi observed. "I wonder what kind of evidence they would need."

"And who is going to make the announcement," Adam pointed out. "Jurisdiction may be a bit tricky."

Parked at the site were police cars, vans from neighboring universities, and an uplink truck from CNN. The off-camera reporter was withering under the heat, taking surreptitious sips from a cold beer. The crew was panning across the site and the assembled crowd.

"Time to see the arena," Adam said, "Too much scrutiny here."

"Did you come up with a code name yet?"

"Yeah, I was thinking something like, 'Elf.' "

Sammi gave him a sour look. "Maybe something less obvious?"

"Oh, all right. How about, 'Dallas'?"

"Better."

A banner announcing the "Grand Opening" had wilted over the glass doors. A young kid in a purple Lazerwarz shirt handed out pink passes as people entered.

"A free pass," Sammi said, taking hers. "The Bureau gave me several."

"We might need them," Adam said, glancing sideways at the kid, a plump teenager with no magical traces about him whatsoever. An icy blast of cold air nearly knocked them over when he opened the glass doors; inside lighting was subdued, but elven eyes adjust quickly to darkness.

"This is it," Sammi said. "Looks pretty much like the other arenas." The lobby, seething with young humanity, reminded him of the arcade in the West End Marketplace, but was darker, cooler, and louder. An airbrushed alien landscape incorporating Tulsa's skyline covered the walls, and in one corner was a big screen TV showing a demo of the game. An island of benches spray painted with fake granite faintly resembled the Henge outside. All around the lobby were riveted metal panels, airplane parts and industrial junk, either painted, polished, or wired with a blanket of flashing LED lights. Behind the main counter a severe-looking youth gazed into a computer screen.

"Wonder where the manager is," Adam said, noticing the assistant manager's name tag on the kid behind the screen. Knowing who was operating the place, even if they were fronting for someone else, might offer clues to whoever was behind it.

The teenaged clientele buzzed about with unrestrained enthusiasm, biding time at shoot'em-up arcade games, a pool table or a big air hockey table in the back. Adam had thought the hairstyles in Dallas were weird, but that was five years ago, and trends among youth changed quickly. Now it wasn't the color of hair but the lack of it: near-baldness seemed to be in now. And the last time he had seen this much metal in someone's face was in a torture chamber.

"I'm afraid I see a problem with our cover already," Sammi whispered under her breath as they took a place in the short line in front of the counter.

"Maybe if I shoved a bronze nail through my nose?"

"No, that wouldn't do . . ."

"A silver one? Through the eyebrow?" He wasn't joking. His suggestions were tame compared to what he saw walking around.

"Don't be silly. The few grown-ups I see here are with their kids."

Adam saw that she was right. "I don't look *that* old, do I?"

"Maybe if you shaved your head . . ."

"No, no. And no. *That* is where I draw the line." He pulled out a wallet and began fumbling for his human currency.

"Don't worry. I think we'll pass. And put that away. I've got passes."

They stepped up to the counter. The kid didn't look up from the screen.

"Code name?" the boy asked.

"Dallas," Adam replied, feeling vaguely silly, and not knowing exactly why. Sammi signed up with her code name of "Isis." For their passes they received an electronic tag, and instructions to wait for the "gamma" game, which would start momentarily.

Meanwhile they used the time to explore. A hallway in the back led to two restrooms and a door with a sign, "Employees Only." If anything was going on back there, Adam could not sense it, and short of opening it he saw no other way to investigate. *Best not to push our luck right away.*

Over the PA a loud voice said, "Good evening and welcome to Lazerwarz. If you are holding a gamma game key, line up at station door. Your judge will be with you in a moment."

Half of the crowd in the lobby surged toward a conspicuous door that looked like a submarine hatch.

"Here goes," Adam said to his sister, as a sudden wave of apprehension seized him.

✧ ✧ ✧

In the Lazerwarz control center, Mort stared in disbelief at the monitors.

What in the seven bloody hells is King Aedham Tuiereann doing here?

Not just Tuiereann, either; his sister had come with him. Mort first spied them at the standing stones, pretending to be humans, yet failing to conceal their auras. The King's shone like a bonfire on a moonless night, while hers, though detectable over his magically tweaked video system, was hardly noticeable. The glamories weren't all that good either; even on video Mort saw the occasional appearance of a pointed ear, flickering like a badly tuned TV channel. Of course the arrival of Stonehenge had broadcast a blast of node energy to the far corners of this continent like a nuclear detonation. That emissaries from Underhill would arrive to meddle was no surprise, but the King of Avalon?

Avalon always had a soft spot for the humans. Then his thoughts darkened, considering. *Especially for the children. Have they come to investigate the stones or the arena?*

Or both?

Whatever their motives for the visit, it could not be tolerated.

He turned to a panel on the control board, made a few queries on the server, and saw that the Gate function was ready to go. He preferred not to start harvesting until well after the first day of business, but this was no harvest, it was a quick fix for something that should never have happened.

By a partner I should never have made an alliance with!

He spoke briefly into the radio headset to Yuaroh Dhu. "We have a situation. Notify the kingdom they will be receiving a very special gift."

Then he shouted an order to the slave boy Alan standing at his elbow. "Pennzoil! 20-50. Straight up. *Now!*"

✧ ✧ ✧

The "judge," a young guy in a flashing Lazerwarz pack who looked to be about fifteen and stood under five feet, ushered them into a dark room illuminated with black light and glowing fluorescent paint.

Appearance was the only thing small about the judge, though. When he opened his mouth to speak, Adam thought he was talking over a PA turned up way too high. But he wasn't; his voice was naturally loud, instantly stopping conversation and seizing the attention of everyone present.

"Gooood evening! My name is Space Demon, and I will be your judge this game . . . !"

In a well-rehearsed and lively speech he explained the vest's features, where the targets were, how to fire the gun, what the screen on the back meant. It was a fairly simple point-and-shoot affair, and the small display kept the player abreast of who was winning the game, and who was not.

"Now, we will go into the station," Space Demon continued, and let them into another darkened room with vests lined up on the walls. A group of apparently experienced players began suiting up in vests. Adam and Sammi followed, activating the gun with the electronic tag. The vests lit up, and an ominous beep sounded from each gun as a large metal door rolled up, and a waft of misty fog drifted in and started pooling around their feet.

Players began filing into the arena, and when Adam saw how big it was, took Sammi aside. "We should split up if we're going to cover this whole place."

She looked doubtful. "Are you sure?"

Adam wasn't, but considered the time factor. The sooner they knew what this place consisted of, the sooner they would prevent it from swallowing up more kids. "Yes. You go left. I'll go right."

Sammi didn't argue, but looked like she wanted to. "Meet you back here when the game's over."

Space Demon took their tags as they entered, and

Adam made a sharp right into a dim, misty world that reminded him uncomfortably of Underhill in some of its darker, less formed areas. Techno music thundered from unseen speakers, reaching deep into his diaphragm, thumping away. Conscious of the countdown beeping away from his rig, he opened up his mage sight and sent it forward, probing the darkness where his eyes couldn't see. Nothing suspicious, so far.

The countdown ended, and Adam guessed from the explosion of laser blasts throughout the arena that the game had officially started. Even though this was a search for evil forces first, and entertainment second, he didn't want to come out too badly on the score sheet. *Besides. I have to blend in. If I walk around without shooting anything it would look odd.*

He intuitively stayed near the outskirts of the arena, zig-zagging through surreal hallways until he heard a blast overhead, and his pack went down. On the level above, peering down through a metal grate, a ten-year-old grinned triumphantly.

He fired back, but the kid danced just out of range. Adam proceeded under the level, looking for another grate to shoot through, but found something better: a ramp leading up. He followed this until he passed an opening, and beyond the wire mesh covering it was a lively battle. It was dark in here, which only emphasized the blue-red-yellow targets on the vests.

He shot one, then two, and with extreme pleasure watched the packs turn dark, then return with a minimum of lights. *Score.* The display on his gun told him he was 17th, and even *he* knew this was pretty pathetic.

The two he'd hit fired back, and killed his vest, which emitted a painful, electronic wail as it faded to black. Adam proceeded up the ramp, followed it left, then left again, taking him to the second level of the arena. He saw from the intense laser fire criss-crossing like spider webbing that this was where the real action was.

I am not going to rank 17th to a bunch of human kids!

Never mind that the human kids clearly had more experience at this than he did, he was an *elf*, and could see better than any of them. In a niche in the upper level, isolated from the main portion, Adam found a good location to shoot from. At shoulder level was a circular hole, giving him a good view as well as good cover. Firing into the battle, he tagged the lights on someone's gun, deactivating the pack, then peered around the left wall, where three players were in the middle of a free-for-all. They didn't notice him until he had tagged all three. Now slightly wiser, Adam pulled back into his protected position. They didn't seem to know who'd hit them.

Shooting through the hole again, he tagged the other player, who looked around in futility for the culprit. In the darkness, with his lights behind a partition, he was invisible. Adam caught himself smiling.

On his gun, the screen told him he was tenth. *Better.*

A stampede sounded from the level below, and a cluster of lights surged up the ramp. Adam turned the gun loose on the group, blotting out the vests, one by one. Finally one of them looked up, shouted, "He's up there," and the seven or eight of them started running the remaining leg of the ramp.

They must have known exactly where he was, Adam surmised, since moments later they had swarmed around him like flies, knee high little munchkins jumping up and down and plinking out his targets, over and over. While one of them poked him repeatedly in his unprotected groin with the gun muzzle, the rest barbecued his elven butt in the cross-fire, giving him no chance for his pack to recover.

Hey! What is this shit! Adam thought, looking for an escape, and finding himself cornered instead. He began to reconsider his race's deep reverence for the lives of children.

"*Hey over there, break up that team!*" shouted the voice of God, but it was only the judge Space Demon shining a flashlight into the brouhaha. "Or I'll take you out of the game!" Like roaches with the light turned on, the swarm evaporated into the darkened nooks and crannies of the arena.

Once they were all gone, Adam's pack came back up. *Great.*

"Feel free to go after them," Space Demon said as he walked off, apparently in search of more vermin.

Don't mind if I do, Adam thought, following the pitter patter of fleeing footsteps.

He pursued them back to the ground level, tracking them easily by the sound, and when three came into view their backs were to him. *Target acquired.* He picked the three of them off, two with one shot, being in line with his sight. *Sweet revenge.* When they saw who was after them, they squawked and scampered ahead, looking for cover. There was none. He tagged them again the second they had their vests back. They jumped with each shot, as if the vests were zapping them with an electrical shock. *I can only wish.* Intent on escape, the munchkins took off at a dead run. Adam was laughing too hard to keep up with them.

He ventured a glance as his ranking. *Hmmm. Fifth. Spite can be productive.*

As soon as the retreating footsteps faded away, Adam felt something change around him, a moment later the music increased in volume dramatically, until the *thump thump thump* of the bass drum shook the walls. *If someone screamed right now, no one would hear it.* Contemplating this notion, Adam began to feel uneasy. *Maybe it's time to look for Sammi.*

He had no idea where to go, so he picked a direction

and started walking. The arena's cinder block wall, painted in black and green, with fluorescent swirls, rose up on his right.

The wall caught his attention, and as he stopped to study it further a familiar blast of node energy struck him from behind. Even as he fell he knew it was levin bolt-induced paralysis, skillfully administered, as it didn't kill him instantly.

There's still time for that, he thought morosely, furious with himself for his carelessness but too stunned to think beyond that. He heard his gun clatter to the concrete floor, out of sight. Lying face down on the concrete he perceived a change in the cinder block wall, then a Gate flashed into view. From the luminous circle came dark figures, not Unseleighe elves, but the unmistakable outline of gargoyles.

Mercenaries. For whom? he wondered as clawed hands grabbed his arms and pulled him up. A foul-smelling bag dropped over his head, blotting his vision, and he felt the unmistakable disorientation of a Gate taking him somewhere else.

Sammi followed the sounds of laser fire through the middle of the maze, and found herself in the worst imaginable position. From two upper levels on either side of her, snipers tagged her, repeatedly. She was a sitting duck.

She was more annoyed than angered. *All this male testosterone crap. Over what, toy guns?*

She walked nonchalantly out of range of the young bucket-o-hormones gleefully firing away at her, to a relatively quiet area under one of the levels. So far this strange place had offered no hints to the sinister activities she was certain was in progress, but that didn't mean much. At the Baltimore arena signs of Underhill magic didn't appear until after the disappearances, and even then there were only traces.

Good thing Adam came along to help out. If anyone

can bear down and do the serious work of rooting out evil powers, the King can.

Just then a horde of small boys, maybe eight years old, stampeded past with expressions of utter terror. Alarmed, Sammi looked to see what was chasing them, wondering if they were about to be kidnapped. *Over my dead body, they are!*

She had half expected an Unseleighe Lord or a human henchman to be chasing them with a net or something, but no, King Aedham Tuiereann, ruler of elfhame Avalon, was in hot pursuit with a plastic gun.

Sammi shook her head. *I don't believe I'm seeing this.* The last time she'd seen him in this state he was fighting Zeldan Dhu for his life, with a *real* laser weapon capable of boring through thick gauge steel.

So much for some serious recon, she thought, as Aedham and his young prey vanished into the maze. Sammi followed halfheartedly, but got turned around, and found herself going in circles. To worsen matters, monotonous techno that had been beating away at her elven senses increased dramatically in volume. Now she couldn't hear her own footsteps. But over the loud music, recognizable only because she had heard it before, came a noise she'd hoped to never hear again, either here or in Underhill: the report of a levin bolt, somewhere nearby.

Adam . . .

The air filled with the power, which was everywhere at once, no surprise in an enclosed environment like this. She pushed forward, taking random turns, finding places she had already covered. The maze was maddening, and she thought it might have been designed to confuse elves in particular.

A new element joined the fray. *What's this now, a Gate?* It was the phenomenon she had expected, but still it caught her unbalanced, and a bit of panic crept into the search. *No one can summon a Gate but a Mage . . . or a god. Is that what's so terrifying to me?*

She had no time to ponder these notions. Her duty was to find the King, but the search was proving to be futile. As she discovered a hallway she knew she hadn't seen before, she felt the Gate vanish, along with any signature of magic which might have led her to its source. *And where is Adam? I don't sense him . . . anywhere.*

The realization sickened her, but presence of mind prevailed. *Am I next?* She now wished she had the Glock she'd left in her room. *Not that it would stop a Mage. It would be . . . something. And the steel jacketed rounds would seriously damage anything second cousin to an elf.*

The game appeared to be over. Players, until now invisible to her, came out of the maze and trudged towards a flashing yellow light.

Game . . . over. She shook her head against the thought. *No, game just getting started. They haven't won anything yet.*

At the station where they began, players were filing in, commenting on the game, who got hit, by whom—innocent talk that had nothing to do with the abduction that had she knew had just taken place. The judge was standing by the door, looking pleased.

"Did you have fun in there?" he asked sincerely.

"Had a blast." Then she remembered the music. "Did you turn the volume up there towards the end?"

"I would if I could," Space Demon replied. "That's all handled in the control center."

She reholstered the gun and started removing the vest. "Where's that?" she asked calmly.

"Upstairs somewhere. We never see it. I don't even know how to get up there."

That seemed to be the only explanation necessary to the kid who was, Sammi knew already, completely unaware of what was *really* going on here.

She lingered in the lobby, waiting for the rest of players to come out, hoping for a betraying expression, a clue, a hunch, anything. Under a large computer display, their scores popped up. Dallas' name didn't show up anywhere.

As if he never existed, she thought, wondering why they hadn't grabbed her, too. *Perhaps they still can.* She surveyed the lobby with her trained eye, seeing nothing that would betray an Unseleighe presence, and considered asking to see the manager. She had done so before, in the other arenas, and had always been met with unquestionable evidence that nothing out of the ordinary had happened in there. *That was the problem. This isn't out of the ordinary, here.*

And they can still get me.

She didn't want to leave without Adam, but if they caught her too, no one would be left to report to the elfhame.

What would Adam do?

He would warn Avalon. If it's not already too late . . .

In the control center, Yuaroh Dhu did not look appropriately chagrined.

Perhaps he doesn't understand yet what he hasn't *done*, Mort thought. He whirled around on the big swivel chair and regarded his henchman with a hard, dissatisfied stare. At length, he said, "The kingdom has received only King Aedham. What of his sister?"

"But, master, we only saw one Mage. And that Mage was Aedham."

"The other *elf*! The woman with him. *Are you blind?*"

The Unseleighe's eyes turned to the floor, but not as quickly as Mort would have liked.

"I saw only the one," Yuaroh replied.

I must watch this elven Lord, Mort thought. *This was a peculiar oversight. I can't believe he didn't see the two* sidhe *in the arena.*

"So be it," he muttered, making no effort to disguise his displeasure. "We have other matters to deal with. Return immediately to Underhill and proceed with the next plan in our conquest. And do *not* fail me in obtaining the Avalon technology I seek. Our kingdom's future depends on it."

Chapter Five

It felt strange, quitting his job. Dobie had wanted to go in and give them notice or something, or at least show up in person. It seemed the decent thing to do. But Morgan had convinced him that that wouldn't be necessary, that he was better than they were and he was only starting to realize his potential. What felt stranger was *believing* her.

He called the Mega Burger to tell them he quit. In words bathed in acid his boss informed him that the cost of his uniform would be deducted from his last paycheck, and had hung up on him. After a few moments of staring at the receiver with the bell tone blaring away, quitting didn't seem like such a bad idea after all. He felt liberated.

On the suite's couch, they both enjoyed the glow of the night before. Morgan cuddled him as if he were a teddy bear, and reclined in the couch with his legs across her lap; he felt rather special. She could lavish whatever attention on him she wished, and did.

Dobie had quit asking himself what she saw in him. Obviously, she saw *something*. Who was he to question her?

"Let's go shopping," she announced, and in a fluid, magical motion plucked him from the couch and led him out of the hotel to her Corvette, which was waiting for them, door open and engine running, precisely where they'd left it. The valet was different but his smile was the same. She tipped him another hundred dollar bill.

On the road in full daylight they drew even more attention. High schoolers maybe a year older than him blared horns and gave him the thumbs up. If he hadn't felt godlike the night before, he did now. She drove directly to Woodland Hills Mall in expensive South Tulsa, and in the ensuing shopping rampage Morgan bought him an entire wardrobe, from casual to formal, a mountain of clothing he couldn't even see over. As soon as he started to wonder how it was going to fit in the 'Vette, Morgan said, "I'll have it delivered to the room."

Dobie tossed the orange polyester Mega Burger uniform into the trash with no regrets. Morgan had promised him a job which would pay much better than fast-food, though she hadn't specified what it would be. Right then, it didn't matter.

Morgan had made a point of stopping by the sporting goods store, which Dobie found puzzling at first. She assured him he would want to wear shorts and sneakers to Lazerwarz, and he shrugged and agreed, not fully understanding. It took some searching to find spandex running shorts in a size 28 men's, but they did, along with a $200 pair of futuristic Nikes that looked liked they were designed for zero G.

Finally, they stopped in at a hair salon. By now the day had developed a momentum of its own, and he didn't question the haircut, or the instructions Morgan gave the girl with the scissors. "Long in the back, short on top, leave the wave." Afterwards, seeing his new image in the mirror, he felt transformed. He caught himself wondering how he was going to fit his new hair into a hair net, then he remembered there would *be* no more hair nets.

Back in the Corvette, Morgan told him to open the

glove compartment. Inside was a folded black Lazerwarz T-shirt and a member's game key on a ball chain. With the key was a silver medallion with the Lazerwarz logo.

"With that member's key you can play as many games as you want, for free," Morgan said cheerfully as she pulled out of the parking lot. "No questions asked."

All the kindness of the day, the clothes, the attention, and of course the sex, was all just too much . . . he didn't know what to say. No one had ever done so many nice things for him before, and he felt unworthy of it all. Somewhere amid the confusing emotions tears began to well in his eyes, and he looked away.

"Thanks, Morgan," he said, after a long struggle with his feelings. He wasn't *about* to start blubbering right there in the seat . . . she might misunderstand. "I mean, thanks a *lot*." He managed to look at her, but her eyes were on the road. "You didn't have to do all this."

"I *wanted* to," she replied, glancing his way with a bright smile. "You're *special*. You deserve it."

He wanted to know what made *him*, a geeky, hamburger flipping, deformed teenager without even a *car*, so special, but thought that asking would be a mistake. He didn't.

"I'm not sure about that, but thanks anyway," he said, turning the member's key over in his hands.

When he looked up again, they had stopped in front of the Lazerwarz arena.

"I have some business to tend to," Morgan said, and Dobie's door popped open, again, by itself. "Go in and have some *fun*. I should be back by closing."

Slightly mystified, Dobie got out, and with a start realized she was *leaving*. He didn't like that at all, because he would be alone, and would have to fend for himself in what promised to be a terrifying social situation. Then he remembered what he looked like, rather buff in his sexy Spandex and new haircut, and she said he was cute, which he was beginning to believe; and in spite of his hands, he would survive.

The Corvette sped off, and Dobie felt an all new longing. *Will my heart grow fonder? You bet it will.*

His bike was where he'd left it, locked to the gas meter. When he had stood here the night before, an outsider looking in, his only ambition had been to get through the day without burning himself with grease. Now the bike represented everything he *didn't* have before, a sense of self, and a hint that maybe he might worth something after all.

He went into the Lazerwarz arena a new man.

The lobby was as he remembered, except now it was a human beehive boiling with activity, and despite the brisk ride in the Corvette he welcomed the cold, comfortable air. Dobie assumed a place at the end of a line that snaked up to "Stage One," while casually scouting out the scene. It felt like high school all over again, in line in the cafeteria or a pep rally, only the kids seemed more enthusiastic about being here. He also noted the dark colors everyone was wearing, black being the favorite, and realizing he was dressed like everyone else his anxiety levels dropped. One or two others had noticed his black Lazerwarz shirt, but habits die hard, and he found himself balling his fists to hide his fingers. In the past this had gotten him into trouble, as many saw this as a challenge to fight. But they just looked away, evidently thinking he was an employee or something. *If they just don't look too closely at my hands . . .*

No one else seemed to have a special silver Lazerwarz key and logo, something that also attracted a few glances. A moment later he considered a humiliating scenario: what if the tag was no good? He had no money, and no ID, and no key to the bike lock. He'd be stuck here until Morgan showed up. Which brought to mind the question of his status: if he were dating the manager, would he get preferential treatment? The advantages to being Morgan's new boyfriend seemed endless.

Now it was his turn, and he stepped up to the counter and cautiously offered the silver key to the guy behind the computer, whose name tag said Pyro.

"A *member*," commented Pyro, with vague overtones of awe. "With a *silver* membership. Look, you don't have to wait in this line. Next time just go to Stage Two," Pyro said, holding the key to an electronic thingie on the counter. "Code name?"

"Pardon?" Dobie said.

"Code name, you know, your handle. This key doesn't have one yet."

Under most circumstances this would have been an awkward moment for him as he stumbled over a half dozen unintelligible words by way of explanation. This was no ordinary circumstance, and his mouth worked admirably, as if by itself.

"The Hound," Dobie heard himself say.

"The Hound it is," Pyro replied. "Get ready, the beta game is about to start. That door, over there," he said, pointing to the station entrance. "Get a jump on everyone. Get in line now," he added with a wink.

Dobie smiled and pretended to know what he was talking about, and got in the new line as Pyro announced over the PA that the beta game was about to begin. A mass of black clad youth swarmed towards the station door.

The judge was a loud mouthed kid named Space Demon who demonstrated the vest and gun with practiced ease, then led the thirty or so players into the main room with the vests. Dobie held his breath as he put his vest on and activated the rig. *There's still time for this key to* not *work!* But no, the vest bleeped to life. In the little computer screen appeared the words, "The Hound."

The Hound . . .

Again, Dobie found himself standing straight up, giving him a better view of his opponents. Space Demon had explained this was a solo game, no teams, but already Dobie saw a team in the making. A huddled conference among four or five, there in the corner. Their worried glances in his direction suggested he might be a . . . *threat*? Having spent his life on the bottom of the social food chain, the notion was alien to him. He had played this game only once before, and it looked like these punks had been here all day.

The judge activated the game. On the gun screen a thirty-second countdown began, and the arena door rolled up. Players scattered quickly into the mist with whoops and hollers. This time the place reminded him of a large boiler room, like the one in the basement of his high school, with passages and tunnels leading into even darker places. Instinct told him to avoid the center this time; he kept to the right, hugging the main wall, finding a mostly direct route along the edge of the maze to a ramp. From beyond the walls came a *thumpety thump* of running feet. *Didn't the judge say no running?* Dobie suspected he would soon find out just how well the rules were enforced.

The countdown on his gun ended with a long *bleeep*, and the game erupted all around him. Up the ramp . . . up the . . .

His vest uttered a mournful wail and died; someone had tagged him. Lights blinked at him from the second level; he'd had a perfect shot of anyone coming up the ramp. *Better keep going.*

Bathed in black light, the second level was its own miniature maze. Sniper holes lined the wall facing out, towards the rest of the arena, where a cluster of players were showing their back targets to him. They were taking potshots at the players below in what was obviously a group effort, and they hadn't yet noticed him.

Dobie ducked back to the rear, where the maze became much tighter, but had interesting shoulder-height sniper holes giving a clear shot at the team. He let loose into the island of flickering lights, and one by one the packs went down.

He pulled back, out of sight, and listened to anguished groans.

"Hey, you tagged me!"

"No I didn't, that was . . ."

"Who's *The Hound*?"

"Dunno . . ."

They resumed shooting below, and Dobie took great pleasure in nailing them again, this time all four of them. Then another player came up the ramp, oblivious to the carnage in progress, followed by another, shooting everywhere and nowhere as if the sheer quantity of shots would win them the game. From his niche in the maze Dobie picked them off, then repeated the process. In the confusion no one noticed him lurking in the rear, as he raked his ruby-red beam across the battle. The gun screen said RANK(4). 734 points.

"I'm fourth?" he muttered aloud. "Guess so." The exhilaration of *not* coming in last gave him new fuel to burn. From his spot he continued to score, and the once-tight huddle had begun to scatter throughout the maze. They must have realized they were not getting tagged from below.

"Hey Hound, come here doggie doggie . . ." one of the twits shouted. "I know you're back here . . ."

The taunting was like lighting gasoline with a match; perhaps it was the doggie part that did it. A wave of adrenaline flashed through his system, and he stepped out from his hiding spot. The periphery of his vision was blurring to red.

"I'm not a doggie . . ." Dobie said, tagging the other's chest target. The scene felt childish, infantile even, like bickering kids in a playground. But beyond

that he felt a lust rise up within him. It wasn't the lust for sex; after a night with Morgan, he was completely depleted of *that*, at least for now. No, it was the lust for battle, for inflicting injury, for scoring the highest score, for *winning*.

Is this what testosterone feels like? he wondered, amazed at the concept.

They sparred back and forth. The player was Gelcap, his gun screen told him. This one had an aura of confidence about him, as if he'd lived in this maze all his life. Dobie blasted away at him, but hit him relatively few times; Gelcap had an infuriating technique of approaching sideways, gun pointed up, which presented *no* targets to shoot at. Yet it was a legit move, he wasn't covering anything, and The Hound wasted no time copying it. The stances reminded him of fencing. *Touché.*

"You're good," Gelcap muttered while his pack was down.

Then why doesn't he go somewhere else? The Hound wondered, but he was having too much fun racking up points. Perhaps Gelcap needed a challenge. If so, he'd found one.

The others joined in, shooting from a distance, sending four separate beams his way, blasting his targets, killing his vest. The Hound was instantly outnumbered. The red at his periphery deepened to a darker color, the color of blood.

He pulled back, just to give his pack time to come back up. He glanced at the gun screen: RANK(3). 923 points.

Five, four, three, two . . .

And came out shooting, pegging two right off. During their five second downtime The Hound advanced on the others, surprising them with his beam. More were stampeding up the ramp, a tight little grouping of targets which he promptly extinguished. He didn't look at his score, he didn't have time. . . . From behind him came the bleep of Gelcap's pack coming back up, and The Hound took a chance and fired blindly, backwards over his shoulder. The chance paid off; Gelcap went back down.

"How the hell did you *do* that?" Gelcap wailed, but by then The Hound's attention was elsewhere. Targets were everywhere, some more competent than others, and The Hound resumed his concealed position in the rear. Here he scooped up more points, tagging, ducking, tagging again; they had no idea where it was coming from.

"I'm not impressed," Mort commented, whirling around on the control center's chair to confront Morrigan, who stood sneering at him, with her hands on her hips. He was not going to let her intimidate him, not now, not ever—and if his horns grew into foot-long spirals, as they were on their way to doing already, then so be it. The young human in question was a shadow on the monitor, highlighted by his targets. His performance during this game had been above average but not spectacular. "Why do you think there's something unique about him?"

"You don't see it? Of course you don't, not on these terminals," Morrigan screeched. "The aura. A *god's* aura."

Mort glanced at the wimpy, skinny human on the monitor, and fiddled with the controls. When he picked up the snooping elves earlier, their bright, shiny auras were obvious, but this kid . . . there was nothing there.

"I suppose we're just not seeing the same thing," Morrigan spat. "In time, you will see who we have with us." She spun on her heels and stalked out, leaving an acrid scent in the control center. Mort rolled his eyes.

She must have seen something. It's not like her to be enamored with anything, much less a human*!*

He was considering going down there in some passable disguise to investigate this lad directly when he remembered the key word: *god.*

"Well, hell's bells, of *course* I can't see a god on these screens!" The video went through an image processor, for which he had made, at no small expense and trouble, a special set of programs to fine-tune the reception of underworld beings. The ability to ken solid gold in any quantity had enabled him to buy not just the best technology humans had to offer, but the best humans to set it up. Mort didn't really think he would see a god in his arena, but just in case one came calling he had had a god program created.

On the server he clicked on the image processor icon, dragged down the screen and clicked the "god" icon.

Do you wish to terminate the sidhe task? it asked.

Yes, Mort entered impatiently.

Terminating the sidhe task will erase any unsaved data.

"I don't give a shit!" Mort shouted at the screen.

Do you wish to continue?

Yes.

Are you REALLY sure you wish to continue?

"No, I wish to sit here with my thumb up my butt. *Yes,* I wish to continue!" Mort clicked *yes.*

As the hourglass appeared he contemplated the deals he'd made to set up this system, and wondered if the one with Gates was worth the trouble. Anyone, it seemed, could be bought if you had enough gold.

There were only a few minutes left in the game, and Mort considered switching to a lobby camera when the hourglass disappeared, and the god program popped up. By now the kid had moved, and he would have to go clicking through each of the hundred monitors to find him; to save time he clicked on the *god scan* option and let it go.

Five seconds later the monitor filled with a view

of the kid in question. The banner *Godlike being found* scrolled across the bottom of the screen. Sure enough, this was no mere pimply human adolescent. His aura blazed *crimson*. Mort had to dampen the brightness to keep the image from burning out the screen.

"She was right," Mort whispered in awe. "This is no elf. This is an older power, from beyond Underhill."

He looked up his code name. *The Hound?*

The Hound had won the game. He'd beaten Gelcap, a budding talent Mort had considering harvesting a bit early, but with all the publicity buzzing around in the parking lot (damn her!) he hadn't dared.

Mort sat back in the huge chair and steepled his fingers. If Morrigan had managed to snag a *god* for this endeavor, she would have more than compensated for the trouble she'd caused. The only problem now was determining which god this was, or at least figure out his lineage.

Take by force or by guile? His identity will have to determine the path.

Mort chuckled to himself, amused at how this was starting to play out.

Suddenly, it was all over. Overhead lights came on, turning darkness to a murky dusk. The gun screen read, <GAME OVER>.

Game . . . over? At first the notion was incomprehensible. He wanted to keep going, keep scoring, and keep *winning*. But alas, pulling the trigger produced nothing. *I guess it* is *over.*

In the lobby the players were clustered around the big screen, waiting for the scores. *The computer must still be adding it all up.* Dobie was dripping with sweat, but the berserker rage was thinning, and he started to calm down. Gelcap and his buddies were under the screen, casting furtive scowls in his direction.

Then the scores came up. The Hound won the game with 1100 points. Gelcap was second, with 909.

Half the players looked his direction now; they knew who The Hound was.

Pride threatened to burst through his chest, like the little lizard thing in *Alien*.

Gelcap came over and extended his hand. "Congrats, Hound," he said, and Dobie saw this was another small, geeky kid, much like himself. "You play a mean game."

Dobie extended his hand, without thinking. Gelcap hesitated before shaking it; he saw the seven fingers. But he shook it, anyway, and smiled. "See you in there again."

Dobie didn't know what to say. Not only was he victorious, his seven finger deformity had become irrelevant. He realized then this was what he wanted all his life, just to be acknowledged as a peer. Being a *triumphant* peer was icing on the cake.

Life is good.

"You even got third high score of the day," Gelcap pointed out, as the screen switched to the daily tally. "Hot *damn*. You must play this a lot. And you're a member, too," Gelcap said, and scrutinized the member key hanging around Dobie's neck. "A *silver* tag?"

Dobie contemplated telling him he was boink—er, *dating* the manager of this place, but stopped himself. It wouldn't be cool, and besides, the kid probably wouldn't believe him anyway. He would be surprised if Gelcap wasn't still a virgin.

Like I was once.

"They must be expensive," Gelcap commented.

Dobie didn't know, and didn't say. "You can get the silver tags at the desk," he suggested, though he wasn't sure if this were true or not. His impulse now was to divert attention from the silver member's tag; it might seem like an unfair advantage to the others.

That seemed to be all the explanation necessary. Gelcap shrugged and wandered off with his buddies, in search of a silver tag, or another victim.

Thirsty, Dobie went over to a water fountain and drank. He looked up, conscious that someone was looking at him. He wouldn't be at all surprised if someone had it in for him, even if that someone was Gelcap. But no, Gelcap and his buddies were now at the air hockey table, intent on slamming a plastic puck into a goal. Perhaps it was paranoia, he reasoned, but the feeling persisted, and at one point he felt a warm itch on his spine, between his shoulder blades.

He turned around expecting to see another teenager, but instead he saw an older gentleman standing off in the corner. At first glance he didn't seem to be with anyone, though if he were with friends, or his children, they could have been playing in the arena. There was no doubt in Dobie's mind that the older man was staring directly at him.

His look was not stern or angry, but slightly bemused, the kind of look one would expect of an older, distinguished gentleman in a room full of noisy teenagers.

Is this a come on? wondered Dobie, but only briefly. The overtones of their silent exchange were anything but sexual. Deep in the man's gaze, Dobie felt like he was at the outskirts of yet another universe, looking in, much as he had done here the previous evening at the glass doors. Yet this world which lurked beyond this man, wherever it was, was nothing like this one.

How do I know this? How can . . . ?

A glimmer in the man's expression, a subtle change that, by itself, amounted to little. Yet it had the effect of changing the man's appearance.

I know him. I've seen him before. He must be a teacher, but from what class? Yes, a teacher. From sometime before, perhaps even long before.

With some apprehension Dobie watched the man slowly meander through the crowd, towards him.

Maybe I'm about to find out.

✧ ✧ ✧

Alfred Mackie arrived at Tulsa International earlier that day, jet lagged and fuzzy, but coherent, excited, and ready to go to work. The local universities who had already set up shop at the Parking Lot Megaliths, as they were starting to be called, had little experience with European archeology, and had welcomed Alfred with open arms. Also, having been the discoverer of the theft in England gave him enormous influence, not to mention the jump he had on the other British archeology schools; Alfred was on a jet bound for the states before half the British population knew what was going on.

Officially, they weren't calling the site Stonehenge, though the Americans had said openly it could be nothing else. With the help of one of the TU professors, Alfred delivered the textbooks he'd found in the severed Subaru to the befuddled law student, questioned him briefly about the night in question, and then came directly to the site.

It was a most uncomfortable situation. By the time he reached the site, word had spread that an expert from Britain was en route, and reporters mobbed him before he had even set foot on the lot. Once the media realized he hadn't seen the site yet they got out of the way, but stayed close behind, recording every move he made. Amid flashing strobes and whirring cameras, Alfred Mackie made a slow walk around the megaliths. Once he completed the preliminary inspection he declared that this was, indeed, Stonehenge.

"How did it get here?" a reporter shouted.

"Who bloody knows," came his reply.

He was ready for a bit of jet lag, perhaps even two or three sleepless days, but he was not prepared for the ghastly humid heat. One of the locals noticed his discomfort and pointed to what he had thought was a closed shopping mall. One store, Lazerwarz, was open. It had air conditioning and water fountains. That was all he needed to hear.

Before seeking sanctuary however, Alfred scanned the skies for any raptors that might be about; Lugh had chosen to appear as a golden eagle, but he could just as well be anything else. He was, after all, a god.

He recalled his excursion to the former Stonehenge site on the Salisbury plain, and the conversation he'd had with the god of light.

The Foevors are intent on setting fire to the realms, Lugh had told him. *The Foevor Morca is their leader. They seek to conquer the underworld, and this realm . . . to rule, without question, without responsibility.*

And then, the strangest part of all: *My son is in danger. You know my son, druid. You are part of his past, you are part of him. You helped make him what he is, you are what he is. He needs your help. I need your assistance, Cathad.*

Go to the stones, and you will find him. Aid him. Fulfill your duties as a druid. Help him remember who he is.

It was a request no druid could refuse, even if he wanted to.

Lugh said he would be here, with the stones. An incarnated human. How am I supposed to know which one he is?

His confusion on this point concerned him greatly; he was out of practice.

And I am an old man.

These depressing musings ended abruptly as he entered the store, and the ice-cold air took his breath away. He had been out in the heat too long, he knew, and decided to stay here as long as he could. It would not do to faint on international television. As he glanced around he saw this wasn't really a store, but an arcade of some kind. A demo on a video screen gave him additional hints to what this was all about.

Most interesting. A laser game. Laser is . . . amplified light. What an ideal place for the god of light to manifest!

He'd heard the rumors that this arena had just opened, and the stones had been brought here as some sort of publicity stunt. He wondered now if perhaps there was some truth to this. Business didn't seem to be hurting, that much was certain. And the youth here seemed as fascinated with piercing their flesh with steel as those in his homeland, without the Midwestern, American accents he found himself surrounded with, the scene might just as easily have been in London. But if Lugh was running around here in jeans and a Mossimo T-shirt, his presence wasn't yet obvious. Alfred remembered his thirst, and searched the premises for the promised water fountain. Wasn't that one over there, in that dark hallway?

Someone was standing next to it. Alfred's eyes blurred as his latent druid sight returned, and as he focused on the young lad he saw something odd about him . . . or rather, his aura. In a crowd of mortals it is easy to detect a person with divine origins. The lad's aura blazed like fireworks. When their eyes met, he shuddered as he recognized him.

Lugh was right, he thought excitedly as he made his way towards the water fountain. *His son Cu Chulainn* is *here, with the stones. But is he in trouble?*

Would a god ask a mere druid for help if he wasn't? What if the lad doesn't know who he is?

Highly likely, that. But how to approach him without scaring him off? In another time and place, it would have been perfectly acceptable to openly discuss druidry, magic and gods, but such was not the case here.

First things first. I can't converse with a god's offspring with a dry throat. The boy watched warily as Alfred went over to the water fountain and took a long drink of cold water. Afterwards he felt revived, as if this were a sacred spring, and turned to the lad who thankfully had not scampered off.

"Hello," Alfred said congenially. "I'm with the

archeologists out there, investigating the megaliths. Do you know about when this happened?"

The boy considered the question carefully before he replied "The stones? Everyone knows it happened a few days ago. Where are you from?"

"Britain," Alfred replied. "My name is Alfred Mackie, and I am a professor of archeology in England."

Now that Alfred's name and identity was confirmed, the lad seemed to relax. "I am The Hound," the boy replied.

Alfred stared at him. *Perhaps he knows who he is after all. Few young men of this culture would know that Cu Chulainn translates to "The Hound of Culann."*

"Are you really here to study the stones out there?" The Hound asked. He gestured towards the site, and in that brief movement Alfred saw that the lad had seven fingers on his hand. "You would know if that's Stonehenge or not."

Alfred forced himself to not stare at the boy's hands; he probably got enough gawking anyway. "It *is* Stonehenge," Alfred replied with certainty. "What remains to be shown is how it happens to be here. Do *you* have an explanation?"

The Hound shrugged. "I haven't really given it much thought, lately. I suppose a group of college students might have done it in the middle of the night," he suggested, with a deadpan expression.

Alfred couldn't help but laugh. "If a freshman class *could* figure out how to do it, they would. Are you attending school?"

The Hound seemed surprised. "Me? No, I graduated." To Alfred's puzzled look, he explained, "High school. Haven't gone to no college yet."

Alfred nodded, but cringed inwardly at the mutilation of the King's English. *An earthy type, like he's always been. But is he a warrior?*

"So tell me, what is this game all about, then?"

A broad grin spread on the youth's ruddy face. "Why don't you sign up for the next game and I'll *show* you."

"You will? How kind of you. I think I will. Do you have . . . what I mean, is there a currency exchange?" The youth's blank look answered the question. "Never mind, I believe I have a few U.S. notes."

"Here," The Hound said, pulling several pink slips of paper out of a pouch. "Free passes. First day they're open. They give 'em away."

Alfred was relieved; he hadn't really wanted to use school expense money for the diversion, even if it was to study the present day incarnation of Ireland's greatest mythological hero. Some board members just wouldn't understand. He had more cold water, and queued up for the next round, the delta game.

When the delta game was up the judge called them into the small darkened room. The Hound hurried in after them.

In the presence of the divine offspring Alfred felt things change around him.

Lugh is here, after all.

The god made his presence known by pulling Alfred back to another time and another place, long ago and distant. The players faded from sight, and the station became a round room with wattle and daub walls. A cold wind blasted and shook the lodge. In the center an iron spit brandished the remnants of a boar over a smoldering fire pit. The thatched roof tapered to a smoke hole at the top, where melting snow dripped and hissed on dull, red coals sunk below in the pit. The place smelled like sweat, winters-old animal remains, and burnt meat. Spring was long overdue.

The lodge belonged to Cathad, Chief Druid of the court of Ulster. The vision of Alfred's former life took over and conquered his senses—soul memories were like this, the druid knew, all encompassing and total.

Around him were sleeping bodies huddled together

for warmth. That year Cathad had welcomed two other families whose house had collapsed under the snow. On hearing of this the King's nephew, The Hound of Culann, went into the lowlands to hunt. He returned with the boar, some rabbits, and the news that the ground was thawing to the south, a good sign that winter was nearly over.

As a druid, Cathad's responsibility was to stay in touch with the Otherworld and communicate with the gods. He had appealed to them on the tribe's behalf, and on spring equinox he'd performed a special ritual which his own teacher had used to banish winter. The results of his work were already evident. Again, the Order of the druids had turned the wheel of the seasons . . . spring had reached the lowlands!

In the doorway of the lodge the air was still frosty, but Cathad felt the changes in his spirit, which was opening up to the Great Mother stirring beneath his feet.

The valley lay beneath a blanket of snow, yet there was The Hound, out hunting again; the druid wondered if Lugh's son was making the wheel turn. His presence commanded the attention of every living thing, and while his intense body heat was not melting the snow from his path, as certain bards were starting to proclaim, to behold The Hound of Culann was to feel the presence of someone more than mortal.

Only thirteen, and the boy not only had a man's strength, but could wield a spear, sword and sling better than any Ulsterman. That he was a direct cousin of their King, Conchobar mac Nessa, was incidental to his spreading reputation, which had begun with his first battle: the smith, Culann, had accidentally left a fierce guard hound outside his lodge when Setanta, as the boy was then called, was due to arrive. The smith remembered the boy only too late, for the hound was already attacking him. Afterwards they found the dog dead, suffocated when Setanta shoved a shinty ball down its throat—Setanta apologized for the loss, and volunteered to protect the smith's herds and property himself while he raised another pup. Thus Setanta became Cu Chulainn, The Hound of Culann.

Cathad saw the omens, and as The Hound continued to grow into a mighty warrior his strength and abilities knew no limit. As a druid, Cathad's duty was to impress upon his tribe the knowledge of reincarnation. To know that you never truly die can make for fierce fighting men. The Hound was already fierce; what could he gain from knowing there is no death? The tribe as a whole would reap the benefits.

To know there is no death, thought Alfred as all around him the soul memory evaporated, and he found himself in the darkness of Lazerwarz. But The Hound was still with him, ready to play laser tag.

"I'll show you some place most people don't know about," The Hound whispered.

"Yes, I'm sure you can," Alfred replied as The Hound helped him with the vest. It occurred to the druid that since he was about to go into battle with Cu Chulainn he should be concerned for his physical safety but no, the rules seemed clear on that point. No physical contact was allowed.

Kids swarmed towards the rising door as the game countdown began, and The Hound led Alfred to the right, into the darkness.

"You get to the upper level down here," he continued, in the solemn overtones of a shared, important secret. "You want to get off the floor as soon as possible. Down here you're an easy target," The Hound explained as they wove swiftly through the maze, leaving the other acolytes stumbling around behind them. Then up a ramp, to another level. Alfred saw the players wandering aimlessly down on the floor below.

"See," The Hound said, pointing at the sea of

lighted targets. "Easy meat. Now, have fun," The Hound said, and was gone.

The game began, and once he had a live weapon, Alfred started shooting at the targets below. In no time they returned fire, and now *Alfred* was the easy meat.

The Hound had moved to the other end of the upper level. Silhouetted by blood-red light beams, the warrior incarnate fired with great accuracy at the five opponents teaming up against him. The druid remembered what happened to The Hound when he was outnumbered unfairly, and stepped back, watching from a discreet distance.

As expected, a fighting fury consumed The Hound; in the dim light his face was hard to make out, save for a few hideous expressions distorted with ultraviolet light. Yes, this was the Cu Chulainn he remembered, and if by chance the lad had anything more lethal than a toothpick they were all in terrible danger.

As Alfred observed it occurred to him that he was seeing a rebirth of sorts; before the game the youth had been a modest adolescent, unimpressed with his own abilities. Perhaps this laser tag was a long awaited outlet? If so, this would make the sacred task of bringing The Hound to an awareness of his past life easier. Or, The Hound's success here might bind him even deeper to this culture's ignorance of the matter. Why believe an old man that he was a great warrior in the distant past when he was becoming one in the present, with all the attention and adoration that goes with the honor?

In any event, he would have to try.

Towards the end of that game, something *changed* in The Hound.

Yet another team was taking him on, five this time, and they were good. There was something viscerally threatening about the vest going down, as if one's manhood had suddenly failed at a crucial moment, pushing buttons he didn't know he had, prodding him into a murderous, fighting frenzy. It sharpened his vision and focused his mind like nothing else. An absolute concentration, an absolute Zen. A piece of a puzzle clicking violently into place.

With lightning-quick moves he hit the team and kept them down, discovering that in these tight quarters holding the gun overhead made for easier shoulder target hits. Also, the fencing stance, with a mock parry and thrust, could be pretty damned intimidating when they weren't expecting it. After keeping their packs down for three or four cycles, they started to scatter, their team cohesiveness coming apart at the seams. The Hound understood the word *victorious*; he felt the meaning throughout his being, and it felt *good*.

He'd completely forgotten about the peculiar man from England until he saw him come out of the arena, flushed but with a smile The Hound was starting to recognize as the look of surprised joy. Laser tag was something that had to be experienced, describing it did no justice. And experiencing it was so much unexpected fun . . .

He'd even forgotten, briefly, of the events that brought him here, and the lady he was seeing. Thinking of her made him wish she was here, to see how well he was doing. He won this game, too.

Hot damn, I'm getting good at this.

"That was a spectacular game you played in there," the archeologist said, walking up to him. All of Dobie's initial wariness was gone now, replaced with the spontaneous camaraderie present among players after even the most vicious of games.

"Thanks, uh, Alfred was it?" The Hound replied. He found this man strangely intriguing, even if there was no chance he could have been a former teacher. The question *Where have I seen him?* continued to nag him.

Alfred nodded, handing him a slip of paper. "Here is the number where I am staying. Your thoughts on . . . the Henge, outside, would be appreciated."

Dobie frowned, not fully understanding. "I don't really know anything about it."

"You will have a dream about your past," Alfred said, with an intensity that was startling. "Tell me about the dream. It is so important."

Under other circumstances he would not have taken the slip of paper. "Sure, I'll call you," Dobie said, unsure where the words were coming from. "It *is* important. I don't know why, but I believe you."

Alfred nodded, handing him a slip of paper. "Here is the number where I am staying. Your thoughts on [illegible] would be appreciated."

Dobie frowned, not quite understanding. "I don't really know anything about it."

"You will have a dream about your past," Alfred said with an intensity that was startling. "Tell me about the dream. It is so important."

[illegible] the slip of paper. "Sure, I'll call you," Dobie said, unsure where the words were coming from. "If it's important. I don't know why but I believe you."

Chapter Six

This feeling that something is wrong here is becoming unpleasantly routine, Sammi thought morosely as she stepped from the gate. The castle was absolutely silent, and no one greeted her when she arrived in the great hall.

"Hello?" her shout echoed, unanswered, throughout the palace. As she ran upstairs to check on Ethlinn and her child, she found Aedham's apprentice, Llanmorgan, lying unconscious in the hallway just outside the King's solar.

A brief examination revealed the reason. *Someone has cast a sleep spell on the palace!* She shook him, with no result. Holding his head up, she shouted into his face, "Llan, wake up!" He came around, slowly, mumbling something about nubile maidens at a bale fire.

"*Today!*" she screeched.

His eyes shot open. "Lady Samantha!" he exclaimed, and got up off the floor. "What has . . . ? What . . . ?" He looked around, stunned.

"A sleep spell," Sammi said, and started up the remainder of the stairs.

Llan followed her into the chambers, where Ethlinn was sleeping on their large canopy bed, and the baby was doing likewise in the cradle.

As everything should be. Or is it?

She woke Ethlinn, gently at first, then with the same method she used to rouse Llan. She sat up, groggy and confused, but otherwise unhurt.

"If this is a sleep spell, I'm getting Niamh," Llan said, and darted off in search of the Engineer.

"Samantha?" Ethlinn said, getting to her feet. Confusion turned to fear, then anger. "What's going on?"

"Sleep spell," Sammi replied.

"Traig . . . ?"

"Is in his cradle. The whole elfhame seems to be affected." Avalon roused itself as the call-to-arms bell began clanging down on the grounds; Niamh must have dismissed the spell. Traig started crying, and Ethlinn numbly went over to the cradle.

Niamh and Llan burst into the chambers, frantic and concerned. "Milady, are you all right?" Niamh said, his short, rounded form bustling up to the queen, who was soothing the crying prince. "We've been attacked with a sleep spell."

"I know," Ethlinn replied grimly as she picked Traig up from the cradle. "I need to know why. *Right now.* See if anything is missing."

"Missing?" Niamh said, with a pale, sickly look of someone considering an unpleasant possibility. "Certainly, not my research!"

"What research?" Sammi asked, but Niamh ran out without her. She caught up to him in his workshop, where chairs, books, and an entire shelf of glass bottles and their contents lay scattered and broken on the floor: sure signs of burglary in any realm. Niamh stared in apparent disbelief at an empty table, which according to his demeanor, should not be empty.

"They've stolen it!" Niamh exclaimed in anguish.

"Start talking, Niamh," Sammi said, switching over to cop mode. "What did they steal? And who are *they*?"

"The King's weapon," he bemoaned. "With which he slew Zeldan . . . *and* the elvenstone generators needed for it to work in Underhill!" He slowly righted an overturned chair, eased into it, and buried his face in his hands. "As for who, I don't know," he mumbled through his fingers. "Their spells walked through our wards as if they didn't even exist."

The revelation chilled her. Aedham had cast those wards himself, and had strengthened them tenfold before leaving. Which reminded her why she returned: she still had to inform the Queen that her husband had been kidnapped.

The simultaneous disappearance of the King and the laser rifle. Coincidence? Not likely.

Sammi found Ethlinn sitting on the bed, holding the prince. "Samantha, where is my husband?" she asked woodenly, not looking up. "Why isn't he *here*?"

Sammi sat in a high-backed chair across from her. "He didn't Gate here with me. I believe the King has been taken hostage, but I do not know by whom."

The Queen did not seem surprised as the story of the Lazerwarz arena spilled out of her. Sammi left nothing out, and when she finished the Queen stood and returned the prince, who had stopped crying, to the cradle.

"Right before the spell struck us, I knew something had happened to him. It wasn't clear what." She turned, and looked directly at Sammi. "Unseleighe?"

What to tell her? "I don't know, Ethlinn. I really don't. The power did not have an Unseleighe feel to it, but it did have an *Underhill* feel to it."

"Perhaps the gods are involved," Ethlinn said with short, sad laugh. "Why would they want us? Nothing has changed in the structure of things among the elfhames."

"Maybe we should contact the other elfhames and find out for sure," Sammi suggested.

"Yes, of course." Ethlinn seemed shaken from a trance. "I will do that now. The communications crystals are in Aedham's solar. And we will both inform Avalon of the King's disappearance." The crystals were gifts from other elfhames, to be used to contact them if something should threaten Avalon, Sammi recalled. It was an act of unity brought about by Avalon's original downfall, which had resulted indirectly from the elfhame's isolationism. With the crystals, they were isolated no more.

Llan appeared at the door as Ethlinn was leaving.

"Milady?" the boy asked.

"Llanmorgan, the King has been abducted," the Queen said gently. "We don't know by who, or how. Or why."

"The humans? Have the humans taken him?" he asked hungrily.

Sammi couldn't help but be amused. *The humans take the King? The lad has an underwhelming opinion of the King's abilities . . . or an overblown concept of what the humans can do.* Which was a typical attitude among elves who had never been above.

"The humans did not kidnap the King," Sammi replied.

The news did not assuage him, and his pained expression intensified. "It's my fault," he said, staring a the floor. "I should have sensed something was wrong . . . I might have . . ."

"You could have done nothing to stop this," Ethlinn replied, "and I wonder if even the King could."

This seemed to be no consolation, and perhaps was even an affront to the youth's perception of his own abilities. Anger flared briefly in his eyes, then his features relaxed into a doubtful calm before he replied, "I will go and get our King back, Milady!"

"No, you will not," Ethlinn replied sharply. "You have never been among humans. You have no idea how to behave among them."

"Lady Samantha does," Llan pointed out.

"You have not been tested."

"Perhaps this is his test," Samantha said. She seated herself comfortably in one of the high-backed chairs, letting her plan come together on its own. "While he is not a proven Mage, Llanmorgan does possess some qualities I would find useful."

Ethlinn made no attempt to mask her skepticism. "*What* other things?"

"It would take little work to disguise him for a good cover."

Ethlinn rolled her eyes. "Which would be, pray tell?"

"An impulsive, teenaged human," she said in English.

Llan's reaction to this observation was mixed. "What does 'impulsive' mean?"

Ethlinn was evidently seeing the wisdom in Sammi's notion. To Llan, she said, "Impulsive means 'fearless warrior.' "

"Aie!" Llan stood at attention.

"It will be a good cover," Sammi continued.

Llan seemed ready to explode. "Milady? What . . . what say you?"

The Queen seemed ready to give her approval when a bright, white light appeared outside the chamber's window, drawing everyone's attention. To Sammi it resembled a car's headlights sweeping across the window, only much more intense, with a tangible heat. Llan rushed to the window first, placing himself between the women and the outside.

"We are under attack!" Llan warned, but his resolve wavered as he took in the scene outside. Sammi joined him at the window and regarded the source of light. Silhouetted in the white light was a large, white eagle, kiting gently above the grounds. It hovered for a moment before continuing a graceful descent. Guards on the ground milled uncertainly, not yet knowing if this was a threat or not.

"I know who this is," Ethlinn said gently, sounding relieved. "I must go down there and warn the men not to fire on him. It would *not* do to start a war with the gods."

Shimmering like light on water, the entity had touched down to a quiet landing by the time they reached the palace grounds. The guards, evidently sensing no threat, stood at ease nearby, shielding their eyes from the brilliance. Fascinated, Sammi watched as the eagle transformed into a figure in a long, white robe. He was not of the *sidhe*, but was no human, either. The light faded, and his features became clearer—he was an ancient entity, a leader, with an aura of tranquility that visibly calmed everyone present. Llan had followed them both down to the grounds, and stood silently beside her.

"Lugh, Lord of Light," Ethlinn finally said, uttering his name for the first time. Her deferential tone told everyone this was a god to be respected. "You are most welcome at Elfhame Avalon. To what do we owe this extreme honor?"

Lugh stepped closer, diminishing his brightness even more; now one could look directly upon him without squinting. His face sharpened into a pleasant smile. "Many things, Queen of the Sidhe. I understand that your King, Aedham, is not here?"

She sensed something beneath the words, as if the god knew already the King had been kidnapped.

"Our elfhame is dealing with its own set of difficulties now," Ethlinn replied. "Our King has been seized by unknown forces, and we of Avalon have just been assaulted with a sleep spell. While we were sleeping, unknown elements have stolen certain magical tools we have been refining. We have just discovered the theft."

The god's face darkened at the mention of the tools. "The tools were weapons, Queen. I have been observing their construction from afar, as I would anything that would threaten the stability of the underworld."

"Did *you* steal them?" Ethlinn asked defiantly.

The god did not appear to take offense. "No, I did not. I know who has, and they have also abducted your King. Do you recall, in your recent conflicts with the Unseleighe court, a certain demon named Mort?"

Sammi rolled her eyes. *Do I ever. What does he have to do with this? I thought he had vanished once Japhet was beheaded.*

"The name is familiar," Ethlinn replied evenly. "What does a minor spirit have to do with this?"

Lugh looked amused. "Everything, Queen of the Sidhe. Mort is no minor spirit, though this was the impression he conveyed, with great success, I might add. No, Mort is an ancient evil, a Foevorian, of the conquered race of Eire your people displaced long, long ago."

Ethlinn hissed at the word *Foevorian*. Sammi was not certain she had heard correctly. *The Foevorians died out long ago!* she thought, remembering half-forgotten stories her parents had told her. Her people, the Tuatha De Danaan, eliminated the Foevors long ago, but it appeared now they were not completely extinct.

"Your surprise is understandable," Lugh said. "They have kept themselves well hidden. They are the scourge of the underworld, and have always been seen in my court as a nuisance, annoying but harmless. Until now." Lugh paused, letting them all absorb his news before continuing.

Sammi remained silent, although she deeply wished to comment on what Lugh thought of as a "scourge." *What of the Unseleighe? Does Lugh care what Zeldan's court did to the humans? Their specially tailored drugs were designed to invoke terror while imprisoning its victims with addiction. They very nearly tainted the water supply of the entire Dallas metro area with their hideous drug, and would have succeeded if not for Aedham's leadership.*

Lugh continued, "While Mort was in the employ of the Unseleighe Court he was studying their tactics. Mort has been a student of the *sidhe* art of conflict since before this Avalon existed, when the *original* Avalon stood."

"And the Foevorians are among us again," Ethlinn said as her eyes drifted downward. Hers was the most intense look of consternation Sammi had ever seen on an elf.

"They never left," Lugh said. "They once ruled everything. They wish to rule everything again."

Sammi's mind raced. *But why the Lazerwarz arenas? Why the kids? Why . . . steal the laser rig, the elvenstone technology . . . ?*

Her thoughts ceased abruptly as it all fell into place.

"They're building an army," Sammi whispered.

Ethlinn turned to her. "They're *what?*"

"The kids, the arenas, Niamh's tools." Sammi turned to Lugh. "Am I wrong?"

"That is their plan," Lugh replied. "Though it is more involved than that. My son, an incarnated human, has become a warrior of these arenas. The Foevorian camp is courting him. They wish to make him their champion."

Elvenstone weapons capable of delivering levin bolts in the hands of the mightiest Celtic warrior who ever lived! This was a threat to be taken seriously.

"My son knows not who he is. Like many of us who go on to become mortal for a time, he has forgotten his true nature. His origins will remain hidden from him, until someone reawakens the memories."

"I assume such is the case," Ethlinn said. "Or this conversation would not be taking place."

"I have dispatched the druid Cathad to contact my

son. As he is a druid, I do not rule over him. What he does is his responsibility, not mine. But the druid's duty is to impart knowledge of one's previous lives."

"How do you know this druid will guide your son wisely?"

"Cathad has done so before, and he will again," the god replied confidently. "I would seek your counsel in any event, as this is a serious threat," Lugh said. "It involves you as well, your King in particular. And, of course, the weapons you have developed." Again, that expression of disapproval.

"You seem displeased with our work," Ethlinn said. "Do you deny our right to defend our home?"

"I deny no one that right," Lugh replied. His glowing aura had dwindled to a mere flicker, and his features had softened to a mask of subdued but tangible desperation. He looked rather ungodlike then, and it occurred to Sammi that anything that would affect a god in such a way should be dealt with carefully and decisively. *And the King is in peril.* "A careful balance has existed in Underhill since your people have taken residence here, and I wish for that balance to remain in effect. Your weapons, particularly in the hands of a human army, threaten that balance. I intend to see the matter corrected."

"Do you seek our apology for this?" Ethlinn asked with a bit of defensiveness.

"I seek your assistance. My son, also, is in peril."

"What of our King?" Ethlinn asked.

"I will help you free him," Lugh replied. "If you save my son. This has become an Overworld matter as well. My powers there have become stagnant with disuse. I am no longer close to the humans who live there, and they are not what I remember. The polarity between us is too extreme for me, or my court, to compensate for. You, however, know the humans and can live among them. And you can reach my son, who is now also human. I cannot."

"What of the other elfhames? Have they been made aware of this threat?"

Lugh nodded. "They are assembling their armies as we speak. I would suggest you do the same. This is not a threat you should take lightly."

It looked as if Ethlinn wanted to digest this information before making any firm agreements. But Sammi saw that a quick decision was required here and looked to Ethlinn with eyebrows raised.

"We shall fight together," Ethlinn said, sealing the pact.

As the gargoyle mercenaries dragged him through the Gate, Aedham's paralysis turned to unconsciousness, then to Dreaming. He felt his body no more, and became, once again, spirit. He returned to the home of his family, the ruins of Castle Tuiereann.

The King regarded the remnants of the home of his youth with curiosity, not pain. He knew this was a dream, that the message he would receive would have nothing to do with the fall of the elfhame, or of his family's deaths. The humans called it lucid dreaming. The elves called it collecting information directly from the source.

Amid the fallen stones of the south wall, Aedham picked through the rubble, finding a relic of their former glory here, and there. A wall decoration, a piece of armor, a smashed chair. All reminders of an innocent past, when the primary challenge to elfhame Avalon was finding something to break up the predictable daily routine. Enemies capable of subduing them were a distant memory . . . until he came here.

The memory was not so distant now, the King thought, contemplating Zeldan Dhu's work.

He did not notice the golden eagle perched on the jagged section of fallen stone until he was within a few paces of it. It was amid these ruins that another eagle, a black monster big enough to carry him off, had attacked him; the eagle was Zeldan's Dhu's spirit, waging war in elven dreaming. This eagle was something else altogether. Aedham relaxed.

"You are a god," the elf said at last. Aedham already knew this conflict of Sammi's extended well beyond the elven lands of Underhill, and had wondered when the rulers of the other realm would show themselves. The time had come, and he was grateful; now he felt progress might be possible.

The Lord of Light greets you on this neutral, and sacred, ground, spoke the god to his soul.

Aedham appreciated the god's reverence. So many others had defiled this site. The golden eagle, a dark brown raptor about half his height, was only one of the forms Lugh had been known to assume. As a god, Lugh had many choices. Perhaps this was the least intimidating? Aedham did not know, he had never had cause to speak with these gods before. They seldom left their own realm. Thorn, the Rider Guardian brought into the Underworld by the Lord of the Land of Shadows, moved freely among the gods and the *sidhe*. Thorn and his ancient Harley bike Valerie were, until now, the most exotic spirits to contact him in his homeland.

Aedham briefly reviewed the sequence of events so far, to try to get a hold on this entity's vantage point. Japhet Dhu had brought in other spirits to fight their battles, and had even sought to enslave a half-human, half-elf for his own purposes. The gods had remained distant even from that, perhaps even looked upon the conflict with amusement. The death of Japhet Dhu had been the end of that battle; afterwards, the elves of Avalon had gone about their business.

Until the Lazerwarz arenas started snatching children. Straightforward Unseleighe tactics, save for the level of energy used in moving the megaliths. The

Unseleighe Court had not the power to accomplish something like that.

But the gods did.

Aedham wondered, *Is this the god at the center of this conflict? Did he initiate the battle, or is he simply reacting to its effects?*

The eagle cocked its head and studied him with a single eye. A singularly raptorlike gesture, which gave the King pause to reconsider: am I in danger here?

I am not here to harm you, but to enlist your aid, Lugh said. *You have been drawn into a conflict not of your making, yet its outcome will determine precisely what form you and your people will choose forever after.*

Aedham surveyed the god evenly, looking for signs that this creature was not what it seemed, but finding only truth.

The King spoke, "I have been taken prisoner in the Overworld. Are you my captor?"

If anything, I will be your liberator. But you must help me. I am struggling to understand this struggle just as you are. In that regard we are similar.

In Aedham's mind he saw the conversation the god had with his wife, Ethlinn. The transfer took only an instant. In the vision he saw Niamh, distraught over the theft of . . . *the elvenstone technology? Great, just great! The enemy, armed to the teeth, with our weapons!* While not pleased that his kingdom had been violated once again by hostile forces, and robbed of its powerful technology, he was grateful none were injured. The thieves must not have had time to divert themselves from their main mission.

I will help you, Lugh said. *If you help my son. He will be an asset, or a liability, depending on the swiftness of your actions.*

Aedham spread his arms, palms up, a universal gesture of helplessness. *I am a prisoner. I cannot yet free myself, much less be of help to my kingdom, or your son.*

The eagle spread his wings in apparent imitation of Aedham's gesture, presenting a span of about twenty feet, but this conveyed anything but helplessness. *Your imprisonment is temporary. Your captors are imperfect. You will find a way to escape.*

The King was not so certain. *Who are my captors? Not the Unseleighe.*

Lugh gracefully tucked his wings at his sides, then replied, *They are the Foevors.*

Aedham stared, holding back an involuntary shudder. The Foevors were a distant memory in the family of elves, a powerful race the Tuatha defeated only at the greatest cost. The Unseleighe's evil paled in comparison to theirs. In his mind's eye he picked up the image of the Foevor in question.

He blinked in disbelief. *Mort?*

As many things are in the Underworld, Mort was not what he seemed. The Unseleighe Court of Aoncos are the Foevor's hired mercenaries. You have dealt with the Unseleighe many times before, and you know their weaknesses.

Aie, I do, Aedham replied. *I've not heard of Aoncos before.*

Lugh seemed apologetic. *Nor have I. I believe they are the remnants of all the Unseleighe tribes your court has defeated. However, their numbers are few.*

Aedham sighed inwardly. *I knew they must have gone somewhere. It shouldn't surprise me they have overcome their greed and power lust to form a cohesive band, but it does.* Then he looked on the bright side. *Their actions will be easier to predict than those of the Foevors. But do you know what they want, what they will gain from all of this? How can I trick them?*

Lugh spread his wings once again, flapped once, then leaped into the air. *You know them better than I do, King of the Sidhe. Exploit them.*

The eagle circled once then set off to the north. Lugh sent the parting words, *We will meet again.*

As Aedham came to from his restless dreaming, he found himself in a square dungeon, barred on two sides with cold iron. He moved away from the iron's painful heat, and took in his situation. Indeed, he was a prisoner. He reached for node energy but found only a tight, magical wall surrounding the dungeon, severing whatever contact he'd had with the nodes. He retained a bit of Mage sight, and with it explored the caging spell carefully, admiring its simplicity and utter effectiveness. He was without magical defenses, and was as vulnerable as a human.

I have no magic, no weapon, but I do *have information. Lugh was kind to give me that much.*

The walls and floor had a recently kenned feel to it, and within the cell lingered a trace of unformed mist which hadn't settled yet. This was his first clue as to where in Underhill he might be. Some time ago Japhet Dhu had claimed a pocket of the Unformed, the King remembered, a territory on the fringe of populated Underhill which became his base of operations. Here he had imprisoned Wenlann and a young human named Lucas; Aedham and company had crashed the party to free them, but Japhet had escaped through another Gate. Since Japhet's defeat, the King had dispatched a few guards to this place to see if anyone had returned, but after a while he slacked off. After all, there was no need to police every square inch of Underhill, especially when so much rebuilding was necessary at home.

He cursed himself. Now, it seemed, he would be paying for his lack of vigilance.

Aedham was not the only one in the dungeon. His cell was only one of many, and in the one across from him were *humans* . . . young kids, dressed like the teenagers in the Lazerwarz arena he had just been seized from. This was where Sammi's missing children had been taken.

Not wanting to brave the cold iron just yet, he called out to them from where he sat. "Are you hurt?" There were three or four sleeping to a cell, or sitting up looking about in a stupor. They had been bespelled into submission, and had none of the built-in defenses of an elven Mage. Flickering torchlight cast shifting shadows over them. If they'd heard him, they did not respond. Aedham wondered if anything was left of their minds; they looked like vegetables.

An old song from The Who began playing irritatingly in his head. *It's only teenage wasteland* . . .

From around the corner came a loud *clang* that could only be a cell door slamming shut. Then footsteps, getting louder, drawing closer. Aedham stiffly got to his feet; he might be defenseless, but he didn't have to confront his captors sitting down. When the source of the footsteps came into view, he relaxed. It was another kid, smaller and less threatening than the others. A child, sixteen maybe, wearing a dirty tunic of some thick fabric that could not have been of Underhill origin. He held a tray with a chunk of mutton and a wooden stein. Dinnertime.

The boy slid the tray under the door and regarded Aedham inquisitively. His eyes flashed with intelligence. Clearly he wasn't as trashed as the other youths. When he turned to leave, Aedham saw a flat, red jewel affixed to his temple, reflecting torchlight.

Aedham knew exactly what the jewel was. Zeldan had enslaved a Seleighe technician with such a device. But the boy's expression was defiant, as if the ruby had not completely extinguished his will.

"You're not one of those bastards, are you?" Aedham tested, taking a few steps forward.

The boy stopped, and turned around.

Aedham continued, "They're trying to manipulate

you like a puppet. But they can't. You're too smart for that. I can see it in your face."

Aedham knelt and reached for the tray, braving the heat. Food was the last thing on his mind, but he saw an opportunity to establish trust. Taking the food without question might just make the right impression. Aedham sat cross-legged, and set the tray on his lap.

"Mutton," he commented, holding joint up by the bone. "It's what's for dinner." He sniffed at the stein before drinking from it.

"It's just water," the boy said, and Aedham looked up to see him holding the bars and peering intently into his cell. "I saw them moving it through the gate in large casks. I guess they can't make it here, or something."

Aedham tried not to look too surprised. "Water doesn't exist in this part of Underhill in any quantity, no. Who are you, by the way?"

The boy looked furtively right, then left, before answering. "My handle is Joystik. My real name is Alan Barker. I was playing Lazerwarz in Baltimore when . . . well, something pretty weird happened."

"Let me guess," Aedham said conversationally. "In the arena a big yellow circle opened up, and a bunch of bipedal lizards grabbed you and took you away. I'll bet you even won that particular game, too."

"Yep, that's what happened, all right," the boy replied, warming up him. "I win all the games, or most of them." He peered closer. Aedham became conscious of his own pointed ears, which without the glamorie, were plainly visible.

"*You're* not one of them, are you?" Joystik asked cautiously.

He had to be honest. "Well, yes and no. I am from this land. But they are my enemies. That's why I'm here, behind these bars."

"You're a faery," Alan observed. Without a doubt

Aedham heard the *e* in the word instead of the *i*, and his respect for the kid's education went up a notch. "And this," Alan said, looking around him, "Is the underworld. *Isn't* it?"

Aedham stared him with unconcealed amazement. "Yeah, that's it. You're the first human I've never had to explain it to."

"I read a lot," Alan said. "Celtic mythology is one of my favorite subjects. I read the *Book of Invasions* in the fourth grade." He amended, "The English translation, of course."

"Then that will simplify things," Aedham said, then considered: *he has the human side of the story. It's not altogether accurate, but it will make a convenient head start.* "I am of the Tuatha De Danaan, the people of Danu, and I am King Aedham Tuiereann, ruler of elfhame Avalon."

In spite of himself, Alan was grinning widely. "I thought Avalon referred to the entire land?"

"A long time ago, it did. Avalon changed most dramatically when our people split into two groups. My ancestors, the Seleighe court, wanted to make peace with the humans. The opposing court, the Unseleighe, wanted to wreak havoc on them for exiling us to this world within a world."

"So who won?" Alan asked, without a hint of sarcasm.

"I would say *we* did, but as I am now their prisoner that cannot be entirely true. But I don't think the Unseleighe have the ability to create all this," Aedham said, indicating the dungeon in general. "The gods have told me some things," he continued. "Perhaps you can confirm a few of them."

"Which gods?" Alan asked excitedly. "Dagda? Danu herself?"

Aedham sighed, wishing his people's namesake *were* involved. It would sure tip the scales in their favor. "Dagda fathered many of our gods, but he doesn't exist in his original form, nor does Danu. Gods live a long time, but after a while even they change, become different thought forms. Some of these forms we can no longer communicate with; we have become alien and unrecognizable to each other.

"I had thought such was the case with Lugh, the god of light. But Lugh is still among us, in fact is a central player in this mess. As is his son."

"Cu Chulainn? The *warrior*?" Joystik pressed his face through the bars, eyes wide with amazement. "How is *he* involved?"

"According to Lugh, he is a reincarnated human. And is playing in the Tulsa Lazerwarz arena, and getting pretty good at it."

"Holy shit," Joystik commented. "I'm not so sure I'd want to play against him. The son . . . of the God of Light? A hell of an advantage in a game of laser tag, if you ask me. Who's side is he on, anyway?"

The words hung heavily in the air; Lugh's warnings notwithstanding, the boy had a point. "The Foevors seem to have their claws in him. To what degree, I don't know."

"So *that's* who's running this place. I thought it was a demon . . . he calls himself Mort, but others have called him Morca. Morca was a ship's captain in one of the battles over Ireland. He must have been around a long time."

"Do you know where Mort is?" Aedham asked eagerly.

"Not right now. There is a royal chamber of some kind, which is in this world and my world, depending on his mood. I wait on Mort. He thinks this ruby has total control of me. It doesn't. You already knew that."

Aedham paced slowly in the cell, touching the cold, moist walls. "Can you get me out of here?"

Joystik frowned, shook his head. "I don't have a key to the cells. Mort has all of them, and watches them carefully. And there are elves, watching this place, and they can't handle the keys, just the lizards, as you called them."

The king's hopes sank. "As I suspected. There are other ways I might be able to gain freedom. I have done it before, in situations more dire than this."

"It's a really big place," Joystik said. "The elves, they say they're of the clan Aoncos. That's not your clan, is it?"

Aedham looked away, trying to hide his despair. "No, they are Unseleighe. Mercenaries."

"Well anyway, they're all spread pretty thin. There are hundreds of these cells, most of them unoccupied. I get the idea that they're still building their army." He turned, pointed to the incapacitated youth in the neighboring cell. "They grab good players, blow some sort of magic smoke in their face that puts them out or something, then give them jewels to control their minds. Like mine," he said, tapping the red stone at his temple. "Every once in a while one of the stones don't take and they put a double whammy on them that, well, you see the results." Again, he indicated the youths behind him. "Looks like they're on thorazine or something. The rest, they train like they're in an army. But it looks like . . . they think they're playing Lazerwarz."

Aedham perked up at that. "Like Lazerwarz? What are they using for weapons?"

"I think they're real lasers. Only they don't work down here very well—they're just training with them. But I heard Mort say something about getting the right technology from the Seleighe so they can work here." He paused, considering what he had just said. "Is that something your clan has?"

"Lugh just informed me that the technology had been stolen from my palace. Looks like they got what they wanted, too." The King's thoughts darkened as he imagined an army of human youths blindly attacking Avalon forces. *How long would my army hesitate before firing? Long enough to be leveled by the levin rifles?*

A sound from down the hall interrupted him. Voices, then footsteps. Joystik looked alarmed. "I have to go. I've been gone too long."

"Keep pretending to be stoned," Aedham said to his retreating back, and groaned at his own pun.

The boy grinned at the weak humor. "I'll come back as soon as I can. With a key, if I can swing it," and he disappeared into the dungeon.

Chapter Seven

Mort surveyed the Dallas skyline from his twentieth story corner office, smugly warming up to the notion that what he surveyed would some day be all his.

But first things first. Underhill must submit to me. Then we'll go from there.

In this human seeming he was a silver-haired, fiftyish man in a blue three-piece suit. Moments ago he'd finished a two-hour teleconference with the electronics and plastics firms who would make the parts for his new, modified gun design.

It was the perfect front for manufacturing his weapon, Mort decided, right here in the middle of Dallas' high rise, high-tech neighborhood. Lazerwarz, Inc. was already making laser tag guns in this facility, and now that he had Avalon's elvenstone technology the next stage of his plan could begin. When the new parts arrived in the next twenty-four hours, Mort's existing laser tag toys would be converted into lethal rifles capable of firing levin bolts, by anyone, human or non. In the assembly plant one floor down, the works would start churning out the guns at a rate of fifty per hour.

Before him on an enormous oak desk lay the prototype of the new rig, its design quickly cribbed from the crude gear stolen from King Aedham's palace. The principle was so simple he wondered why no one of Underhill had come up with it before. Odras, an Avalon Mage, had originated the concept and had first applied it using the wheel of a BMW motorcycle. Three Underhill rock formations—amene, topolomite and diaspar—were arranged on the wheel and opposing forks to induce node energy; the faster the wheel spun, the more node energy was generated. This was a first for Underhill; until now, magic existed as pools of energy, or *nodes*, lurking beneath the ground.

The existing Lazerwarz pack had a round target of lights on the front, covered by a plastic housing. This would be replaced by a spinning disk assembly which contained the three-stone configuration. Node energy tended to track along electrical pathways, and the existing laser beam array acted as a pointer, like the laser sights for human handguns.

An hour earlier, Mort had tested the device in an improvised firing range. The target was a three-foot-thick slab of concrete the size of a ping-pong table, turned up on end. One blast had put a three-foot hole in the concrete, and had damaged several walls beyond it. The weapon's recoil was comparable to a .22 handgun. Mort had to remind himself that the device *did* obey the laws of physics . . . but of a different, magical realm.

With this weapon he would conquer Underhill. The AK-47, the human weapon designed to be fired by peasants, was mass-produced, imprecise, but absolutely reliable in the worst conditions. The USSR, may it rest in peace, had been built and fortified by such arms; Mort would do the same with his weapon.

But what to call it? Mort thought. He needed a name for his creation. It was shorter than a regular rifle, but longer than a handgun.

Two great tastes that taste great together!

Hadn't the Uzi been named after an Israeli commander?

Hell. Let's call it the Mort. The Mort Short.

The phone buzzed. Mort hit the handsfree.

"Yuaroh Dhu on line one," the secretary announced. Mort picked up the phone.

"Have you raided the mines yet?" Mort demanded.

A bit of static garbled the response. The connection to Underhill had always been a bit fuzzy, but after a fashion Yuaroh's voice came through loud and clear. "Aie, commander. As you warned, there was resistance at the amene mines—Elfhame Outremer took exception to our presence—but we seized enough unworked stones to fill your order for this lot."

The news was a blessed relief; it was the last link in the production chain. Now he had the means to manufacture the first few hundred Morts.

"That is good news, Yuaroh. You will receive my highest award, once I decide what it is. Transport the stones to the palace immediately for gating."

He frowned, knowing he was forgetting something. "Oh, yes. Question our prisoner, King Aedham Tuiereann. Claim that *you* are responsible for his capture, and this entire operation. Negotiate a 'cease fire' of sorts, but try to get whatever information you can from him. I'm particularly interested in the communications network the Seleighe courts have created with their amene crystals. We must find a flaw to exploit, so we can disrupt their early warning system. I want the invasion to be a *complete* surprise."

"Aie, commander. Consider it done."

"Oh, and Yuaroh?"

"Aie?"

"Don't fuck up."

Mort hung up.

As soon as Joystik scampered off Aedham heard another set of footsteps coming down the dungeon's hall. It didn't take a Mage to predict that the following conversation would not be as cordial as the one he'd just had.

An Unseleighe Lord flanked by two guards stopped in front of his cell. The Lord had a long, thin mustache, and a human Asian look that made Aedham wonder in what part of Underhill this elf had originated. He held a long, pretentious scepter crowned with a silver gargoyle. Under long, black cloaks all three wore unadorned fur tunics; simple, straightforward, and practical. Their odor suggested they'd just returned from a long journey, and their faces, the leader's in particular, betrayed weariness.

Aedham sensed nothing particularly magical about the Lord, who probably was not the source of the levin bolt which had laid him out. But that didn't mean they weren't a force to contend with; his being on the wrong side of the bars more or less mandated that.

"I was disappointed that you didn't put up more of a fight," said the leader, sneering at him through the bars. "King Aedham Tuiereann, leader of Avalon, the elven prince who grew up *as* a human, *among* humans, thinking he *was* human. Somehow I was hoping that a *sidhe* who had survived such an ordeal would have more . . . character."

Aedham shrugged impassively. "Happy to disappoint you."

"And those pathetic wards you put on your palace . . . they were simple enough to walk through. There, I would have also expected more."

"You did not dismiss those wards," Aedham said. "I doubt you could even manage a simple Mage spark to start a fire."

The leader threw back his head and laughed raucously. "Of course I didn't. I am Yuaroh Dhu, Lord of the Aoncos clan. I represent the Unseleighe bands you've defeated, as well as those who've never challenged you. I am no Mage, as you have already deduced, but I *am* a warrior. And I am, of course, an elf. An elf who would like to see the elves remain in power in Underhill."

"Provided they are Unseleighe, of course," Aedham said. "How do you think Mort and his merry band of Foevorians would react if their mercenaries turned on them?" Aedham folded his arms, and met the Unseleighe's hard gaze with one of his own.

The Lord did seem taken aback; he must not have known the King of Avalon could figure things out so quickly. "I admire your clear vision. My employer underestimated your ability to see the true nature of things. Yes, the Foevors are moving to take Underhill." Yuaroh stepped away from the bars and paced a short distance down the hall.

"Mort was one of your own minions, was he not?" Aedham asked.

"I never hired him. Those who did are dead. But of course, you know that. You killed them."

"Just Zeldan," Aedham said, with a yawn. "One of my men killed Japhet."

Yuaroh ignored him. "I sought to annex myself to Mort's plan once I saw how powerful he had become. Zeldan, Japhet, and others—they are to blame for Mort's rise to power. Not that I think it would have mattered if they had ignored the sniveling little Foevor." He stopped his pacing in front of the cell's door and looked up. "Mort sent me here to mislead you, King. I was to tell you that I am your captor, and the mastermind behind this plan."

Now it was Aedham's turn to laugh. "I would never have believed that. I think you know that."

"No, you wouldn't. Yet the request did make me consider, does this Foevor *really* understand us? If he thinks you so dimwitted, what must he think of me? Much worse, I wager."

Aedham was starting to get the drift. *This Unseleighe wants to turn against Mort. Would that be stupid?*

What if the Foevor is underestimating our entire race as dramatically as it seems?

"We stole some important equipment from your palace while we were there. The node generator, with the diaspar, amene and topolomite configuration. Mort has it now. He is mass-producing a weapon capable of using the generator to fire levin bolts. No Mage required." He paused, and motioned to the sleeping youths behind him, in the other cell. "*They* could wield it most effectively. And how many Seleighe elves would fight human *children*?"

It *was* the most unpleasant part of the problem—elves fighting children who are armed with such lethal devices. Even if the kids didn't mow entire elven armies down with the levin rifles, they were entirely expendable so far as their leader was concerned.

"That's not a comfortable thought," Aedham admitted. "So what do you want from me?"

"I would make you an offer. An alliance. Soon Mort will be preoccupied with the coming invasion of Underhill. The mass production of levin rifles has already begun in the Overworld." Yuaroh leaned closer, and said in a near whisper, "How would you like to even the odds?"

Aedham's first thought was, what would be "even" to the Unseleighe? Their sense of fairness had always been, at the very least, warped. *Asking is free.*

"What did you have in mind?" Aedham asked, trying not to sound too interested.

"Your engineers have developed the weapon. My men have delivered the stones needed for their manufacture. It only follows that we should both benefit from the weapons, don't you think?"

Aedham was starting to see what Yuaroh was steering towards, but remained mute.

The Unseleighe continued, "The weapons will be stored in a part of the palace which is *not* subject to the spell which prevents node power from entering."

Aedham feigned boredom. "Go on."

"You could construct a Gate. My men are waiting, in another portion of Underhill. We shall steal the rifles!"

"Mort will only make more," Aedham pointed out. Yet the plan had a great deal of merit . . . for the Unseleighe, that is. "And I am to trust you to share the plunder, I take it."

"Trust works both ways, King. As a sign of good faith, I let your sister go free when we captured you. And remember, you will have access to node power."

"And what would keep me from nailing your whole tribe with a levin bolt of my own making?"

Yuaroh's expression turned faintly amused. "I am no fool, King. We will *escort* you to the location. You will have, at all times, three blades to your back, and one at your throat if I feel inclined. If you could summon such a power undetected, and attack us before we run you through, it is unlikely you would be here in Mort's dungeon."

Yeah, right. And what happened to "trust"?

Aedham considered his options. He was absolutely powerless here, there was no debating that. If he had a chance to get out, even on those terms, he knew he had to take it.

"If I refuse?"

The Lord was unmoved. "We'll kill you trying to 'escape.' Mort wouldn't mind."

Aedham shook his head in amazement. "And this is how you seek alliances? At sword's point?"

Yuaroh shrugged most unapologetically. "It's all we know." The three started to leave. "When it is time, we will return."

When it is time, Aedham thought, as he heard the Unseleighe walk down what had to be an extremely long hallway. Then, moving silently, like a wraith, Joystik popped into view.

"I thought you had left," Aedham said.

"I just went around the corner to listen in," the boy replied. "So this gate thing, you can make one?"

"Outside this dungeon I think I can. If there are no surprises. Foevors handle magic differently, and in some ways better than I. Blocking it from me is easy for them."

Joystik nodded thoughtfully. "I get the feeling you don't trust them."

Aedham fought back the anger rising in the back of his throat. "They killed my family. I will never trust them."

Chapter Eight

"You can see it from here," Sammi said as she pulled the carriage to a stop. "That large, white building, near the circle of stones. Just go on in like you own the place."

Llan was still getting over the ride in the carriage, which had just hurtled them through the Overworld kingdom of Tulsa at a dizzying speed. Elvensteeds traveled far faster, granted, but Llan had never ridden one, and now he wasn't certain he wanted to.

"Why are we stopping here?" Llan asked. They were still quite a distance from the arena, in a clearing covered with smooth, black stone painted with white lines.

"The arena has special scrying eyes that can see us," Sammi said, pushing something down with her left foot, making a ratcheting sound. She was dressed like a human, in a "suit" which had something to do with "checking in with the office." Llan sensed the weapon she kept beneath the suit, a nasty tool of cold iron surrounded by some other substance that allowed her to carry it. "We have to keep our distance from it. They may recognize me, as I was with Aedham when he vanished." Of course she had mentioned this before, but there were so many rules to remember about this strange world: Try not to stare too much at the sky, which seemed endless compared to the high ceiling of mist in Underhill. Use the gloved hand to touch iron, which was to be found everywhere; he flexed his right hand in the thin leather glove. When he asked why Sammi didn't wear a glove, she replied that she and Aedham had gotten accustomed to handling cold iron when they couldn't avoid it altogether, having spent a good amount of time here. It had something to do with turning off the pain when they came into contact, though *extended* contact still left marks on their skin. Until he had the glove, Sammi had to open the carriage door for him, which had made him feel less than masculine; he'd looked furtively about to see if any humans were watching.

The most important rule was *never use magic*. Ever. For any reason. If the humans saw him use it, they would know he wasn't human, and would seize him and strap him to a table and cut him open and examine his entrails. He was *not* going to let that happen. His entrails were private, and he would keep them to himself.

"Remember to come back here when the medallion on your wrist starts making noises," Sammi said, and Llan glanced at the non-iron item in question, which was strapped around his arm. It flashed numbers when you squeezed it a certain way. The King had taught him the rudiments of human numbers and writing, and he could read, though with difficulty. "I will be right here."

"Aie, Lady Sam—"

"No, call me Sammi. Do not use my title. The humans wouldn't . . . understand."

So many rules! But it was for his King, and he would put up with far more rules if it would rescue him from his captors.

"Now," Sammi said sternly. "Where are you from?"

"England," Llan replied. "In Britain."

"And what is your name?"

"Colin Downy."

"Good. Do you have your ID?"

Llan pulled out the thin leather pouch which contained all his documents. The humans, he had learned, placed much importance on these strange little cards.

"That's your driver's license. Now give me . . . sixteen dollars."

Llan counted out three of the sheafs of paper in his pouch with the number five, and one with the number one. The humans depicted on both notes looked the same.

Sammi seemed satisfied and gave the money back. "That will do. Don't worry if you get confused. Just tell them you're from England if they seem suspicious. But if you get into some serious trouble, and you think you are in real danger, push the button on the device." Llan touched the small black box in his pocket, making sure he still had it. "It will tell me, and I will come in the carriage and we will leave."

"Aie . . . I mean, okay, Sammi. I will not fail you."

"I know you won't. Just remember, it's not the humans we are fighting. Something from *Underhill* has seized the King. Find out what you can, and return when your medallion says so. Now *scoot*."

Llan got out, careful to handle the door with his gloved hand. He started off towards the arena, past a grove of trees growing up through the smooth black stone, and towards several rows of the different human carriages. His glamorie hung discreetly and invisibly about his head, making his pointed ears appear short and human, and gave his eyes rounded pupils instead of the slitted ones of the Fey. The smells were so strange, and the heat of their summer day was heavy and oppressive. The clothes they had given him were strange as well, but fit him like the glove on his hand; the jeans and T-shirt had belonged to Aedham when he was Llan's age. He also wore the King's strange ny kees, and now that he had them on he knew why

Aedham cherished them so. They were the most comfortable boots he'd ever worn, and gave spring to his step. Though he was glad that his long golden hair could remain as it was, he would have surely shaved it off if it would help get the King back.

If I can get the King back.

The doubt came unbidden and unexpectedly, and Llan quickly shoved it aside.

I will *get the King back.*

He found himself in front of the arena, past the horde of humans who were gazing at the circle of stones. Sammi had told him to avoid going to the Henge—it was not important to the mission, and might attract unnecessary attention. The frame of cold metal that was the door stood forebodingly. Two humans burst through it, talking excitedly.

While the door was open, Llan walked in to the darkened, cold interior, and looked around. Lots of humans here, with more colors of clothing than the elf had thought possible.

Now, where is . . . there it is, Llan thought, finding the line of humans at the counter. When it was his turn Llan stepped up with his leather pouch in hand, as instructed.

"Code name?"

Llan hesitated.

"Don't got one? Here, look at this list."

Llan fumbled with the piece of paper, suddenly afraid for his cover. *They forgot to tell me about this!* his mind raced, but the words came into focus, and the hours the King had once spent teaching him reading paid off. There were sacred names like Zeus and Mercury . . . how could they be so brazen with the gods?

Llan had no qualms about his selection. "Elvenmage."

"Sorry, someone already has that. Try another."

Curious that humans would select such a name. Llan made something up. "Elven . . . boy."

The human did something behind a glowing screen; this must be what the humans called a computer. "Elvenboy it is. Your game will be up soon. Six dollars."

Llan gave him a one and a five, for which he received a bright green tag. He inadvertently touched the metal button with his left hand, but hid his pain, and managed not to drop it.

He moved towards the big door on the right. Sammi had gone over the layout of the place on the chalkboard in Niamh's workshop, and what he saw in here was, fortunately, no surprise. The door was right where it should be. The place had the feel of a great hall, in a lesser palace, with no manners; these humans talked loudly among themselves, with no hierarchy visible among them. Sammi had warned him about the metal piercing their flesh, but the phenomenon was still disturbing, particularly close up. The young ladies here were attractive, he noted before reining his thoughts back in.

I am here to find the King!

"I'll bet you get your ass kicked in there," said a voice behind him.

Llan whirled around defensively, forming a half-dozen retorts, all of which only another elf would understand.

"It is my first game," Llan replied. "I doubt that I will win."

The boy was tall and menacing, but thin as a rail, with black clothing from head to toe. At first glance he had an Unseleighe look about him, but he was most assuredly human, with no magical traces about him. And he had an odor. And no hair. When he spoke, Llan saw a metal stud in the middle of his tongue.

"You sound kind of funny," the kid said, his face wrinkling suspiciously. "Where you from, anyway?"

"England," Llan replied glibly. "In Britain."

The kid rolled his eyes, an exaggerated move which

felt patronizing. "I *know* where England is. So you never played before?"

Llan gazed at him evenly. At least he knew when he was being made fun of.

"Oh, leave him alone," a thin female voice said from behind the kid, who turned and wrapped his arms around a young lady, a child even, dressed in black as well. "You were new here once."

"Tell me about it," he said with a laugh, nuzzling the maiden with abandon. They started kissing, right then, right there. Beneath the glamorie, Llan felt his ear tips burn with embarrassment. *Randy, mannerless humans!* It looked like they were going to devour each other's faces. The elf half expected them to disrobe and fornicate right there on the floor.

The kid came up for breath. "My name's Zeus. See that guy over there?" He pointed to a tall, older man with silver hair standing at the end of the line. A set of goggles hung around his neck.

"That's *Elvendude*. Stay away from him. He'll kick your ass."

"I thought this was laser tag," Llan said, in proper, cultured tones. "As I understand it, the kicking of asses is not allowed here."

Now the girl let loose a peal of laughter, then looked as if she regretted her outburst. "In America, 'kicking ass' means conquering or winning, as well as other things. That's what numbnuts here is trying to tell you."

Zeus ignored the jibe. "And that one, over there," he said, indicating another youth, who had something different about him. "He's The Hound. Between you and me, you should go find some easier targets. The Hound gets kind of weird. Eyes get all strange. Face gets all radical. Sometimes it looks like there's light coming off him."

The Hound looked as alone as Llan felt right then; he was human, yes, but something different about him, intangible but there, definitely there . . . what was it? *Why can't I see auras like the King can?*

The door opened suddenly, and the line of kids streamed into the still more darkened room. Here a human, called a judge, instructed them in the ways of laser tag. The device looked something like a suit of armor, but with the electric lights that were everywhere in the human's world. Next, the judge led them into a place where rows of the laser rigs hung on the wall.

It was a strange way to fight war, Llan mused as he entered the maze. Fighting everyone but yourself, no armies, no commanders, and above all, no *swords* . . . but this was a game, one these humans took seriously. They scattered into the arena, a dark maze that at first glance looked like *Underhill*, complete with mist. The game started, and around him laser beams sought their targets. Amid the web of light one of the beams hit him, extinguishing his pack like water on fire.

Into the arena. Find the King, he reminded himself, chanting the mission's directive as he plunged into the darkness. Weaving through the maze, Llan tried to imagine what the King would do, what path he would take. To make it look convincing he fired at some of the moving targets in the distance, hit one, and moved on. Sammi had said it would look suspicious if a kid his size came out with the lowest score of the game.

Then the human called The Hound came into view, moving through the maze like a wraith, tagging Llan casually as he moved. A swarm of kids led by Zeus pursued The Hound with undisguised glee. Suddenly the game had turned into something else, something dishonorable. Sammi had warned him of this dark side of the human character. They outnumbered The Hound five to one.

Intrigued, Llan followed, tagging a few from the rear, undetected. The Hound stopped and faced them down, shooting in a frenzy of laser that, for a moment, looked like a spider web of light, touching all of the targets at once. Nothing short of a Mage could do something like that, unless this was a warrior of warriors with divine powers. Llan had seen such warriors Underhill; they were not Mages, yet they worked another, powerful enchantment, from a fierce inner fire that crossed from combat to magic.

The gang of youths stood quietly, and darkly, until one by one their packs returned to life. Llan had his turn with them, but soon found himself overwhelmed. The elf retreated into a dark corner, waited for his pack to come back, and reemerged. He was alone. The others had moved on.

He took this opportunity to explore the maze a bit before the end of the game, but found no traces whatsoever of the Gate that had whisked his mentor away. It was frustrating, for Sammi had insisted it was here, she had seen the power herself. But there was nothing, just this strange human environment with peculiar odors and sounds.

At the game's conclusion Llan hung his pack on the wall and joined the others outside beneath another screen. Groans erupted in the crowd when the scores appeared. The Hound was number one with 1320, Elvendude with 1233, and Zeus with 905. Llan was down near the bottom with 500, but by no means in last place.

Llan spied the winner talking to someone over by a water well. Until now The Hound didn't appear to have any acquaintances, but this man seemed rather familiar with him. His father? Perhaps, but it didn't really seem that way. He sensed the same sort of distant magic about this man as he had The Hound, with a hint of Underhill somewhere in the mix.

Are these the ones responsible for the King's disappearance?

This was the what Llan had come to learn. But

despite the vague magical impression they had both made, he did not feel any danger or threat about them. Perhaps they were connected, in some obscure way, to the standing stones outside.

The older man glanced up and looked directly at Llan. The gesture froze the elf where he stood, and for the first time since gating here Llan thought that his identity had become known. The elf didn't like the idea of humans reading his entrails, but he didn't want to bolt for the door, either. Not yet. Instead his hand moved toward the pocket where the little black box with the button lurked.

Finger poised over the button, Llan moved towards the water fountain. The Hound had gone elsewhere. Activity buzzed around them, from loud blinking boxes with controls that had the kids mesmerized, and from unseen voices called *speakers*, some human technology which Llan had become familiar with in Aedham's solar.

Llan drank from the well and stood, regarding the man quizzically. He was still gazing directly at Llan. *He must know I'm an elf!* Yet, his instincts told him there was no danger, and his hand moved out of his pocket, away from the black box. This, he felt, he could handle without Lady Samantha's intervention.

"I know you are of the *sidhe*," the man said with an aged, gravelly voice.

What a disconcerting way to begin a conversation with a human, Llan thought. He met his eyes evenly. "How can you know that?"

The man smiled, reminding Llan of his own grandfather, long dead. "Not all humans are blind to the other worlds," he replied, then nodded towards the front doors, beyond which stood the Henge. "Even when the other worlds come directly to their doorstep. My name is Cathad," the man said, extending his hand. As Llan took it he felt a power which went far beyond his humanity. "I am a druid."

A human Mage! The elf believed him without question, though reason would have insisted he investigate further. Again, his instincts spoke from his gut—the man is who is says he is. The druids were one of the few groups of humans to actually reach the elves in Underhill, but that was an eternity ago. Their brief visits were described in dusty old elven legends, told to littles at bedtime. The druids were the kind ones, the wise ones who offered magical protections to their tribe, who tended battle wounds and healed the sick, and who beseeched the earth and sun for food, water and warmth. The druids had vanished long ago. Or so Llan had thought.

Druid. A human who knew magic. But can a druid be behind the evil that kidnapped untold hundreds of human children, and the elven King, Aedham Tuiereann? Hardly.

There was also the feeling this had more to do with the visit Lugh made to the elfhame. *What exactly did the god say?* The memory lurked just beyond reach; perhaps this conversation would bring it closer.

"Let us discuss this privately," Cathad said, and Llan felt an invisible shroud surround them, and blocked most of the sound from getting inside it. The ambient noise of the Lazerwarz lobby had become a distant murmur, and it was obvious the shield worked both ways. Their words would remain in the shroud.

"My druid name is Cathad. My name in this life is Alfred Mackie, and I have come from Britain to examine the stones which have so mysteriously appeared outside," the wise man said. He was well advanced in years, but had that glow of eternal youth common to most human Mages. To think him an old man would be a mistake, Llan knew; the elf hoped Cathad would not misjudge him because of his obvious youth. "I did not expect to find a faery here, so far from my homeland."

"Nor did I intend to be spotted by a human," Llan

replied. He surreptitiously probed the area around them for hidden traps, in case this druid was not as benign as he seemed, but found none. "I would think that my purpose for being here might have some connection with yours."

"It would seem the obvious conclusion. Tell me, does the name Cu Chulainn mean anything to you?"

"It's old Gaelic, I think," Llan said. "Someone's hound. Culann's?"

Cathad smiled appreciatively. "And beyond that?"

The Hound. Wait, isn't that . . . Llan scanned the lobby before replying. The Hound who had won the last game was standing in line to sign up for another. He seemed timid out of his element, and was clearly trying to hide his hands for some reason. Llan peered closer, venturing the use of his Mage sight, and saw why. The youth had seven fingers on each hand.

Llan remembered an old tale about an Irish warrior who had the same deformity, who slew armies single-handed, and was the son of the God of . . .

It fell into place. The revelation shook him to the core; the memory of Ethlinn's conversation with Lugh on the palace grounds surged to the surface.

Lugh's son, the incarnated human, a warrior of the arenas.

Llan hazarded another glance at The Hound, who was still in line. Yes, the spark hung about him still, as likely unseen by the humans around him. *The son of a god. And he doesn't know it.*

"Lugh contacted us," Llan said to Cathad. "He even mentioned you, in part. The task of the druid includes teaching the humans that there is life after death, many lives . . . that's why you're here. The Hound needs a teacher."

"Indeed, he does," Cathad admitted, with an air of futility Llan found unbecoming in a wise one. "His past is buried so deeply into his soul. I don't know . . . if I can reach the divine part of him, with what I have.

I have been separated from the Old Order for a long time. My skills are, alas, rusty."

Llan tested the muting shroud. "It seems intact to me. This is excellent work, for a human."

Alfred's eyebrow arched, as from a mild insult. "Thank you. I think. So, when have you last confronted a Foevorian?"

"I never have," Llan admitted. "Our realms don't overlap as much as you might think." By now The Hound had made his way through the line and was waiting for the game to begin. "The Foevorians want him for their army, don't they?"

"For all we know, they already have him. Either way, he doesn't know much of anything of his origins." Alfred shook his head sadly. "The poor lad has trouble holding his head up among his peers. If only he knew who he was."

"Perhaps we can both bring him to this knowledge," Llan said, as a plan began shaping up before him. "I think that is what Lugh had in mind for us all."

Sammi waited patiently in the Caprice, the car running to power the air conditioner. She hadn't counted on such a hot day, and her fuel tank was running low. At the corner of 41st and Yale was a Texaco, in full view of the arena; she decided to go fuel up, keeping an eye on the arena, and an ear to the pager connected to Llan's black emergency box.

She pulled around to the parking lot, and was waiting for traffic to clear so she could pull onto Yale, when a red Corvette whizzed past, going south at a high rate of speed.

The Corvette's top was down, and driving it was a woman with long, red hair, who for some reason possessed a divine aura which did *not* belong in this realm.

Let's check this out, she thought, already certain that somehow this had something to do with the King's kidnapping.

Sammi turned south on Yale, and followed.

She was no traffic cop, but as special agent Sammi McDaris she had the authority to pull over pretty much whoever she wanted. On the floor was a red, rotating cop light that plugged into the cigarette lighter. Keeping a steady eye on the 'Vette, she fumbled with the light and plugged it in, hoping it worked.

It did. She pulled up right on the tail end of the 'Vette, and in lieu of a siren, honked once.

That's right, I'm right on your tail. And the spinning cherry is in plain sight.

The redhead looked up, and their eyes met briefly her rear view. But the 'Vette showed no intention of slowing down. Instead, the driver used the rear view to send a blast of . . . something, directly at her.

Sammi suddenly couldn't see.

She slammed on her brakes, feeling the Caprice fishtail under her. Cars behind her honked and swerved, but the impact she expected next didn't happen. Slowly, her vision returned, and when she could see enough to drive she restarted the stalled engine and floored the accelerator. Pulling on the scant reserve of node power at her disposal, she constructed a crude shield between her and the 'Vette, and hoped it held up against whatever else this *bitch* sent her way.

The 'Vette was well ahead of her, but was stopped behind traffic at a light. It looked like it was trying to nose past a pickup and flee onto a service road on the right. *Oh no you don't, not on my watch you aren't,* she fumed, riding right up to the Corvette again.

The traffic moved ahead leisurely, and the Corvette, evidently surrendering to the pursuit, drove slowly onto the service road, pulled over, and stopped.

Sammi pulled up behind her, calming herself. The redhead was sitting casually in the driver's seat, her arm hanging over the door, as if she were drying her nails.

Sammi held the Glock down, at her side, but plainly visible. Her shield, with some careful maneuvering, traveled with her. And she made sure her badge was visible from her lapel.

Sammi walked briskly up to the 'Vette. "I'm Special Agent Samantha McDaris. Who the *hell* are you?"

The driver looked up casually. There was nothing here to identify her as nonhuman, except for her use of magic. Even a good human Mage couldn't have temporarily blinded an elf.

"Would you like to see my driver's license and insurance verification?" the driver asked in an oily, patronizing tone.

Sammi had heard this voice before.

"Yes, let's have it," Sammi said, checking out the car, the driver, the whole weird situation.

The driver searched through a red purse; Samantha leveled the Glock at her. If this *was* a god the gun wouldn't be very effective, but it did make her feel better.

"Special *Agent* McDaris," the driver said conversationally. "You really are moving up in the world. You were a homicide detective, I think. The last time I saw you was at the New You Fitness center in Dallas . . . moments before it imploded."

Sammi didn't have to search her memory very hard. "My dear Morrigan. I didn't recognize you."

Sammi kept the gun aimed at her, and hoped the scene wasn't attracting any unwanted attention. To say the least, this would be difficult to explain if it came to the attention of her boss.

"Interesting little realm you have here. The sun is a very interesting feature. And the youth of this place . . . I understand they are drafted at an early age to fight wars."

Sammi let this pass without comment, keeping her

focus on the gun and what Morrigan was doing with her hands.

But she couldn't resist a comment or two. "You look, well, *different*. Sexy. Big breasted. And dare I say, promiscuous? What, you didn't like the 'Snapple Lady' look?"

"It didn't suit my purposes," Morrigan sneered. "For this project."

Sammi lined the Glock's sight up with her face. "Where is our King?"

Morrigan made an impatient gesture. "What, you've misplaced him again? How should I know where that silly Seleighe has run off to?"

"You and Mort have him," Sammi stated. "You're involved in this Lazerwarz arena. And I'll even bet you're the one who moved Stonehenge to its present location. What*ever* were you thinking?"

"Business," she said severely. She put the purse away. "Samantha, do yourself a favor. Stay out of this. It's more than you and the entire Seleighe court could ever handle."

"You know I can't do that. Shall I take you in for questioning?"

The peal of laughter was piercing, and unexpected. And backed with a great deal of confidence.

"You're welcome to try," Morrigan said, as she and the Corvette vanished in a bright flash of light.

Whenever Dobie entered the arena at the start of a game, he felt a change sweep over him, a metamorphosis into The Hound. It felt good, and right, and somehow overdue. Dobie knew intuitively that The Hound always had been a part of him, but had remained hidden until he'd discovered the arena.

And Morgan.

The third day now after meeting her his life was nothing like it had been before. For most of those three days, secreted in her hotel suite, they made wild, passionate love, for hours on end. She introduced him to the Kamasutra, which had quickly become an aerobic workout, and they weren't even halfway through it. Now he was dehydrated most of the time, and had to guzzle Gatorade by the liter just to keep up with her. And as soon as they finished . . . she was ready to go again! He obliged her willingly, drawing on some untapped pool of energy he still didn't understand, thrusting into her with ever harder and deeper strokes. And still it didn't seem to be enough.

Finally, when she dropped him off at Lazerwarz today, with kiss and a slap on his spandexed butt, he discovered he was in *pain* down there. He walked with a funny gait which he hoped was not noticeable, but probably was. "Please, just let me recover, for Pete's sake!" he wanted to wail, but to do so would break whatever magical spell had created this situation in the first place. And he didn't want it to end, not yet. He comforted himself with the knowledge that every male in that arena, from puberty on, wished they had *his* problem.

And this guy, this Alfred, the archeologist. He didn't seem to be studying Stonehenge very much. The older man seemed inexplicably interested in him, though not in any sexual way (thank God). Alfred had a power about him, which at times triggered memories which bore a striking resemblance to his dreams of the old civilization.

But today Alfred was talking to another player, one The Hound had never seen before, who went by Elvenboy. The kid was about the same age as himself, and clearly new to the game. Waiting for this seventh game to start, Dobie watched them from a distance as they discussed something rather enthusiastically. If he focused his eyes a certain way it looked like a translucent bubble was surrounding them. The image was brief and fleeting, never staying put for long, and no one else seemed to notice it; Dobie decided he was seeing things.

Today Zeus and his band of bullies had been coming after him every damned game. The first time The Hound had nearly lost his first place position because of them, but in every game after that he learned to milk the situation for points by mentally timing each pack, and nailing them a half second before they came back up. After all, the targets were all right there in the same place, and he didn't have to go far to find them. They found him. *How convenient.*

The next game started out slow; after the gun's countdown, The Hound found himself completely alone, with nothing to shoot at. All around him he heard points being made. It was infuriating to know they weren't *his* points. Up the ramp to the unoccupied second level, The Hound scanned the floor for targets, started picking off the few wandering lights down there. Across the arena, at the other, larger second level, laser mayhem was taking place. He found a clear shot over there and started dropping packs; they soon saw where the fire was coming from, and moved out of the way. *Damn! Nothing to shoot at again!*

He would have to get to the other level. It took about sixty seconds to get there, valuable time when he wouldn't be scoring. *I'm not scoring anyway. Better go there now.*

Nearing the other second level he knew he had made the right choice. It sounded like a hundred people stomping around up there. And who did he find, at the top of the ramp, but Zeus himself. All alone, too.

The kid looked alarmed, and started firing at The Hound, who turned sideways, gun up, then dipped the barrel, tagging the chest target.

"So where are your friends?" The Hound asked. "I don't see them anywhere."

"Quit tagging me, goddammit!" Zeus said, holding his hand over his chest target. A major infraction of the rules, and no judge was around. It didn't matter. The Hound got the shoulder target, then took out a few of the targets Zeus was after, deeper into the second level, and swung around to take Zeus out the moment his pack was up.

"It's not fair! You're cheating!" Zeus wailed.

"Then go somewhere else," The Hound said. "Go find your buddies if you can't handle me by yourself."

"Go screw yourself!" Zeus said, walking right up to The Hound, holding his gun right at The Hound's chest target while his pack was counting off the seconds before it came back.

"You're a little too close," The Hound said, backing up, and turning sideways, then nailed Zeus again. *If he doesn't like it, why doesn't he go somewhere else?* The Hound thought, before deciding to go after more sporting targets. He tried to squeeze past Zeus, who stood in his way.

In a broad arcing motion that could not have been an accident, Zeus swung his gun around, hitting The Hound soundly on the side of his head.

It was not a move The Hound anticipated. The gun connected with his skull soundly, sending an explosion of light through his brain that had nothing to do with lasers. He fell backwards, down the ramp, hitting his head again against the wall.

The light turned to darkness, and he entered the world of his soul.

Chapter Nine

Chulainn rose from a fitful sleep, sore from the previous day's battle. He sat up and surveyed the Valley of Athebern, at the edge of the kingdom of Ulster. The dull glow of dawn rose in the east, burning away the mist of the sleeping land. The warriors of Ulster had camped here the night before, hoping to put as much distance as possible between them and their stronghold, Emain Macha. There it was said a terrible curse had been cast on the Kingdom, and their chief druid, Cathad, had said that if they traveled far from it they might escape it.

The warrior saw the army sleeping soundly, and as he tried to wake his men he saw that the curse was as strong as ever. Most remained sleeping, and those who did wake were as weak as newborns. Though they were far from their home, the curse remained in effect for all but Cu Chulainn, whose divine lineage made him immune to it.

The warrior sighed and took up his arms—a bronze sword, a barbed spear called the *gae bulga*, and his shield—then hitched his light wooden chariot to his war horse. It was not the first time he would fight an army single-handed, and he knew it would not be the last. He marched to the battlefield, shaking his head in amazement at the events which had brought him here: Queen Maeve of Connacht, Ulster's neighboring kingdom and rival, wished to borrow a divine brown bull from Cuailgne, a district of Ulster. In spite of their usually bloody rivalries, the two kingdoms sometimes traded livestock for breeding, and all would have gone well if the bull's owners hadn't overheard the Queen's men claim they would steal the bull if refused. This soured the deal, and Queen Maeve declared war on Ulster.

Cu Chulainn, the champion of Ulster, found the dispute rather ludicrous but yearned for a fight nevertheless. With his men down with the curse he feared for the safety of their cattle, which grazed in a nearby valley. What was he to do, herd cattle or fight? The answer was simple. Though only seventeen summers old, Cu Chulainn had only one calling in life, and that was to wreak havoc and spill blood.

While immersed in these pleasant thoughts, Cu Chulainn drove the chariot out of the camp, past a treacherous canyon. Suddenly two warriors jumped out from behind bushes, and one dropped down from a tree; they were Maeve's soldiers, hoping to surprise him.

Cu Chulainn leaped from his chariot and landed on the ground with a war cry that echoed through the valley; he would fight these men on their terms, afoot. Swords and shields clashed, and Cu Chulainn buried his sword halfway into a bronze helmet. The other fled for his life. Cu Chulainn calmed his horse and resumed his journey to the battlefield, unperturbed, as if he'd just swatted at a couple of annoying mayflies.

The battlefield was a clearing at the base of the hill where his men were camped. At the other end of the clearing the army of Connacht lined up on chariot, horseback and on foot. Infantry, archers, cavalry. One Cu Chulainn.

Queen Maeve sent one chariot to the field, and Cu

Chulainn quickly engaged him, thrusting at an angle, severing the man's arm in an instant. As the opponent lay screaming and bleeding, the archers let loose a volley of arrows, and Cu Chulainn stopped each of them with his shield. Next, two chariots attacked the warrior, and one suffered the barbed spear, the other the sword; both chariots returned to the army without their warriors.

Then an unarmed messenger came to him from the opposing army, frightened of the mighty Cu Chulainn.

"The Queen wishes to declare a truce," the messenger stammered, a youth no older than himself. "She would offer her love and friendship to the Champion of Ulster."

Cu Chulainn sneered at the messenger. "At what price?"

"If only you would join the army of Connacht against Ulster," the youth stammered, "you would be a prince."

"I have no time for insults," Cu Chulainn replied. "Go. Return to your army. Tell them they will have to kill me to get what they desire."

The day progressed much as it began, with Cu Chulainn slaying all the Queen's best men, into the night.

Then the next morning the men of Ulster were still bespelled, and the fighting began all over again. Morrigan, the goddess of war, whom he'd insulted by refusing *her* favors, landed on his horse's head in the form of a crow, and spoke with the voice of the war goddess.

"I said that you would pay someday for refusing me," the crow said. "Now is the day!"

Before his eyes the crow turned into a long, writhing eel, which slithered down the horse's tack and up Cu Chulainn's arm. He flailed ineffectually at it, just as another chariot charged. The eel grew until it was as large as he, and wrapped itself around his waist.

Before the warrior could reach him Cu Chulainn cut the eel in half, then kicked the two pieces out of the chariot. As he turned to the oncoming chariot, a throwing shield with sharpened edges flew through the air and struck him on the side of his head. The impact caught him off balance, but he didn't fall. His vision cleared, despite the blood flowing from his wound. Cu Chulainn charged the remaining line of infantry, and the whole lot ran like cowards. Queen Maeve's army retreated to the next valley, and Cu Chulainn returned to camp, weary, wounded . . . and, as usual, triumphant.

He fell off the chariot and landed on the ground, weakened by the loss of blood. He peered up, through the trees, as the sun set on another bloody afternoon in Ulster.

As the last traces of the memory faded away, The Hound opened his eyes and saw another player leaning over him. His targets weren't flashing. Evidently, this game was over.

"That," the player said, "was *completely* uncalled for." He held a hand out, and as The Hound took it, he saw the gray hair tied in a pony tail, and the goggles hanging around his neck. *Elvendude.*

The Hound sat up, then stood, with Elvendude's help. "You have a nasty cut on your temple," the older player observed. "You were out cold for about two minutes. Do you feel dizzy? Sick?"

The Hound reached up to his throbbing head, and his hand came away with a bit of blood. But not as much as it had . . . when the throwing shield hit him.

Not a dream. A memory.

"I think I'm fine," The Hound said. Then, cheering up, added, "We'd better get out of here. There's another game coming up."

The Hound moved towards the exit, followed by Elvendude, who seemed overly concerned. His injuries must look worse than they were. The judge, Crazylegs, was waiting for them.

"Zeus smacked him with his gun," Elvendude explained. "Have you . . . seen him anywhere?"

Crazylegs took their packs and hung them up. "He and his buddies left the arena just soon as the game was over. Now I know why. You gonna be okay?"

The Hound was starting to wonder why they were fussing over him so much when he remembered he had the special member's key. "Really, I'm fine. Thanks."

If only that were true. A massive headache had started pounding at his skull, as if it were trying to get out. He went into the lobby, and squinted at the bright sunlight pouring into through the front doors.

Father? The thought came unbidden, unexpected; the memory remained fixed in his mind, and he reviewed and explored it. Something about the eel he had cut into stayed with him, nagged at him like a troublesome splinter in his skin. *The war goddess. So familiar. Who is she?*

He went into the bathroom to have a look at the cut. In the mirror was a thin crescent where the gun barrel had hit him. As he dabbed at it with a wet paper towel, he became aware of someone else in the bathroom with him.

"You came in second place that game," Alfred said gently. "I came to see what was wrong."

"They can't all be gems," Dobie said with a forced laugh. He just about had all the blood mopped up. "Some ding-dong in there decided this was a contact sport."

"Maybe I can help," said another, younger voice.

Dobie jerked around in surprise to see a young blond kid who for all the world looked like Zach Hanson.

But Zach Hanson didn't have pointed ears and slitted, catlike pupils.

"What the fuck!" Dobie said, backpedaling into the corner. Then, in a resigned tone, "*Now* what."

"He will help you," Alfred said calmly, and Dobie believed him. The kid came up closer to him and looked at the cut, then held his right hand a few inches over it. Dobie's eyes remained fixed on the kid's eyes, which could not belong to a human. Yet all the fear had left him. Dobie found himself trusting this strange creature.

A warmth emanated from the hand to the cut. Soft yellow light branched into tendrils which flickered over his temple. The headache subsided, and the creature withdrew his hand.

In the mirror Dobie examined the cut, which had healed completely with only a slight trace of a scar.

"How did . . . ?" Dobie said, but the creature was doing something to make himself look normal. The ears and eyes looked human. *Shape shifter?* No, if he looked a certain way by unfocusing his eyes, he saw the outline of something covering these features, making them look different.

Dobie came away from the experience inside the area with enough awareness to know that Llan was connected to that other world, and that something in this world, he didn't know what, was threatening him. Another one of these creatures? His gut told him it was much worse than that; the arena didn't feel safe right now.

"We have some things to explain to you," Alfred said. "It would be best if we did so away from the bustle of this place."

"Far away," Llan said.

Dobie believed him. "Can you give me a ride home?"

"Yes, I can," Llan said, pulling a black pager out of his pocket and pushing a button. "We have a ride coming right now. Let's go."

They moved through the lobby, ignoring the sea of

stares aimed their way. Evidently word had gotten out that The Hound had been injured. Some looked away in obvious disappointment; they must have been expecting a bloody mess.

They left the coolness of the lobby for the scorching heat outside, and Dobie winced at the sudden brightness. Moments later a black Chevy Caprice roared up to the front doors with just a hint of a screech coming from the tires as it stopped. A lady in a dress suit and a badge looked up at him quizzically.

"Are you the cops?" Dobie asked.

Llan shrugged. "Sort of. We'll explain. Get in up front."

Dobie got into the front seat of the spacious car. There was an empty gun rack on the front dash, and a cop light on the floor.

Without a word spoken among them, the car took off the moment the doors were shut.

"Okay, Llan. Who are your friends?" the driver said with a bit of well-concealed suspicion. The cop was a rather attractive lady, in a no-nonsense sort of way. Her eyes didn't leave the road; she was intent on getting them out of there as quickly as possible.

"Lugh asked us to find his son," Llan replied smugly, sitting behind the driver. "And the druid, Cathad. I obliged him."

The driver turned slowly to Dobie on the front seat. She blinked, and then suddenly her eyes were slitted, and her ears were pointed. Alfred inhaled suddenly in surprise.

"*You're* Cu Chulainn?" the driver asked Dobie.

The name sounded so very familiar. *Coo Hullin.* Not an English name, that was certain. But was it his own?

Then, louder, "*Are* you?"

"I don't know," Dobie finally replied. "I'm not real sure who I am right now."

"The lad is . . . rooted in his present incarnation," Alfred offered. "But yes, if you are of the *sidhe*, and

I am sure you are, you will see the divine lineage in his bright aura."

"I offered to give him a ride home," Llan said. "That might be a good place to start."

The driver smiled, but the pointy eared creature looked uncomfortably carnivorous. "Where to?"

Though it seemed like an eternity, Dobie knew it had only been a few days since he'd last seen his home. He led the strange assortment of beings into the front room and turned on the large window air conditioner; it belched musty air before the cool came through. Nervously, Dobie addressed his visitors.

"Have a seat," he said, waving toward the ancient sixties vintage living room set with kidney-shaped coffee table and pole lamp. Under a bay window looking over the front yard was an enormous Magnavox TV-with-stereo console, and an old top-loading VCR on a shelf with his collection of tapes. The old beige cable TV channel changer sat on the floor, neglected. These had been the furnishings in this room since before he was born. Having had a taste of the good life, he now saw how depressing his home was.

"I have no family," Dobie explained. "My mom died last year. I live here by myself."

"I see," said Samantha, whose name he learned on the ride over. She seemed sad for him, and for a change the sympathy was welcomed. On the vinyl upholstered sofa, Llan and Cathad sat on either side of a long gash in the cushions. Dobie had mended the tear with duct tape, but the heat, in his absence, had reopened it.

"Cathad, you'd said that I would have a dream, and it would be important. When I was knocked out, I had it."

The druid incarnate glanced knowingly at the two elves, then, to Dobie said, "Tell us about it."

Dobie described his dream, a day in the life of Cu Chulainn, the fighting, the crow, and the eel; the blow to his head had evidently triggered this memory, which had ended with the throwing shield striking him.

"Then I came to, and well, you know the rest of it," Dobie said. There were still some major pieces missing in all this, he could feel it in his gut.

"The Morrigan," Sammi said softly, looking at Cathad. "Do you know who she is?"

"I do indeed," Cathad said. "What has she to do with this?"

"We are acquainted with the Morrigan," Sammi replied acidly. "She has been involved in Unseleighe doings before. I know for a fact she is involved in this one."

"How so?" Cathad asked, alarmed.

"I saw her here. Driving a red Corvette. Just a block from the arena."

The news made Dobie feel weak. *Morrigan? Morgan? Are they the same?* If so, then why hadn't Alfred-Cathad mentioned it, unless . . . he hadn't seen her. Alfred was always inside the arena, and Morgan always dropped him off, and left. *He wouldn't know.*

"So this was all from a previous life?" Dobie asked. Reincarnation was something these folks seemed to take for granted, but it was a new concept to Dobie. His family had always been ambivalent towards religious and spiritual issues, and even after his parents' deaths he hadn't considered where they might be besides their graves.

"*Your* previous life," Cathad replied as he sat forward eagerly on the couch, his hands gesturing as he spoke. "You are an invincible warrior, Cu Chulainn. Everything is connected. Your past, your present, and your future."

"Yeah, but the present is a little murky," Dobie replied, after a pause. "I wish it felt more real than it does."

Cathad, Samantha and the elven kid Llan all exchanged looks.

"I think we can oblige you," Cathad replied. "With your permission, of course."

Dobie nodded tentatively.

"Close your eyes," the druid commanded gently. "And we will take you back to another place, and another time. Know that which was, so that you can be again, now and in the future."

Cu Chulainn woke at the sound of a crackling fire and the aroma of cooked meat. The warrior found himself in the Ulstermen's camp, lying on the ground next to a small fire pit with rabbits on a stick.

He rose to a sitting position, puzzled over the lack of his physical injuries; the last thing he remembered was fighting Queen Maeve's army and taking quite a few wounds. Gashes to his arms and face where a Connacht sword had found his flesh, and half a hundred bruises from sling-thrown rocks. All had healed mysteriously.

"Combat had taken a toll on you," a voice spoke from behind him. A wise looking man stepped closer, carrying an armload of firewood. "You have slept for days. I saw to it that you did."

Cu Chulainn was suspicious of the stranger. He was no druid, the warrior saw as he dropped his load of dry deadwood. He wore a divine aura, and under that a green cloak. A gae bulga that was not Cu Chulainn's lay nearby beside a foreign, black shield. The warrior knew he might have been anything, evil or wicked, a demon from the underworld . . . or a benefactor.

"I sleep when I choose," the warrior proclaimed proudly. Now he recalled nodding off on watch, his hand on his sword, sitting on a hill overlooking the valley. But he hadn't fallen asleep, had he? The Ulster men continued to sleep, their still forms lying everywhere about him.

"Then you must have chosen to sleep for three days and nights," the stranger replied, the twinkle in his eye flashing brightly, further convincing Cu Chulainn of his divine origins. "For that is how long you have slept."

Cu Chulainn was furious; this was an insult. Three days? Only the sick or bespelled slept that long, and the warrior was neither. If the stranger had bespelled him, he had also healed his wounds, something no enemy would do knowingly. True, he felt renewed, to such a degree that only a long sleep would explain it.

"Where is the army of Connacht?" the warrior asked. They would not have been idle during those three days, he was certain.

"They are encamped in the same place you saw them last, afraid to approach us here, for fear of meeting you," the stranger said evenly. "But, truth be told, that is not the real threat to you now." He spread his arms wide, a graceful gesture that reminded Cu Chulainn of an eagle spreading its wings. "As Cathad has taught you, everything is connected. Past, present, future . . . what you see here is but a memory. Your future is here," the stranger said, as a scrawny youth wearing a strange tunic stepped into view, transparent like a spirit. Cu Chulainn recoiled from the sight; without a druid present, the warrior did not wish to deal with anything from the spirit world, not by himself.

"This is your future, my son, and your future self is in trouble," the stranger said.

Son? "You are Lugh, god of light. My father?"

Lugh nodded; the aura flared in confirmation. "The Morrigan has courted this young lad, who knows not who she is. You have spurned her once, for good cause. She is persistent, for she has pursued you across time in order use you as her warrior, and once she is finished with you, she will destroy you."

Cu Chulainn regarded the youth with mild contempt. He would not have willingly chosen to become such a feeble looking being. Perhaps in this future world, the rules were different. That tunic, and what had to be a weapon at his side, perhaps his future self was skilled in such weapons. Whatever the situation, the Morrigan would easily devour him in his ignorance, and that he could not allow.

"The druid Cathad has sent you here for my instruction," Lugh informed him. "He has joined you in the next life, as he promised you long ago. Cathad will counsel you wisely, as he has in the past. Do what you know is right. Choose your battles wisely."

The warrior stood, knowing intuitively what to do. He looked again at his arms and hands, and saw that he also was spirit. The two warriors walked slowly to each other, then fused together in a flash of intense whiteness, becoming one.

Dobie came to sitting in his chair, then leaped to his feet as a something akin to a lightning bolt struck his soul.

"It's all right, it's all right," he heard someone say, as he stood shaking. Phosphenes of brightness drifted in his vision, then faded. Alfred was holding his arms at his sides, and Dobie was dimly aware of him and others urging him to sit back down.

Then he remembered the elves, and they were right here, helping him. They'd given him a ride here, to his house. He was breathing hard, and his heart was pounding away in his ribcage, like he had just played a savage game of Lazerwarz. Gradually he relaxed, caught his breath, felt his heartbeat slow.

He looked at them, one by one, and saw friends he could trust. Cathad in particular—he had a track record with him.

"I remember everything," Dobie said.

Cathad's relief was evident in his eyes. Samantha smiled, and her features no longer frightened him. And Llan beamed happily, almost with the brightness of Lugh's aura. Yes, he could trust them.

"So now you know who Morgan is," Cathad said.

The question brought a wave of grief. Dobie closed his eyes and held his face in his hands, willing the tears away, to emerge at a later, more appropriate time. His lust had turned to love, and it was his first love, as Dobie—and the love was misplaced. But how could he break away from her? She had done so much for him, and in that moment Dobie realized what a double edge the gifts had. They brought guilt, a sense of obligation he hadn't asked for, and certainly didn't want now. The gifts were, if anything, an emotional weapon, intended to keep him in her debt.

So was the sex a gift, too? A pity fuck for a skinny kid with nothing going for him. . . .

Dobie pushed the old pattern of thinking aside. It mattered not what he looked like now, or what he had done (or didn't do) as Dobie, in the past. The visit with Lugh had shown him that. *It's what I am now, not what I was.*

"I can't see her anymore. But I have to go tell her myself," Dobie informed them. "Now, I can do it."

They didn't seem to think this was a terrific idea, the elves in particular. Llan looked downright grief stricken. But it was the only way he could do it: in person. "Look. She didn't get me before, but this time she got what she wanted. I'll be all right."

"So be it," Samantha said softly. "We cannot fight her—only you can do this. But be careful. Shall we give you a ride back now?"

"Yes," Dobie said, standing again. "Take me back to the arena now."

Before I change my mind, he amended to himself.

Morrigan burst into the Lazerwarz control center, unannounced, and unwelcome. Mort turned around in the big chair and scowled.

"What?"

She walked up to him, her heels click clacking on the linoleum floor, and folded her arms.

"The Avalon elves are here."

Mort nodded thoughtfully. "And I'm supposed to give a damn?"

Morgan made a loud, exasperated sound as she exhaled dramatically. "Samantha McDaris is an *FBI agent*. Unless I miss my guess she is investigating the disappearance of several hundred kids in Lazerwarz arenas around the land."

The Foevor found the news alarming, but not disastrous. "Soon it won't much matter. The weapons we will need for success are manufactured. As we speak they are arriving in the palace. The army is trained. They are ready to fight." The calm he exuded surprised himself. "Now tell me, what contribution do you have to make to the war effort? So far all I have seen is a useless collection of megaliths in our parking lot. And lest I forget . . . the human lad you have been diddling."

Morgan's expression turned triumphant. "The human lad is a warrior of warriors. You've watched every game he's played, you know what he can do. And who he is." She nodded toward the rack of file servers. "The God program is still running."

Mort conceded the point. "He's Lugh's son. And he is quite a good player . . . but unless we can control him, make him fight for us, what difference does it make?"

Morgan smiled in a most disarming way. "I have him wrapped around my little finger. He'll do *anything* I say."

Chapter Ten

"Wake up, King," the Mage heard through the gray mists of his fading dream. "It's time."

Aedham rose from the hard, cold floor and regarded the Unseleighe gathered at his cell's door. Joystik was with them; evidently the boy was given the honors of opening the cold iron door for them. As they escorted him from the cell he had the uncomfortable feeling they were leading him to his execution.

Joystik lingered behind them, putting on a good "stoned" routine, moving lethargically like the other rubyheads in the cell, drooling a little for good measure. The kid must have been doing this for a while, the King decided; he was quite convincing.

"Just remember the two swords behind you," Yuaroh said, without looking back. Aedham felt two jabs on either side of his spine. "We just spent the last candle mark sharpening them."

"It's a shame we have to do it this way," Aedham commented. "I'm on your side, you know."

The comment went without reply. Either they didn't believe him, or they were mulling his words over. After a long walk past several cells, Joystik scampered ahead of Yuaroh and opened another, larger cell door. They climbed a flight of dark, damp stairs, which led them to a spacious area resembling an empty warehouse;

it was a long, unfinished section of the palace. The smooth, gray surfaces looked like perfectly carved granite. *This castle must be as large as a city!* Aedham thought as he surreptitiously checked for node access. There they were, deep under the palace: three nodes within his reach. The dungeon's barrier that had prevented him from feeling them had vanished.

Two sword tips jabbed him, again. *A reminder.*

"You have probably found the nodes by now," Yuaroh said. "There is no need to reach for their power yet. I would know, and my men would know, if you did. So don't. If you want to live."

"Of course," Aedham said. "It's not time to build the Gate anyway." Joystik wandered on ahead, apparently knowing where the Unseleighe were leading him. *I don't want him around when the fireworks start!* Aedham thought, but saw no good way to get him out of the way. *Should have discussed this part of it sooner, when we had a chance.*

The enormous hallway gave way to a smaller one, with a long opening offering a view of the grounds below. The area was larger than several football fields, hell, larger than the Tulsa International airport. Part of the palace wrapped around to the north of it, its stone facade looming over it like a mountain. Down on the grounds were tall, dark creatures that had to be Foevors, drilling several units of young human soldiers. Rubies showed clearly on their temples in the murky nonlight of Underhill. The loose, black clothing they wore as a uniform reminded Aedham of Viet Cong in their silk pajamas. There had to be hundreds of them, moving in perfect rectangles of discipline.

Yuaroh stopped a moment, then turned to regard the grounds, leaning on the long window's sill with both hands. "Impressive, aren't they?" the Unseleighe commented. "The magics they've worked with those red stones have given the Foevors an obedient, expendable army." Yuaroh glanced at Aedham sideways, giving him a sly wink. "And your court developed it. What *were* you thinking?"

While Aedham could not deny that the Seleighe Rathand had developed the ruby technology, he also saw no point in mentioning that he had done so under the orders of Zeldan Dhu. The King merely shrugged a reply.

"Those tall, dark creatures. They're the Foevor officers in charge of the individual units." Yuaroh squinted, as if looking for someone in particular. "And I don't see . . . ah, yes. Here they are. The Clapperlegs."

An enormous palace gate opened up, and out hopped a dozen or so deformed giants. Each wore vests with large, shoulder-mounted laser guns the size of bazookas. They were creatures Aedham knew only from legends, and until recently it had been common knowledge that Clappers, and the Foevors in general, were extinct.

"When the Foevors emerged from the sea, their first land-based form was the Clapper. One arm, one leg, one eye. Taller than three of us put together. See how they move," he said, as the Clapperlegs spread out, and took up positions at each of the units. Their arms were long enough to help them walk, and they did so with fluid, slippery motions that looked like a snake slithering through sand. "They can walk faster than you and I can run. Each unit of humans supports and provides cover for a Clapper. This is the first time I've seen them with the new weapons, however . . . and that *is* distressing. Perhaps we should move along and get our job done, don't you think?"

The sight left Aedham speechless. At first glance this was strongest army Aedham had ever known to exist in Underhill, perhaps bigger than the combined forces of the Seleighe elfhames . . . who didn't have The Weapon. The true magnitude of what they were up against had finally dawned on King Aedham, and his knees were feeling a bit weak at the prospect.

I have to admire Yuaroh's bravery in trying to take this army on, Aedham thought. *Even if I still don't trust them for anything.* Then another thought came, unbidden. *Are the combined Seleighe armies up to this?* It disturbed him that he couldn't even come up with a guess.

They proceeded into another torch-lit passage. The Unseleighe Lord took a burning torch down from the wall as Joystik opened yet another door, this one smaller, like a hatch. Aedham bent low to go in, the swords urging him along. The boy followed and shut the door behind them.

Aedham found himself in a long, narrow chamber. One of Yuaroh's men lit the torches along the wall, and in the new light Aedham saw a long line of brand new laser vests stretching into the darkness. The place had a synthetic smell of newly molded plastic.

"All told, around three hundred so far," Yuaroh said. "Enough to equip the army we just saw outside."

"Where are the guards?" Aedham said, unable to believe such a horde of weapons would be left unattended.

"At the far end. Don't worry, they're my men, Unseleighe."

Seems foolish to trust them, Aedham thought. *Then again, I've had more experience with this lot than they have.*

Yuaroh pulled out a long bronze sword, and held it in front of him, blade down. "As I am not ignorant of the conditions of Gate making, I know that you can conjure an opening here to any location in Underhill. A hundred of my soldiers are awaiting this Gate to open in a location you know all too well."

"Which is?" Aedham asked, but already he had a good idea where it was.

"The former site of Avalon. Where Zeldan Dhu first

defeated you, Aedham. Or I should say . . . your father." With the sword pointed at Aedham, Yuaroh moved around to his right side. "I do realize this is a sensitive location, and my people have defiled it a number of times in the past. But please understand I needed a place you knew quite well . . . a place unguarded by Seleighe. No disrespect is intended, of course."

"None taken, to be sure," Aedham said. "As we are now allies, I have no problem with the choice. What has happened between our two clans in the past is no longer relevant." The lie came smoothly and evenly, and the King delivered it with ease. Yuaroh raised an eyebrow in apparent surprise, as Aedham made a note not to lay it on *too* thick.

Aedham continued, "It will require our combined resources to fight the army I saw just now. If we have any chance in defeating the Foevorian race, we must set our differences aside."

"Well said!" Yuaroh said, and sheathed his sword, and nodded to the two standing behind him. While he didn't hear them resheath their swords, they no longer jabbed him in the back. "Shall we get started?"

"Of course. First, I would like the human over here, closer to me on my left. He will be less of an obstruction to the forming of a gate." Aedham paused at Yuaroh's puzzled look, and with exaggerated impatience explained, "*He's* not from Underhill. He would interfere with the optical orbit of the primary node branch. That could cause some phlogiston problems, and we *don't* want that. Over here," he said, jabbing a thumb toward Joystik, who had shuffled over to a spot on his left, immediately next to him, "The node branch is neutral." Aedham furrowed his brow at Yuaroh. "You mean you don't *know* that?"

If you can't dazzle them with brilliance, baffle them with bullshit.

"The art of Gate making wasn't covered in my

training," Yuaroh replied apologetically. "I shall take you at your word."

"Aie, then," Aedham said, and prepared himself for the Gate making. "Give me a moment." He closed his eyes and sent his Mage sight outwards, to areas of Underhill in question. *The Unseleighe can wait for a Gate to appear at the ruins of old Avalon all they want to. I'm going to find the Seleighe army!* Plundering the elvenstones had to have triggered a call to arms; The mines were well guarded and monitored by all the elfhames. *The foray into Outremer alone would have been enough to stir up our defensive forces. Where are they?*

Aedham's mage sight, fueled with carefully selected tendrils of node power, swept across Underhill with lightning swiftness. He saw his new palace in the distance, but on a hunch directed his vision towards Outremer. Halfway there, he saw what he looked for. Indeed, Avalon's army had joined their brethren, cavalry, infantry, and a few Mages from Outremer for good measure.

"I see the Unseleighe army," Aedham said. "I think I shall put the Gate a bit further down the hill, towards the bridge. In case I misjudge the placement. Anyone standing where the Gate appears will be obliterated."

"Good thinking," Aedham heard Yuaroh say. The Mage pulled out of his trance and opened his eyes.

"Now for the Gate," the King said. "They are rather bright. You might want to look away."

Aedham reached for the nodes beneath Mort's castle, brazenly scooping up huge potloads of energy for the Gate. Joystik watched, wide-eyed, as Aedham focused the power arcing between his fingers to a spot a few paces before him. He ventured a glance at Joystik, who seemed to register the unspoken signal, and went back into zombie mode.

Yuaroh gasped as the vague outline of a circle

appeared, its edges a thin line of yellow light, about the size of a dinner plate. Once that was established the Mage dumped everything he had into it, and the circle expanded abruptly. A bit sloppy, but it worked. He had constructed a Gate in record time.

The Unseleighe stood in stunned amazement, shielding their faces from the intensity.

"What are you waiting for?" Aedham said to all present.

The King grabbed Joystik's arm and charged headlong into the circle of light.

The Caprice stopped a half mile from the arena to let Dobie out. "You don't have to do it this way," Samantha said as he unbuckled himself. "She's not going to let you go easily."

With his hand on the door handle, he hesitated. "This is how I have to do it," he said with as much conviction as he could muster. "It's the honorable thing to do."

The lady elf seemed doubtful, even cynical; she must have been down this road before. "Then take this," she said, offering a business card. "It has my cell phone number on it. *Use it* if you need help. I'd give you protection spells if I could, but she'd be able to dismiss anything Llan or I could come up with."

He hesitated before taking the card. It felt like a betrayal to someone he had come to love, but he took it anyway knowing that Morgan was actually quite dangerous. In the other realm she had pursued him for her own selfish interests. She didn't destroy him then, and she wouldn't now. But as much as he wanted to, there was no reason to think anything had changed.

"We're at the Doubletree. Downtown. The suite's on the top floor," he said. *At least I can tell her that much.* She seemed grateful for the information. Dobie nodded to Llan sitting in the back seat before getting out. The elven kid's expression was as worried as Samantha's, making him wonder if he really was making the right decision.

He walked into the arena lobby, which was bustling with activity. Hardly noticing the looks of admiration, and in some cases fear, he went over to the big screen where the day's scores were displayed. As usual, he had the highest and second highest score of the day.

"Are you The Hound?" a boy of about eleven asked him, looking up with an expression of pure awe.

"Yeah," he replied, but something else was distracting him. An expanse of red flashed by the front doors as the Corvette pulled in. A moment later Morgan stood in the doorway, regarding the lobby as if she owned it . . . which she probably did.

The moment their eyes met, his resolve to rid himself of her faltered.

"There you are," she said, walking up to him. At one time Dobie would have enjoyed the attention they received while they were together, but now it seemed like a curse. And given who he was dealing with, that probably wasn't too far off the mark. She looked at the screen. "As usual, you're doing well," she said. "Care to go back to the room for dinner? I'll call room service."

Everything he'd planned to say to her had inexplicably vanished from his brain. "Okay," he said, and followed her to the Corvette.

"You seem a bit . . . out of sorts," she said as she started up the 'Vette. "Is something wrong?"

What to tell her? *Hell yes, everything is wrong. I shouldn't be in this car, I shouldn't be going back to the room. And I shouldn't be thinking that maybe we have a chance together after all!*

"I'm just really hungry," Dobie replied, and that was no lie. He hadn't eaten all day, and before meeting Llan and Samantha he had played ten intense games. His stomach growled in agreement.

"I see," she said with a distant smile, which didn't seem genuine. She turned left at the intersection of 41st and Yale and went south, to I-44. "Any idea who that is behind us?"

"Huh?" Dobie articulated, looking in the side rear view. The Caprice was tailing them conspicuously, with Samantha clearly visible in the driver's seat. Llan was sitting in the passenger's side. *Shit.* "No. Who is it?"

Morgan didn't reply, and an uncomfortable silence fell on them. Suddenly it didn't seem like a good idea to go back to the room.

"Why don't we stop at this Denny's over here?" he suggested, but her look sent a cold shiver through him.

"Don't be ridiculous," she said. "You deserve better than that," she added, and continued to drive.

He didn't know if he should go with her or jump out of the car. With Samantha so close, he felt less threatened. If only she stayed within sight, and close enough to help him.

This didn't seem to be in the cards. As soon as the Corvette hit the expressway Morgan punched the engine, scratching the road in third. The sharp acceleration pressed him back in the seat, and cars blurred past as if they were parked. The 'Vette's nose seemed to be shifting to the red end of the light spectrum. For a blessed moment all he could think about was not dying.

He risked a glance in the rear view; Samantha was long gone.

"No matter," Morgan said, and a moment later she had pulled up in front of the hotel, a valet took the 'Vette, and they were back in the room, all in what seemed like seconds.

The moment the door had closed Morgan spun around and slapped Dobie in the face, hard enough to snap his head back. He was too stunned to feel it.

She glared at him, all fury and flame, with her hands on her hips. "Now what the *hell* is going on?"

"What do you mean, what's going on?" Dobie said, trying hard not to whine. His new-found self didn't seem to have much useful to contribute, and he found himself withdrawing into the old shell of Dobie the Wimp.

"You left with that elven *bitch* a few hours ago. We have it on the cameras. And then she was following us. What are you trying to do, set me up?"

Caught red-handed, he didn't know what to say, at first. Particularly when he wasn't sure what he was guilty of. *Oh, to hell with it!* "It's nothing you don't deserve," he said, and grabbed the doorknob, expecting it to turn, expecting the door to swing open. The knob didn't yield, in fact seemed to have become one solid piece with the door.

"Try again," she said, with a wicked smile.

It was the only door into the room. He went to the phone, which was dead. The windows led nowhere but down. *Shit. I'm trapped.*

Morgan walked casually into the main living room and flopped down on one of the chairs, kicking off her heels in two fluid motions. "So who got to you? The elves or the druid?"

"Neither," he said, glaring at her. "I grew up."

Her laugh was loud and bitter. "You are a child, warrior. You were before, and you are now. And without me you are *nothing.*"

"With or without you, I'm The Hound of Culann," he replied, but the anger was making him tremble.

Her look was cool and appraising, and bit surprised. "So you finally figured out that much. The druid must have pulled that out of you. He needn't have bothered, I would have done the same. But since you're the perfect boy toy, I wanted to *play* with you some more, first. And I still can."

"It takes two to screw," Dobie said, rolling his eyes. Even he knew that.

"No, it doesn't," she said, with a confidence that

was chilling. "It only takes *one goddess.*" She raised her right hand and closed her eyes as something shuddered through the room, shaking the walls briefly before it was gone. By the time she opened her eyes again Dobie was uncomfortably aware of an unwanted heat in his loins, and a total lack of resolve. He wasn't even angry at her anymore, though something deep within him screamed at him that this was not right.

"Now, I want you to go into the bedroom and wait for me."

With only a vague sense of humiliation, he did as he was told.

With Joystik in tow, Aedham hit the yellow light and waded through the expected disorientation of gating until he found solid ground on the other side. As anticipated, he found himself nose to nose with the Seleighe army.

Of course, they didn't know who had made the Gate, or who would be coming through it. A battalion of archers filled the horizon, two rows, kneeling and standing. The King had counted on their hesitation at the sight of his human clothing, and made the obvious Seleighe move by shielding the human child with himself. He achieved the desired effect; as one the nocked arrows pointed to the sky, away from Aedham.

Aedham scanned the army for a familiar face, and found one.

"Petrus!" the King shouted, and moved towards the army, glancing warily at the Gate behind him.

Petrus, in full battle armor, led his elvensteed Moonremere through the archers and approached the King. The elf had been among the small group who lived with Aedham in Dallas, and had seen more of the human's world than any other Avalon elf besides himself and Samantha; now he was the commander of his army. Still on the youthful side, with long blond hair spilling out from behind his helmet, he could pass as Llan's much older brother.

"Aie, King! You escaped!" he shouted triumphantly as Moonremere gaited to a halt.

"No time! There are three Unseleighe on the other side of that Gate," Aedham said, moving out of the way of the archers. Petrus followed suit. "I suspect they'll be coming through any second now! I must get this child out of the way."

The ranks opened up to allow them past, and Petrus gave orders to the archers to resume their aim on the Gate. Joystik seemed to be taking it all in stride, though it wasn't clear the boy fully comprehended what was going on.

The weapons. We must claim them, Aedham thought, and found a supply wagon. "Stay here," he said to Joystik, and to the puzzled driver said, "Protect this human. I'll return shortly."

Aedham returned to the front line just in time to see a rain of arrows strike three rather surprised Unseleighe as they stumbled through the Gate. He saw with approval that Petrus had ordered elf shot; it made their deaths quick. Petrus was looking to him for further instructions.

"I need . . . all the infantry to line up here," he said, stepping over the arrow-riddled bodies. "We're going to raid the enemy's armory."

A cheer went up as elven infantry lined up as ordered, swords drawn.

"After me," Aedham said, charging back into the Gate. In the weapons room Aedham grabbed eight of the vests, four on each arm, and gave them to the nearest Seleighe. "They're light. And they're *not* fragile. Grab as many as you can and drop them on the other side of that Gate, and come back for more. Now *move* like you have a purpose! We won't go undetected for long!"

Some of the infantry were from Avalon, some

weren't, but they moved as if they all had grown up under his command. The operation went with a minimum of chaos as the King guided the flow of traffic in and out of the Gate, and with growing exhilaration watched the racks empty at a phenomenal rate.

The infantry's movement, not to mention the armor they wore was not quiet, however, and Aedham's anxiety grew. He ventured into the darkness of the weapon's room until he found a door at the other end; on the other side he sensed more Unseleighe. From here the operation was anything but quiet.

Certainly they must hear what is going on in here? he thought, then recalled, *but of* course *they hear an army making off with the weapons. But they think it's their own forces! How generous of them to guard the door for us.*

The operation went smoothly, the only wrinkle being when Aedham saw Joystik walking into the Gate with a dual armload of levin rifles. The King might have objected to putting the boy in unnecessary danger, but the lad seemed capable, and a direct confrontation with the Unseleighe seemed unlikely this round. *I'll have to have a talk with him about obeying orders.*

After several more passes, his men had cleaned out the armory. He looked up to see row upon row of empty racks. Not a levin rifle remained; the King resisted an urge to thank his Unseleighe guards for their loyal assistance, but felt that would jinx an otherwise successful operation. After a thorough search of the now quite empty room, he decided everyone was out and took his own leave through the Gate.

"Is everyone accounted for?" the King shouted to his men, and as Petrus did a head count he looked for and found Joystik, who was grinning like a monkey next to a long pile of levin rifles that was taller than he was.

"Everyone accounted for!" Petrus shouted. "Do we have any more Unseleighe to contend with?"

"Negative!" Aedham called back, and prepared to dismiss his creation. He considered siphoning off the three nodes under Mort's palace to fortify his own, but that would definitely draw unnecessary attention. Instead he quickly shut down the Gate, which folded in on itself quite easily, no surprise given its quick and dirty construction. When the last trace of it was gone, a cheer rose from the army.

"Well done, King!" Petrus said, dismounting Moonremere to slap him on the back. "So tell me, what did we just steal?"

"Remember the work Niamh was doing with the elvenstones? That's what was stolen during the sleep spell attack on the palace. Our enemies have done us the favor of making Niamh's work operational."

The King picked up one of the vests and put it on. The gun was connected to a cable much thicker than the phone coil of the original Lazerwarz rifle, but otherwise was exactly like the "toy" version. *But this is no toy.* The gun was a black tube as long as his arm, and wide enough to put his fist in. On the grip he found a power switch. "Unless I miss my guess, this turns it on," he said, but flipping the switch did not have any effect.

"Yes? And?" Petrus said eagerly.

"Something's not right," Aedham said, with growing unease. He took the vest off, and Petrus held it for him as he examined the back. He removed a panel, which revealed a wheel adorned with elvenstones. *Aie, the node generator,* Aedham thought, but something was still wrong. *What turns the generator? What makes it—* His eyes fell on six empty slots, and groaned as he understood what was supposed to be in those slots.

"Batteries not included," he said with disappointment. "Six of them." He glanced at the mountain of levin rifles, with Petrus and Joystik selected a few randomly and checked the back panels. *No batteries in any of them.*

"We need batteries." *How many of these did the late Yuaroh Dhu say there were? Three hundred? Times six? Damn!* "We need one thousand eight hundred D batteries."

Petrus frowned. "I don't think we have that many at the palace."

"I know we don't," Aedham said. "There's one place that would have that many batteries."

"Where?" Petrus asked.

"Wal-Mart. But we'll need money," Aedham pointed out. "I can ken a big pile of twenties for us, but I'll need an original." He addressed his army. "Does anybody have any human currency?" he shouted. "A twenty or fifty dollar bill?"

His answer was a sea of baffled elven faces.

"What about gold?" Petrus said. "Here, on this sword, on the handle. There's a bit of gold here . . ."

Aedham didn't notice Joystik, who had sauntered up to the conversation. "Why use gold when you can use *plastic?*" the boy interrupted. He opened up a black leather wallet, revealing an impressive assortment of credit cards. "I don't leave home without them."

"Very resourceful," Aedham said, looking over the cards. "Plenty of credit?"

Joystik looked mildly insulted. "Of course. Dad pays them off each month. And one's an American Express."

Aedham saw the green and white card and nodded his approval. "Fine, then. We can do it this way," Aedham replied, but something about the deal felt intuitively wrong. It wasn't how they were going to pay back the money—Avalon would do so at the first opportunity, with solid gold, if that's what the boy preferred.

What's bothering me about this? The ruby on his head? The stone was dark and inert, but it was still attached to his temple. Aedham wanted it removed altogether before they returned to the Overworld.

"Give us a moment," Aedham said to Petrus, and took Joystik aside. "This stone on your head. I think it's time we removed it, don't you think?"

Joystik reached up and touched the flat stone. "Hell, I almost forgot it was up there. Yeah, go ahead and take it off. I don't know how they got it to stay in the first place."

Aedham ran his finger around the edge of the stone, feeling its dark magic but no obvious adhesive, like glue. With the edge of a bronze dagger loaned by Petrus he probed where it connected to skin, but only received painful grimaces from Joystik for his efforts. The unpleasant possibility of having to cut the thing from his skin kept him searching for an alternative.

"It's connected with magic," Aedham decided.

In a mild trance, the royal Mage entered the stone, finding an amazingly complex structure of magical paths. Drawing on a bit of node power, Aedham dampened the paths closest to Joystik's skin.

"Something's happening. I feel it tingling," Joystik said anxiously. "It's not gonna blow up or anything is it?"

"No, of course not," the King said, but he wasn't certain himself. With another push of power, the jewel fell off the side of Joystik's face; the King deftly caught it before it hit the ground.

"It's off," the King announced triumphantly. He held up the round red jewel to show Joystik. "How do you feel?"

"Great. It itches up there though," the boy said. "Okay to scratch?"

Aedham examined the round patch of skin where the stone had been. The only difference was that it was a clean white circle on a dirty, dust streaked face. The King shrugged.

"Scratch away," Aedham said, and Joystik rubbed the area with his fingertips.

"It's not numb or anything," the boy observed. "Feels normal."

"Then I'd say this didn't do anything to you permanently," Aedham said, studying the stone. It looked like nothing from Underhill, and didn't feel like it was from the human's world, either. Then he remembered the path of matrices, and explored it from another direction, until he found what he sought.

It's synthetic! he discovered. *The Foevors made this from . . . who knows what. The matrix is like a code. Chances are the other stones in the other rubyheads are kenned from the same stone. The patterns of power flowing through them would be identical.*

Then he saw a way to break the rubyhead spell. *Send a mild magical blast encoded with the reversed pattern of paths. It might cancel out the other spells, or at least interfere with them enough to make the stones ineffective. The only question is how to do it for more than one person at a time.*

But first things first.

"Let's go get some batteries," Aedham said, and Joystik nodded enthusiastically.

Chapter Eleven

"She must be on an elvensteed!" Llan exclaimed as the Corvette vanished from sight. "It's . . . gone."

"No, not an elvensteed," she said sadly. She slowed the Caprice down to sixty, unable to pursue Morrigan in the thick traffic. "Just a fast *human*-steed." With Dobie in her car there was no telling what she would do to him if Sammi tried to hunt her down. *I should have never have let him go in there!*

As she debated her next move, her cell phone trilled. "McDaris," she answered.

"Samantha? It's Special Agent Hawk," the voice from the Nokia spoke into her ear. "Listen, I know you wanted to go solo to recon the arena, but something's come up I think you'll want to be in on."

"Go ahead," she said, trying to drive and talk on the phone at the same time, an unsettling experience for Llan.

"Bank One of Baltimore just called us with a high priority flag. Someone just tried using Alan Barker's Master Card at the Wal-Mart at 81st and Lewis."

"When?"

"Ten minutes ago. The police are holding them right now."

Holding who? "I'll meet you there."

She took the Lewis exit, then looked over and saw that Llan had reverted to full elf mode.

"*Llan!* Your ears. Glamories, always remember your glamories when you're here!"

"Sure, sorry La—I mean, Sammi," Llan said, flustered. "I thought, since we were in the carriage, no one can see in."

"It. Doesn't. Matter," she replied tensely. "They can always see. And don't argue."

"Aie," Llan said, chagrined. Then, "How's this?"

Sammi looked. "Eyes too!"

"Oh, yes . . . What about now?"

Llan had again become a human teen, with long, blond hair and an adolescent pout. "Perfect. Now don't let it slip."

While she made progress through the thick traffic on Lewis she debated what to do about Llan. *Leave him in the car?* No, at this point she felt like she needed to keep a constant watch on him.

"Yes, Samantha."

"It's 'Agent McDaris' until further notice."

That dealt with, she concentrated on the situation ahead, at the Wal-Mart. Alan Barker was the congressman's son, which was why they were able to get the flag through a usually uncooperative banking institution. Because of the heat from the congressman, others in the Bureau would be interested in this development, and they just didn't need that. Alan had disappeared in Baltimore, and was likely taken Underhill through a Gate. So whoever was trying to use the card must be connected with Mort's operation. The prospect didn't look good for keeping the Underhill angle under wraps, especially if Hawk got there before she did.

She put the red spinning cop light on the roof and floored the accelerator. Tulsa traffic was amazingly blind to anything besides a full blown light bar, and she ended up using her horn more often than not to get cars out of her way.

There was another Caprice with federal plates already in front of the Wal-Mart. *Hawk beat us here. Great.* She pulled up behind it and parked. "Stay close to me Llan," she said, getting out and going straight for the entrance.

Sitting on a bench in the breezeway was a life-sized Ronald McDonald statue with a psychotic grin. Llan did a double take. "Humans are weird," she heard him mumble. She had thought this numerous times before, and knew he was right.

A Tulsa cop stood guard at the entrance, acting rather protective of a shopping cart loaded to the brim with batteries. More evidence of human weirdness; Llan rolled his eyes. She showed her badge to the cop.

"FBI. Where is the credit card perp?"

"Back in the manager's office," he said. "Know where it is?"

"Thanks, I'll find it," she said, and hurried past. Keeping Llan in her peripheral vision she waded into the bustling Supercenter, hoping she would be able to cover up whatever godlike events were transpiring in the manager's office.

An employee directed them to a hallway, then a flight of stairs. At the top was a plain hallway with doors. She knocked on the one that said MANAGER.

Hawk opened the door. "Oh, Sammi. Come on in. You're not gonna believe this."

I'll bet I do, she thought, then turned to tell Llan to stay put.

But the elf was nowhere to be seen.

Shit! Where is he? I must have lost him in the store.

No time to go looking for him now, she sighed and walked into the manager's office. In chairs facing the desk, like two sullen schoolboys caught fighting in the playground, sat King Aedham and Alan Barker, whom she recognized from the file photos. With them was a Tulsa cop sitting at the manager's desk. "I'm Officer

Doyle," he said, extending a hand. "We have ourselves a little situation here," he said as they shook.

"I'm Agent McDaris." She presented her badge and ID. The cop studied it closely before giving it back. "Yes, we do," Samantha said, trying to maintain a calm facade. *Thank the gods the King is unharmed but . . . what the blazes is going on?* Her eyes met Aedham's, which were anxious and eager. He seemed to understand the predicament they were in. *First things first. Let's cover this up.*

"Could I have a word with you and Agent Hawk in private?" she said, motioning towards the door.

"Certainly," the cop said, and they moved to the hallway for the conference. "This isn't about a stolen credit card, is it, Agent McDaris?"

"No, it is not," she said, struggling to come up with some kind of cover story that would fit. *First, let's see what's already gone on.* "What have they said so far?"

"Not much of anything," Hawk said, sounding frustrated and annoyed. "As soon as we started questioning them the older one asked for you by name. Sammi, what *is* going on?"

Good. They've stayed quiet. That will make things easier.

Doyle said, "They were attempting to purchase a large quantity of D cell batteries with a credit card. The bank said it was stolen, but the boy in there appears to be the legitimate card holder. His ID checks out, but the NCIC says he's a runaway."

Okay, now I have it. Let's hope this story stays together.

"The boy is the son of Congressman Barker of Maryland," she began. "He is not a runaway. He was kidnapped."

The cop raised an eyebrow. "By the man in there?"

She shook her head. "He's an undercover FBI agent. He was on a special assignment to rescue Alan, and it appears he succeeded."

Hawk was skeptical. "Then why buy batteries?"

Good question. "Don't know. What matters is we have them. This operation was intended to remain very quiet, you understand. The last thing we need is for this to get out . . . preferential treatment for the congressman's interests, and all that." She looked directly at Hawk as she said, "Now that we have Alan, we probably also have a lead on the *other* kidnappings. If you catch my drift, Agent Hawk?"

Hawk did not seem convinced, but appeared to see the wisdom in discussing the matter without Officer Doyle.

"Agent Hawk?" Doyle asked.

"There is an ongoing investigation into a large number of child kidnappings," Hawk confirmed. "I didn't know the man in there was an agent." He shrugged, with a smile. "Such is the nature of undercover work."

Doyle didn't appear completely convinced, but seemed to give in to her story anyway. "Then I will leave the situation in your capable hands," Doyle said to Sammi. "I don't think I have the full story, however."

"I understand your concern," Sammi said, as diplomatically as possible. She rubbed her temples, massaging a not-so-imaginary headache. "Trust me on this, you don't *want* to know the full story. This investigation is complicated enough as it is." Then she brightened. "This is the first good lead we've had. In a few days you'll probably get the full story on CNN."

Not.

"Then the matter is yours to deal with," Doyle said. The cop shook both their hands and strode off down the hallway. Before his footsteps faded completely away, Hawk eyed her accusingly.

"Undercover agent?"

"He was working in Baltimore," Sammi said. "I don't know how they got here. That's what I hope to find out."

"Look," Hawk said, closing his eyes a moment in concentration. "You've asked for the freedom to reconnoiter the arena alone, and I've given it to you. But we're supposed to be working on this together, and right now I feel left out of the big picture. What gives?"

He doesn't deserve this, she thought. *And I can't help it.*

"I will let you in on it when I can. But not right now. I'm sorry, but this is bigger than you know. You'll thank me for not dragging you into this now. Trust me."

Hawk didn't seem convinced. "I hope I can," he said. "The big boss is going to start wondering, you know."

"I know. But by then the matter will be dealt with." *I can only hope.* "Meanwhile, we can close the book on the Alan Barker case. I'll need to ask him a few questions before we get to the office."

Hawk's look was pleading; he wanted to know more, but seemed to also realize more was not forthcoming.

"You'll know everything when I can tell you. Wait here a moment, would you?"

Hawk threw his arms up in frustration. "I don't have anything else to do."

Sammi went back into the office, where she immediately sensed that something magical had just taken place. Alan had a glazed expression completely unlike the anxious, quizzical one she'd seen on him moments before.

The King zapped his memory, she thought, relieved. At least he had the smarts to do *that* much. "So tell me what happened?" she asked Alan.

"I don't remember a whole lot of it," the boy said, sounding slightly stunned. *As a normal boy would be after a kidnapping.* "I was in the Lazerwarz arena when someone hit me over the head. I woke up in a van. I got out. Went into a Wal-Mart. Then I was here." The lad looked utterly confounded. "Where am I?"

It's the best I could do, Aedham's eyes seemed to say.

"All right, then. Let's go."

Sammi had Hawk take Alan in to the office; this served the dual purpose of safely including Hawk in the case and freeing her to look for Llan. Hawk and Alan went on ahead, while Sammi and Aedham waited behind in the store.

"I'll ask you later what the batteries are for. Now we have another problem," Sammi said. "Llan is walking around here somewhere."

"Llanmorgan?" the King said. "Why is—"

"To look for you in the arena," Samantha said, scanning the store for the wandering elf.

Lady Samantha moved quickly, and Llan followed as best he could . . . but there were too many distractions! He understood this was a merchant shop of some kind, but gods it was *huge*. He stopped at a stall where scrying crystals were for sale, before realizing these were smaller versions of the big scream. And they all had the same visions, a human sitting at an altar, just talking.

He looked up and didn't see Samantha anywhere. Being alone in the human's world felt suddenly intimidating; from all the stories he had heard, Llan had assembled a picture of what this land was like, and what he found was nothing like it.

With a start he saw himself on one of the crystals. *How did they do that?* It was a vision of the present. So it wasn't really scrying, as he first thought. On a shelf in front of him were several shiny boxes with eyes on them, and when he picked one up the vision *moved.* So this was some poor creature's eye, connected to the crystal.

"I tell you, it's *him,*" someone said behind him, and

he turned to see two young girls huddled together, looking his direction.

Have they spotted me? he wondered, and checked his disguise. It seemed to be in place. *What are they talking about?* Whatever it was it couldn't be good news. Attention in general was a bad thing, he had learned. Llan set the eye down, and walked over to another crystal, where two boys were watching with extreme interest. They were pushing boxes, and it looked like they were making things happen on the crystal.

Now *this* he had to check out. Maybe this was the human way of making magic. Instead of scrying visions here, they were making the visions happen. Llan felt like he had uncovered an important secret. And what visions they were: flying chariots sending levin bolts at each other. When the warriors fell, they came right back up. They must have strong shields. But where were the Mages? Only Mages can make shields that strong.

"Excuse me," a small, feminine voice said behind him. She clutched a piece of parchment and a quill. "Are you Zachary Hanson?"

She seemed utterly in love. Llan thought she might melt into a little human puddle right there. For an uncomfortable moment, he had forgotten his cover, and contemplated admitting that yes, he was this human, but the consequences seemed potentially ill-favored.

"No, I am . . ." he struggled to remember his "human" name. "*Colin*," he said at last, but the young girl seemed rather dubious.

"You sound like you made it up," she said, with a shy smile. "It's okay, I won't tell anyone you're here. Just, could I get your autograph?" She batted her eyes. "*Pleeease?*"

Perceptive human; she saw right through his falsehood. *But I can't let them know who I am! It is against . . . against the laws! The humans can't know who we are! Perhaps I should pretend to be this Zachary Hanson.* Every instinct he had told him this was not a good idea, but compared with revealing his elven identity it seemed the lesser of two evils.

"Just don't tell anybody," he whispered, and took the parchment. He scribbled a rough approximation of *Colin* on the sheet of paper and handed it to her. *Now the matter should be resolved.*

But evidently it wasn't. The girl took the piece of paper, held it to her chest and with her eyes closed, screeched at the top of her lungs: "I've got Zachary Hanson's autograph!" Then she ran screaming from the stall.

No! Llan thought, terrified. *The humans will think I attacked her! Took liberties I shouldn't . . . and she's not even old enough to bed! Not even close!*

Then the scream was joined by another, then another. He sensed several young human girls nearby, and he had a dreadful feeling that they would want his autograph, too.

Lady Samantha! Where are you?

Llan felt that it would be unwise to stay where he was, and made good his escape from the stall before anyone else could ask for his autograph. Sammi had gone towards the right, but in that direction lay the screaming girls. Llan went left, seeking safety.

Must hide. Must hide!

But where to hide? He found an aisle which had brightly colored storage containers, but none were even close to being large enough for him to fit in.

From the aisle next to him he heard, "Where is he? He's here somewhere! Zachary Hanson, I *luuv yooo!*"

Llan frowned. *Magic. If I use magic—but no, I can't do that, either. The humans will catch me, cut me open and examine my entrails. Not good!*

Must hide!

Llan doubled back around the stall with the scrying

crystals, averting his look from the human adults who were now starting to notice him.

Lady Samantha! Help!

As Samantha and Aedham passed the linens and bathroom furnishings, the screams of young human girls reached their ears.

"Oh no," Samantha said. *"Llan." His glamorie must have slipped again!*

They followed the piercing shrieks to what had to be the source, but no Llan was to be found anywhere. Five preteen girls clutching posters, *Tiger Beat* magazines, paperback books and a half dozen CDs, looked frantically around the store for *someone*.

"Hey, kids, what's all the fuss about?" Samantha asked.

"Hanson is here! Their tour bus is outside. All three of them are here somewhere." She walked up and studied Samantha closely. "Have you seen them?"

"Seen who?" Aedham wanted to know.

"A singing group," Samantha said, utterly relieved. *Good, it wasn't Llan,* she thought briefly, before her eyes fell on one of the CDs. One of the boys on the cover bore a striking resemblance to Aedham's apprentice.

Whatever caused the excitement, this was attention they didn't want, didn't need.

"Let's find him," Aedham said.

With a renewed sense of urgency, Samantha retraced their route to the manager's office, seeing nothing that might offer clues to Llan's whereabouts.

"He didn't just vanish," Sammi said.

"Maybe he did," Aedham said, and she sensed his Mage sight unfolding, taking in the environment. "No magic. But I think . . . yes, I think I might just have a fix on him."

Aedham led her to the back of the store, turned down an aisle full of exercise equipment. "Too much iron," Aedham said. "But he's close."

Then Samantha heard in a loud whisper, "Sammi! King Aedham! I'm over *here.*"

They both whirled around. Before them was a large wire chute full of multicolored beanbag chairs.

"Llan?" Aedham called.

"Here," Llan said, and then Samantha saw where he had hidden. The elf's face was sandwiched between two beanbag chairs as he peered from beneath them; otherwise he was completely buried.

"What are you doing in there?" Samantha asked, as Aedham tried to keep from laughing.

"They're after me. They think I'm someone named Hanson! I didn't lay a hand on them, I swear to the gods and Danu herself!" Then, "Help me!"

Sammi groaned.

"Bloody hell," Aedham said, and searched the area out for young girls. "Coast is clear. This calls for drastic measures."

Sammi looked up at the brown domes protruding from the store's ceiling. "The cameras!"

"Can't be helped," Aedham said, and helped Llan extract himself from the heap of vinyl beanbags. Llan's glamorie, again, had slipped.

"We can't be running around like this," Aedham said, quickly conjuring a full invisibility glamorie. Llan vanished from sight.

"Now. Follow us. Try not to bump or touch *anything.*"

"Aie, King," said the invisible space that was Llan.

"Why does his disguise keep slipping?" Sammi asked as they started walking towards the entrance. "We've never had this problem before."

"We haven't gone over glamories yet," Aedham explained. "He needs special reinforcement for that skill."

On the way out they passed a battery display, where an employee was carefully replacing row upon row of D cell batteries from a cart piled high with them.

Aedham hesitated over the shopping cart; he looked like he wanted to grab it and run.

"What *is* it with the goddamned batteries, Aedham?" Not knowing was driving Sammi nuts.

"We need them," he said. "Do you have any money?"

"Yeah," she replied cautiously. "Why?"

"I'll explain in the car." Then, to the empty space behind him, said, "Come on, Llan."

Where the hell is Yuaroh Dhu? Mort thought angrily, as he let the Foevor into his chambers. *He should have put one of his warriors here to deal with these visits.*

The Foevor Dubh entered Mort's chambers, head down, with a nervous shuffle; that alone would have roused Mort's suspicion. Only recently he'd felt a surge of node power that might have been a Gate, but because it was so brief had assumed it was only a fluctuation caused by the new weapons. Yet without the shipment of batteries that hadn't arrived, the weapons were inert. Or so he had thought.

Dubh made a puzzled gesture with his hands; like the Clapperleg clan, this clan was learning to speak like their leader Mort, but the transition was moving slowly. The Green clan was hairless and humanoid, with smooth greenish skin that looked like formica. They resembled gargoyles, yet they had no eyes, just a toothless mouth that spoke, and tiny, circular ears that listened. They saw with a third eye located deep in their brains. Telepathic communication was possible only among themselves; Mort kept himself shielded, insisting on verbal communication only. With training some could shapeshift, but only Mort had mastered this skill enough to use it easily.

"Speak," Mort commanded gently.

"The Unseleighe have g-gone," the Foevor said, with some difficulty.

"Yes, they must have gated," Mort said patiently. "All of them?"

"All have left. Some Gated. Some . . . set off across the realm."

All.

"Unseleighe took Overworld weapons. All gone."

Mort stared at Dubh; the temptation to reject his message as mistaken or uninformed was strong. Yet, he had to investigate.

"Show you," Dubh said, pointing to the chamber's exit, and moving towards it. "Show you *now.*"

On the long walk to the armory, Mort remembered why he had found the Green clan unfit for battle, and had opted for the human kids for his supply of raw grunts; they moved awkwardly, visibly unfamiliar with their physical form. They tended to live like wraiths or lost human ghosts, with no hierarchy or sense of territory. In short, they were unambitious. In the brief time Mort had risen to conquer Underhill, he had spread his vision to all Foevorian clans, reawakening a common racial memory. Now their glorious past was no longer just a part of their past; it was their future, as well. With time Mort knew he could breed and train a whole army of pure Foevorian soldiers to fight alongside the Clapper clan; until then the mercenaries would have to do.

As he drew closer to the armory, he wondered if using the mercenaries had been a bad idea. The Unseleighe guards who were supposed to be protecting the horde of new weapons were nowhere to be seen. Mort opened the armory's cold iron door and walked into an empty room.

The racks were still there—that was the only thing that told him he was in the right room in his enormous, unfinished palace. The weapons, whose delivery he had personally supervised mere hours before, were not.

He looked back at Dubh. "All gone," Dubh said, sadly.

"The Unseleighe took them?"

"Over here," Dubh said, and led Mort to the other end of the long, empty room. "Here."

The unmistakable residue of a Gate lingered, but that was all he sensed. Clues to its destination had already vanished.

Only a Mage can cast a Gate. His thoughts darkened. *Aedham?*

With Dubh following meekly, Mort set off for the dungeon to see if his Seleighe prisoner was still in his cell. And if he wasn't, what did that mean? *The Unseleighe and Seleighe working together? Impossible!* It contradicted all he had learned about the elven clans.

Even so, it took everything he had to keep from killing the messenger on the spot.

"Battery powered levin rifles," Sammi said, turning into the Homeland supermarket parking lot. It was the third store they'd stopped at since leaving the Wal-Mart. "Doesn't the concept seem, well, inherently *goofy* to you?"

"It's based on Niamh's analysis," Aedham patiently explained. "We know in *principle* that it works. The same configuration of elvenstones on the front wheel and fork of a motorcycle had the same effect as tapping into a node. The steel of the motorcycle dampened the field quite a bit—these weapons, which are made from composites, won't have that problem."

Parking the Caprice, Sammi still seemed unconvinced. "How do you know the levin blast won't melt the weapon?"

"We should test it before marching into battle. That was next on the agenda anyway."

At Homeland they bought out the entire supply of D cells. From this and the earlier shopping visits they had around three hundred batteries, enough to power fifty rifles. Out of a possible three hundred this didn't seem like enough until the King reminded himself that if the weapons performed as expected, this was the equivalent firepower of fifty *Mages*.

Faith in Niamh's work was one thing. Risking Seleighe lives on unproven technology was something else. The King saw the wisdom in her words.

"Let's take this load back to Underhill and see how these weapons work," Aedham said, grateful for Sammi's input.

"You'll stay here," Morrigan said from the bedroom doorway, dressed and ready to go out. "That should give you time to reconsider your feelings toward me."

From the bed Dobie managed a hostile glare before she left—at least he could look angry, even if he didn't really feel it. He knew he was bespelled; he also knew he couldn't fight it. During the night he was unable to keep from getting aroused, or from feeling some level of warm feelings toward this goddess. Now he felt like a prostitute who had serviced a client. She had complete control over him, and could rape him at leisure.

And when she comes back, she'll do it all over again.

It was all part of her power.

And I can't do jack about it!

Dobie listened for the suite doors to shut; when they did he leaped out of the bed and ran to them, finding them in the same unworking state as before. He banged on them with both fists to get the attention of anyone in the hall, but his efforts made no noise. *Some kind of voodoo magic shit,* he surmised. And again, he tried the phone. Nothing. He tried throwing the phone out the window, but it just bounced back, unharmed.

I'm a prisoner.

Aedham remembered the canyon from his childhood. A tributary of the Aranann river had carved a deep groove into the Avalon landscape, leaving behind a sheer cliff topped with boulders. From a distance it looked like a castle perched atop a hill, and Avalon Mages had wondered if it was indeed a legacy from an earlier clan.

Whatever its historical origins, Aedham thought with mixed emotions, *today it becomes target practice.*

With the entire Seleighe army watching with rapt attention, Petrus handed him Madame Photon, Aedham's first laser rifle, which had been hanging with the rest of the rifles in Mort's armory. The battery was dead. In their frenzy of battery purchases he had neglected to pick up some twelve volt cells for this particular gun. But unless the war spread to the Overworld, he would not be using it here anyway; the rifle didn't work in Underhill. While Niamh's research had not made the rifle usable in the elven realms as hoped, it had produced the levin rifle technology.

He set Madame aside and donned one of the Lazerwarz vests. Inserting six batteries had brought the pack to life, including an LCD display with a gauge of some kind.

"One button here starts the generator spinning," Petrus explained as he pressed it. Short of actually firing the weapon, Petrus had gotten a jump on deciphering the weird technology as soon as the batteries arrived. "Then this gauge starts climbing."

"It's measuring the level of node power," Aedham observed, recognizing the power immediately as it coursed through his soul. He hefted the short rifle with one hand, noting the thick wiring connecting it to the vest.

"Now it's live and charged up," Petrus said nervously. "Are you sure you don't want someone else to test this first?"

"Certain," Aedham said, taking aim at the canyon formation. "I wouldn't ask any of my people to do something I wouldn't do myself."

"So be it," Petrus said, backing away from the rig nevertheless.

The LCD gauge had reached its maximum reading; node power hovered behind him, poised for release.

"Banzai!" the King shouted, and pulled the trigger.

Aedham felt the rig pull on the node power, guiding it over the vest through the thick wire and into the gun. With no recoil, the short rifle blurted forth a large sphere which ripped into the cliff wall. The impact sent a loud report, quickly followed by a shock wave that knocked Aedham back a pace. The blast had taken out half the visible canyon wall; the sequence of events took maybe a second. Rock and debris continued to rain down into the Aranann. A carefully administered levin bolt from a Mage would have performed similarly.

A cheer erupted from the army, and Petrus came forward to examine the King and his weapon. The gauge had dropped down to zero, but as they watched, it recharged. In less than a minute, it was back to full strength. Before the cheers faded, Aedham let loose another blast at the formation, with the same results.

His highest ranking men clustered around the King and the new weapon. Aedham looked the rifle over, feeling the barrel, the wires, and then removing the vest for Petrus to examine. While warm, the barrel certainly wasn't hot.

The realization that his weapon was intended to be used against the Seleighe tempered his otherwise joyous mood; if they were to defeat Mort, they needed to attack before he could resupply his human and nonhuman troops with the damned things. Other advantages to the weapon came to mind; Aedham could use his freed-up Mage resources for making Gates for the army to travel through, a strategy that was until now impractical. A Mage had to spend quality time to recover from gatemaking, in some cases up to a candle mark, before being able to blast anything with a levin bolt.

Now, there was no downtime.

How convenient, Aedham thought, unable to suppress a triumphant smile.

Now let's clean up Underhill for good.

From a balcony overlooking the palace grounds, Mort regarded what remained of the nonhuman segment of his army. Cikal Clapperleg was now his commander, and was addressing the army with much pretended enthusiasm. The Foevor balanced perfectly on his single leg, and gesticulated wildly for effect; the demon had been studying Hitler's oration techniques. Mort hoped it would be enough to get his army back on track.

The Unseleighe's betrayal had shot morale to hell. He still had twenty-five armed Clappers, and a hundred or so from the Green clan, and as many more in wraith form drifting beyond the perimeter. With so large a gathering Mort knew he shouldn't feel the loss of thirty-five Unseleighe, but he did. The Green clan was a wild card; he wasn't sure they could even fight. And the wraiths . . . he wasn't even sure they *wanted* to fight. It seemed they were lurking in the background to see what the outcome of all this would be, a revelation which did not improve his mood at all.

Ah, but we do have the Clappers. And they have the arms, Mort thought, grateful that the large levin rifles, the Mort Longs, had not been stolen. The shoulder-mounted weapons had roughly three times the power and range of the Mort Shorts, and could punch holes in thick palace walls . . . not to mention what they could do to the elves themselves. Mort's own Short remained stashed behind his throne in his royal chambers. The shipment of batteries from the Overworld had arrived, so powering the weapons was no problem. But his attempts at cheering himself up fell flat. Without the three hundred weapons for his human army, victory was no longer guaranteed.

Indeed, he'd found Aedham gone from his cell when he had investigated, confirming the Foevor's belief that the King of Avalon had made the Gate. Mort would never have thought cooperation between the two elven groups possible; in his long existence, nothing had surprised him more. If the elves were combining their forces, he had much to worry about. The Seleighe courts had at least three hundred warriors, and half as many nonwarriors for support. He suspected that less than a hundred Unseleighe remained. *The numbers are rather lopsided,* he considered. *It just doesn't fit that the Seleighe would throw in with the Unseleighe when their numbers are so few. The Shorts must have been their bargaining chip. And what of Morrigan? She has been conspicuously absent during all this. Did she have a hand in the weapons' disappearance?*

Behind him, from the other side of his chambers, he detected another Gate forming. He recognized the node signature as Morrigan's. *Speak of the devil.* He returned to his chambers and awaited her arrival.

As usual she entered his royal space without so much as a knock.

"So tell me, what's new on the home front?" she asked, without a hint of sarcasm. "Are we ready to start a war?"

"We've received the batteries," Mort said, feigning boredom. "The Gate didn't zap their charge like you thought it would," he said. She seemed uninterested. *Does she know there's nothing here for the batteries to power now?*

Mort took a seat on his throne and studied Morrigan through steepled fingers. *Does she know anything?*

"So what's the problem?" she said, evidently sensing his grim mood. For once, she seemed genuinely concerned for the project—and anything out of the ordinary was suspect.

"The problem is," Mort began, with an amazing level of calm, "the Unseleighe have made off with the entire armory."

Morgan uttered a forced, shrill laugh. "Oh, Mort. Such a flair for drama. What is it . . . really?"

Mort studied her further, looking for some sign, any sign that would give her away.

She said, "Are you serious? The weapons are gone? *All* of them?"

Her words sounded sincere, but her eyes, that was a different matter. As usual, they mocked him; that was all he needed to see.

"Don't play games with me Morrigan!" Mort shouted, his words ripping through the palace like an explosion. His vehemence caught her unawares, and she stepped back a pace. She seemed genuinely frightened, for a moment. Then she was back to her old mocking self.

"Don't get snippy with me, your nastiness," Morrigan chided. "I am in the same sinking ship as you, in case you haven't noticed."

Are we really? he wanted to ask, but gave her time to finish.

"The Unseleighe," Morrigan said. Her words became distant, "How very strange that they would do this. But with all those guns, they would be formidable, indeed."

"Aedham assisted them," Mort said. "He set the Gate up, and they left with the goods. As near as I can tell the elves have decided to set aside their differences and take me on." His dark thoughts took control of his expression, and he made no effort to fight it.

"Then you'll have to make more," Morrigan pointed out.

"There's no time!" Mort spat.

"The Seleighe are sticklers for protocol," Morrigan

pointed out. "It is a weakness we have exploited before. Perhaps we would do well to do so again."

"Out with it, then! If you have an idea let's hear it."

"Well," she began, apparently unperturbed by his foul mood. "Do we still have the human children under our control?"

Mort nodded.

"Then we'll use them as shields. To force their hand. To play *our* game for a change."

"Do tell."

"Single combat, you silly Foevor!" Morrigan tittered. "One of ours against one of theirs in the Lazerwarz arena. No magic. Just the game. Winner take all. And if it doesn't turn out the way we want, we can go back on our agreement and be right where we are right now. Don't you think it's worth a chance?"

Her optimism was infectious; Mort perked up. *We own the arenas, and we have the best players.* "Perhaps it is worth a chance, at that. Who did you have in mind to fight for our side?"

She smiled that evil, condescending smile, and Mort's hackles got right back up. "Who do you think I've been grooming for such a possibility?"

Mort's calm evaporated. *So that's what the bitch is after! A monopoly on our champion. The lad she's been fornicating with for the last week! I should have known.*

" 'For such a possibility,' " Mort echoed. "It sounds like you planned for it. Sounds like, maybe, you had a hand in this fiasco," Mort said, his words dripping with acid.

Morrigan waved the accusation aside. "How ridiculous, Mort. I would no more want those pretentious elves in control of Underhill than you do." She took a few steps forward, regaining the territory she forfeited during Mort's initial outburst. "You spent too much time around the Unseleighe, Mort. I have never seen them trust each other. Their suspicion is rubbing off on you."

"Where are you keeping this rodent?" Mort asked. As much as his pride wanted him to turn down the offer, his rationality wouldn't let him: Mort had *seen* what the kid could do in an arena. He was invincible. Single combat would afford drastically better odds, at no risk to himself.

"He's at the Doubletree, downtown. In the suites, top floor. I dare say the wards I put on my rooms there are better than the ones King Aedham managed to slip through."

Mort ignored the jab; he'd seen it coming since the beginning of the conversation, and would have been surprised if she *hadn't* reminded him of his failure. But it would be the last time she would remind him of anything; he realized now that finally, challenge or not, she had outlived her usefulness to him. Now she was a traitorous pain in the ass, and Mort was not going to let that stand. He couldn't afford to trust her any longer; he had a realm to conquer.

"Excuse me," Mort said politely, and went behind his throne to retrieve his levin rifle, and turned it on. The batteries were new. It came online right away. *Haven't really tested this on an Underhill entity yet. Now is the time.*

He stepped out from behind the throne and aimed it at her. The sight of the levin rifle froze her sneer in place. Mort felt her reaching for power, and pulled the trigger before she could summon it. The rifle belched a fireball from the barrel and struck her head on, picking her off the floor and sending her into the opposite wall, quickly, violently.

Mort fully expected the weapon to turn her into a grease ball, or at the very least dismember her into several separate pieces before blowing a hole in the chamber wall. She wasn't moving, but her physical body remained intact, with no other collateral damage to the room. She must have pulled together an emergency shield, which had absorbed the brunt of the blast. He walked over to examine the remains, and found a blackened Morrigan lying in a twisted pile, not moving, not breathing. He toed the carcass with his foot. She rolled over, eyes wide and staring at the ceiling. Shield or not, the levin rifle had clearly gotten the best of her.

There were no life signs. She seemed to be dead.

Mort blew imaginary smoke from the gun's barrel, then returned the rifle to its place behind his throne.

The evening with Morgan had made him feel dirty; her scent was all over him, and he felt tainted. After trying unsuccessfully to get the attention of the housekeeper he heard pushing a cart on the other side of the door, he gave up and poured the hottest bath he could stand and submerged himself. Here Dobie spent a good part of an hour with a washcloth and a thin amber bar of Neutrogena, scrubbing himself down all over, as if the soap alone would banish Morrigan from his life. Even with his limited knowledge of otherworld beings, he knew it would not be as simple as that. But at least it made him feel a little better.

He was about to add more hot water to the cooling bath when he realized he was no longer alone in the suite. Something bright and luminous had silently entered the room. If he was lucky it would be a UFO full of grays, here to abduct him.

Dobie scrambled out of the tub and toweled himself off. His clothes were in the other room. So be it; the new Dobie was not embarrassed about nudity. He remembered fighting armies without a stitch of clothing, smeared from head to feet with blue woad. Brazenly, he walked out of the bathroom to confront the source of light.

What the hell? he thought, taking in the strange sight.

A tall, white-haired man in a green cloak stood in front of the suite's window, looking his direction. Dobie held a hand up against the brilliance.

"Forgive me," the old man said, and the intensity dropped. He was still luminous, as if lit from inside, but was not as bright. Dobie gazed upon him, knowing who he was, and uncertain how to react. *He is the spirit in the vision. The one who healed me. Lugh, Lord of Light.*

My father.

"I forget how bright my light is to mortal eyes," Lugh said, with a sparkle in his face that for all the world reminded Dobie of a benevolent Santa Claus, out of costume. The green cloak hung loosely over him, and beneath that was a white robe. He slouched against a staff; inside the transparent tube a miniature thunderstorm churned and spat lightning through its entire length. Dobie, who was starting to think of himself as Cu Chulainn more and more, didn't remember this particular prop from the vision. Then again, he hadn't been standing naked in an expensive hotel suite. Perhaps the staff allowed Lugh to be in this realm.

"Morrigan seems to have taken advantage of you once again," Lugh said, shaking his head sadly. "A mighty warrior you are, a man you are still trying to be."

The comment stung. Embarrassment reddened him from head to toe. He shrugged and started looking around for something to wear.

"You are not the only one she has made fool of," Lugh continued. "And do not think yourself a lesser warrior, either."

"She controls me with magic," Dobie complained. "I don't know how to fight it."

"Indeed you don't," Lugh said, sounding saddened. "I had not the opportunity to train you as I would like. Such is the disadvantage of having human children."

Lugh stepped closer to him, his illumination flaring somewhat with each step.

Dobie rummaged through a pile of pants, found a pair he liked, and started ripping the tags off of it. Then, with his eyes brimming with tears, he looked up at his father. He didn't care.

"Get me out of here," Dobie pleaded, with the voice of a child. "*Please.*"

Lugh smiled benevolently. "Securing your escape from this place would only temporarily solve your problem, son," Lugh replied. "She would only bring you back. I know of a way to rid yourself of her."

Dobie looked up hopefully.

"Permanently," Lugh said, his smile turning to something . . . slightly *less* benevolent.

"How?" Dobie asked desperately.

The staff flared as a swath of lightning flashed through it. Dobie flinched.

"Listen closely," Lugh said, dropping his voice to a conspiratorial whisper. Dobie didn't know why; they were alone in the room. "There is a war going on, between good and evil. We are at the center of it, whether you like it or not."

Dobie sighed in resignation. "Tell me something I *don't* know."

"What you don't know is this," Lugh said, with a hint of anger. "The elves, the druids, the other humans, and, lest we forget, Morgan, are all against you. They are against the Foevors, the first race of spirits to inhabit the Overworld, the underworld, and everything in between."

Dobie's memory of the distant past was murky, and he had to search diligently for knowledge on the Foevors. When he found it, he replied, "Yes, they were the first race. What has that to do with us?"

Lugh's expression turned proud, and he stood up from his stooped position. His face beamed with brilliance.

"*I am Foevorian,*" Lugh finally said, and looked directly at Dobie. "You, also, are Foevorian!"

Dobie stared at his father, mouth open. "Say what?"

"It was a well kept secret," Lugh replied. "Known only to a few. My father was among the first Foevorians. It was later that he assumed the name of Dagda."

Dobie closed his eyes and shook his head: this went contrary to everything he knew about his lineage. *The gods came before the Foevorians, didn't they?* He looked into his father's face, and saw only truth.

"Yes, I am sure that it is shock, perhaps even a disappointment," Lugh said, apologetically. "But it makes us no less mighty. We are what we are, and when we win this battle, we will be more. More than you can imagine."

He wished that were true. At least it would solve all of his mundane problems. Godhood would do that, he suspected.

"What of Morgan?" Dobie asked. "How do I rid myself of her?"

Lugh chuckled softly. "My son, haven't you been listening? The gods will summon a warrior from each side. You will volunteer to fight for the Foevorians; Mort is your leader. Do as he says."

"That much I follow," Dobie said. "But Morrigan . . . she has bespelled me."

"Not to worry," Lugh said, reaching into a pouch at his belt. He withdrew a gold ring and gave it to Dobie. "Put that on your left hand."

The ring slipped on perfectly. It held a small red stone, perhaps a ruby, and no other decoration. The moment it was on his hand he felt the ring's magic sweep over him.

"This ring will protect you from anything she can throw at you," Lugh said confidently. "But I doubt she is much of a threat now anyway."

Dobie didn't understand, but chose not to ask any more questions. He had enough to digest as it was.

"At the Lazerwarz arena, you will play for the Foevors. Your *brethren*. Take Morrigan's chariot to the arena now; it's waiting for you downstairs." Then the god added, with a smirk that was strangely unbecoming, "She won't be needing it anymore, I wager."

Chapter Twelve

It was not so long ago that Aedham and his warriors had chased a party of Unseleighe into the thick cover of the Black Forest. Though hampered by the close proximity of trees and underbrush, Aedham and his army had waged a bloody sword fight, and had emerged victorious; the remaining Unseleighe had fled through a hastily made Gate.

Now, they have no Mage, Aedham knew with certainty. *They will not flee, not this time.*

The King explored the territory with a squad of fifteen Seleighe warriors, each armed with a levin rifle. Quick studies, all of them; they knew how to operate the weapons, and could in all likelihood take on the entire Unseleighe army themselves. They followed a creek bed for a time, and through the dense forest wall spotted the enemy, which had set up camp on the ruins of the old Avalon castle. The Unseleighe were even using stones from the ravaged site for fire pits; he didn't want to imagine where their latrine was.

But the wry humor of the situation tempered his anger somewhat. *They're still waiting for the Gate to appear. They still think Yuaroh will provide them with levin rifles!*

Levin rifles they asked for, levin rifles they shall receive. From the business end.

Crouched beside him, a Seleighe warrior said, "How dare the bastards."

"That's all I need to see," Aedham whispered, and they pulled back into the dark forest. With a stick Aedham drew a map in the dirt. The elven warriors gathered around him.

"This creek bed is a natural entrance to the forest from the ruins," he said, drawing the creek and the border of the forest. "When the Unseleighe bastards run—and they *will* run—they will come here. This is where they fled before. We will come around the ruins over here, using the hill as cover, so we don't hit each other in the crossfire."

"*If* there are any left to run," said one of his warriors.

"They know what these weapons are," Aedham said. "As soon as they see it in the hands of the enemy, they will turn tail. That is, the ones who don't fall in the first wave."

"Aie," said another.

"Spread yourselves out a bit, and don't be afraid to use the forest for cover. Just remember, that's what they're trying to do when they run here. Don't let them past you."

The King bid them good luck, and at a fast march set off for the main camp.

"If I have learned anything from fighting the Unseleighe," Aedham said to Petrus as they rode elvensteeds at a moderate clip, the army thundering behind them, "it's to never take anything for granted."

Petrus nodded in agreement, as well he would. He had seen as much action with the Unseleighe court as the King. "I still think a guerrilla attack is the way to use these weapons."

Aedham shook his head resolutely. "Not enough cover. Guerrilla warfare works because of stealth; there is no way to sneak up on the ruins. That is why the site was selected."

Aedham and his command stopped at the base of a rise which overlooked the ruins. With a strong sense of irony Aedham realized this was the very rise from which Zeldan Dhu and his army launched the initial assault on Avalon.

"Time to spread out," Aedham said, signaling the ranks to disperse themselves; at his command, the army ascended to its peak, revealing themselves to the Unseleighe.

The commotion in the Unseleighe camp was instant and chaotic. An approaching Seleighe army had been furthest from their minds; they hadn't even bothered to post sentries. A call to arms blared through the camp, and the Unseleighe quickly armed themselves and assembled.

"Keep the rifles hidden until I say," Aedham shouted to his soldiers. Then, to Petrus, said, "They will probably form a phalanx or two along the perimeter and attack. That's when I want the rifles to take them out."

"And after that?" Petrus asked.

"By then those still alive will probably head towards the Black Forest. That's the only way out."

"Then they'll discover our surprise," Petrus said, with a slight smile.

"Look sharp," Aedham said, pointing towards the Unseleighe. "We haven't won anything yet."

Indeed, once the commanders appeared on the field they organized their men into not two but three phalanxes, five abreast.

"That must be most of their army." Aedham was surprised.

"All the better for us," Petrus said.

The King saw his levin rifle infantry in position behind the regulars. Shields hid them from the Unseleighe, and he noted with satisfaction all the rifles were powered up.

Just don't pull the trigger before it's time. Friendly fire isn't.

The Seleighe were getting edgy. An absolute silence fell over the area, a sure sign all hell was about to break loose and rain down on them all. Aedham caught himself reaching for the nodes the old fashioned way, and hesitated. He located the power, but left it untapped. They would need it later for gating.

Then at some unheard command, the Unseleighe army charged. A cheer went up from the enemy, and Aedham saw his own men visibly holding themselves back. The urge to rush the enemy was strong among them all; it was how they were trained.

"Not *yet*," Aedham shouted. The Unseleighe ran down hill at full speed before crossing the dry moat. Regaining their momentum, the phalanx reformed and continued the charge.

"*Ready!*" Aedham shouted, and the infantry parted to give the riflemen a clear shot.

"*Aim!*" Thirty muzzles drew on their targets.

"*Fire!*"

The air filled with blinding light spheres surging toward the enemy; suddenly the three phalanxes were pools of light and smoke. The levin blasts pulverized the Unseleighe mercilessly, and armor and bits of dark elf rocketed into the sky in a gory mess. What remained was a scorched field of writhing, blackened bodies, and shields and armor that had become molten bronze.

Aedham felt it coming first and shouted, "Shock wave!" before he dismounted. The Seleighe dropped to the ground, as drilled. The next second the roar of explosions ripped past them, knocking those off their feet who were still standing. The shock wave blasted past them. Petrus was getting to his feet, but was clearly too stunned to react.

"Attack!" Aedham commanded, and his warriors rose from the ground and formed a line; Aedham mounted his elvensteed and led the charge, sword drawn. The Seleighe forces swarmed over the charcoaled remains of the Unseleighe phalanx, putting the sword to those unfortunate enough to have survived the levin bolts. The remaining Unseleighe had turned to flee—as predicted, towards the Black Forest.

"This way, this way!" Aedham commanded, leading his forces around the castle, away from the line of fire from his men in the forest. A moment later, another flash filled the sky; the resultant shock wave was not as strong, but still a force to contend with. Once it was past, Aedham found himself in the center of the Unseleighe camp, a tangle of tents and armor amid the jagged walls of his former home. The Black Forest spread majestically beneath him. Between the line of trees and the moat, the remaining Unseleighe lay in a scorched pile of bodies. None appeared to have survived the blast.

Then it was all over. If any Unseleighe had escaped, it would have been a miracle. Aedham dispatched his men to search the entire area, ruins and all, for any who might be hiding.

Petrus rode up on Moonremere, evidently recovered enough from the blast. Aedham motioned him to follow down to the Black Forest.

There he found the men he had positioned in the forest among the dead Unseleighe. Aedham and Petrus' steeds gaited up to one charcoal pit.

"It's over?" Petrus said softly.

"For now," Aedham said, gazing at the carnage. "Two volleys, and the fight was over." He turned to Petrus. "Why don't I feel victorious?"

"It wasn't much of a fight," Petrus said. "They didn't have a chance."

Neither would we! Aedham wanted to shout, but he felt empty, as if he'd won a game of poker by cheating. His warriors sensed his bitter mood, and a lull had fallen over the scene.

"This was no honorable way to fight," he announced to his warriors. "No one deserves to die like this."

Nods of agreement among all of them; they all knew about Zeldan Dhu and his son, how they would have gladly slaughtered the Seleighe in the same manner. They all knew Mort would have done this to them had Aedham not stolen this deadly, horrible weapon from them. The Seleighe had wanted to live in peace, always; the Unseleighe, without exception, had forced war upon Underhill.

But none of that would have altered the situation. War in Underhill had changed, therefore Underhill had changed. The King wasn't sure how he felt about being the instrument of that change. *I must take some credit. My people developed this hellish weapon at my request.*

"Sire," one of his men said, gratefully shattering the morose quiet that was smothering them. "Messenger."

Indeed, two Seleighe cavalry were escorting another, darker being, riding a black horse. *A Foevor.* The messenger walked his horse up the king's and waited for a Seleighe to pass a written note to Aedham. He opened it and read:

> To His Majesty, King Aedham Tuiereann, ruler of Avalon,
>
> I hereby challenge your kingdom to a contest of single combat, to be carried out in the arena of Lazerwarz in Tulsa, Oklahoma, at twelve midnight, tonight in the human's realm, under the stipulation that no magic be used, and the victor of said Lazerwarz game be determined by a superior number of points only. NO physical contact will be permitted.
>
> In the event that the kingdom of the Foevorians lose the match, I will without condition release the 287 human youths I have

imprisoned. Remember them? They are also my guarantee that you will abide by these rules. Their lives depend on it. See you soon at Lazerwarz with the champion of your choice.

Have a nice day,
Mort

P.S. Perhaps this will teach you to not take that which is not yours, asshole.

"The bastard!" Aedham said, passing the message to Petrus. "*Now* he's going to play by the rules!"

"He has nothing to lose," Petrus said, reading the note.

"We have everything to win," Aedham reminded him. "Including the lives of those humans. We *must* win."

Stupid, foolish human boy! Mort thought as he returned to his palace chambers, rather pleased with himself that he was able to imitate a god with so much success. *The simplest of glamories, some stock footage of a wizened old man, with lots of light and especial effects. Spielberg would have been proud.* Mort wouldn't trifle with Lugh under most circumstances, but the situation had called for extreme action. And so far the ruse had worked: Dobie was now on his side, and seemed to have accepted everything Mort had told him, without question. And if Dobie *did* question the instructions, the ruby ring Mort had given him was set to squelch any doubts.

Mort saw one flaw in an otherwise perfect plan. Dobie had not arrived yet, and the elves should be here any time. *I must keep Dobie away from them lest they see he's been bespelled. I want my victory to be absolute.*

And fair, of course.

At the console Mort brought up the link to his palace and summoned Dubh. He didn't really want to trust the wimpy Foevor, but his staff of competent Unseleighe were now twisted charcoal briquettes strewn across the ruins of old Avalon. Dubh appeared on the screen, his image broken by the crystal facets on the device on his end. His promptness in answering his call pleased Mort. *Perhaps Dubh has potential.*

"Yes, Master?" Dubh said obediently.

"Have you cleaned up the mess in the chambers yet?" he asked. When he returned home victorious he did not want to be greeted by the rancid odor of flash-fried Morrigan.

The Foevor made a helpless gesture. "She . . . not *here*, Master. Morrigan *gone*."

Someone must have cleaned it up already. At the moment, he didn't want to entertain any alternative explanation. His moment of triumph was at hand, and he didn't want to ruin it with needless worry. "Very well, then. Continue patrolling the grounds. If you catch so much as a *whiff* of Seleighe, sound the alarms. And . . . good work, Dubh. I am very pleased with you."

Dubh's eyeless face bloomed with pleasure before Mort cut the connection and switched over to the local security cams. On the external parking lot view he panned wide, taking in the damned megaliths, which the human police were still guarding. If he were to operate from this location too much longer he would have to get rid of them somehow—and he didn't look forward to diverting his resources to the task.

When this is over, I can level the entire site with the levin cannons. Then the humans can figure out what to do with the pieces!

"Aedham, there is no way this will be a fair match," Sammi declared angrily, pulling the Caprice up in front of the arena and parking. She turned off the headlights. A single pole light cast dirty shadows on the pavement around them. "Mort is in control of the game. He can handicap us and fix the points any way he pleases. Don't you *see* that?"

"Of course I see that," Aedham replied from the passenger seat, more angrily than he intended. "I also see two hundred and eighty-seven youths who have no idea what is going on, and will die if we refuse this challenge. I'd rather not have them on my conscience, thank you."

"We still haven't found Dobie," Llan pointed out from the back seat.

"No, we haven't," Sammi said, sadly. On returning from Underhill, King Aedham briefed Sammi on the new challenge. Then they had gone in search of the best player they knew: Dobie. He wasn't home, nor was there any sign he had returned. The Doubletree hotel was a promising lead, but Dobie was nowhere to be found when they had gone to investigate. The hotel staff was remarkably tight-lipped, even when shown an FBI badge. No doubt Morrigan had greased them thoroughly with lots of kenned Underhill cash.

That left the arena, where they had just arrived. The time was 11:30 P.M. on a moonless night. A single cop was sitting in his squad car, observing them casually as they pulled up before going back to his newspaper.

"They close in half an hour," Sammi said. "When was the challenge scheduled?"

"Twelve," Aedham said morosely. "Doesn't look like Dobie . . ."

As soon as he mentioned the boy's name he saw twin headlights appear from the street. A red Corvette pulled up in front of the arena and stopped.

"It's him," Sammi said, and they both got out of the Caprice.

"Dobie!" Sammi shouted as he got out of the driver's side. Morrigan was not with him.

The boy turned around in midstride as the elves hurried to catch up with him.

"Oh, uh, hi," he said nervously.

He had changed somehow since Aedham had last seen him. *He looks like he fears us.* Aedham peered at him closely, his Mage sight picking up a suspicious aura. *He's been bespelled.*

"We have a proposition for you," Sammi said brightly. "A chance to make something right."

"We need a player," Aedham said urgently, while probing his aura for the spell. It seemed to be centered on his hand. *A ring.*

"I've already picked a side," Dobie said, with a mixture of sadness and fear. *Something haunts him. A ruby ring.* "I know more about what's going on, now," he said, now with a hint of anger. "My father explained it all to me."

"What?" Sammi and Aedham said in unison.

"I'm expected inside," Dobie said, went into the arena.

Aedham stared at the glass door, then to Sammi, said, "What is he talking about? How could he have seen Lugh?"

Sammi shook her head. "Lugh said he couldn't enter the human realm."

"Not without difficulty," Aedham pointed out. "He could do it if he needed to. I mean, he *is* a god. If he did, why didn't he contact us?"

Sammi looked away, glancing back at the car. Llan was walking towards them.

"We need a player," Sammi asked the King. "How many games did you play in there?"

"Just the one," Aedham said, with a frown. "Not enough to really learn anything."

"Well, Llan here, he played a whole afternoon," Sammi said as the apprentice caught up with them.

"I played *three* games," Llan said. "Who's going to be our champion?"

Aedham turned to Llan. "You are."

✧ ✧ ✧

Aedham insisted on being in the control room during the game, and Mort, surprisingly, agreed. Granted, this was no guarantee the game would go fairly, but at least it afforded him a glimpse at the game equipment. It was a rather mundane collection of file servers and electronic bric-a-brac, with a suggestion of magic working beyond it, but nothing solid enough to object to. Mort sat at the console, choosing the form Aedham remembered from Dallas, the spindly black cartoon creature with pointed elflike ears and a long, Zeldan Dhu nose. The King knew this was no accident; it was meant to remind Aedham of the past, and it did. The Mage surreptitiously probed Mort's magical defenses, finding a solid shield surrounding the Foevor. Probing further would not go unnoticed; the King restrained himself, for now. Instead he probed the room's perimeter, looking for magical traps that might deny him access to the Overworld's wild power, and found none. It was there for the taking. If he wanted to pull together the power for a levin bolt and cook Mort where he sat, it looked like he could. The temptation was great. The Seleighe had warred long and hard with the Foevor, and never before had Mort shown the slightest inclination towards honor *or* fairness.

On the other hand, Mort was trusting *him* to abide by the rules as well, and the King's sense of honor would not allow him to do otherwise.

Mort continued bringing up the system, mousing his way through the menus like a pro. It was a Compaq dual processor, running Windows NT, but that's where the King's comprehension ended. "Have a seat," Mort said smugly, pointing to a swivel chair against the wall. "Pull it up here, next to me. I don't want you to miss *anything*."

Aedham did not reply; he was still studying the equipment, looking for something he understood. A row of monitors stared down at them from the wall, each with a camera view of the arena. A large computer screen displayed the game program, a Windows-based interface with lots of fancy graphics. Two names appeared, The Hound and Elvenboy. To the right was a window for their scores, and next to it a clock set to zeros.

"In case you're concerned about me fixing the scores, I can't. Humans designed the software, which I find incomprehensible. I couldn't tweak it to go in my favor even if I wanted to. It will be an absolutely fair game."

"We'll see," Aedham said dryly. "There's a first time for everything."

As Dobie put the laser vest on he felt empty. His father had told him to fight for the Foevors—that *they* were Foevors—but his heart was telling him otherwise. He wasn't sure what the outcome of this game would mean, or what they were really fighting for. There was more at stake than who had the high score, but what?

Not a soul was in sight in the arena. Lugh had told him to report to "Mort," who turned out to be a voice on the speakers, greeting him as he entered, instructing him to suit up, get into the arena, and position himself. He questioned the tactics; it was a huge arena for two people. Precious game time would be spent just locating each other. Yet like a good warrior, he accepted the orders without complaint, and entered the maze.

The Hound stopped halfway up the ramp and peered through holes in the wall, where he had a view of the weapons room. Someone else had entered the room and put on a vest.

Llan?

That was ridiculous. The kid, or elf, was a novice. It seemed like an unequal match; perhaps they didn't have time to find someone else. As he considered the unfairness of the situation, the countdown began on his gun. Thirty seconds.

When he looked up, Llan was gone, now somewhere in the maze. As the seconds ticked he felt the now familiar change, the fighting rage that started from his toes and shot through his entire body, sharpened his senses, and turned his heart into a thundering bass drum.

It's showtime.

There, he heard him, somewhere down below. The unmistakable squeak of shoe rubber on concrete. Llan was on the first level. The Hound moved up the ramp to the second level, peering through the wire mesh screening to the floor below. *There, movement.* The seconds ticked down to zero, the guns bleeped to life, and the packs came up. Llan was a cluster of targets.

The Hound was a cluster of targets, too. The instant the game started Llan aimed and pegged The Hound in the ten point chest target, then ducked out of sight.

Stupid! The Hound thought, no longer feeling sorry for the elves. *Llan knows where I am. I'd better move.* A distant memory from his previous life surfaced: *The elves' senses are sharper than a human's. I wonder if he can hear me breathe!*

There were two ways Llan could come up the stairs; at one the ramp had a good ambush at the top where it entered the level. Dobie silently moved to the ambush, covering his gun's speaker as it bleeped back to life. There was Llan, and The Hound tagged him, and backed away.

Even score now; the elf looked up, saw his opponent, and moved on up the ramp, moving behind a minimaze. The Hound considered taking him face to face, but he was rather enjoying this cat and mouse stuff.

Above the maze where Llan had sought refuge hung a long metal mirror, and the elf's lights were reflected perfectly in it.

The Hound bounced his beam off the mirror, blotting out the pack, and thumped him again as soon as his pack was alive. In the mirror Llan looked around in confusion. *He must not know the mirror trick.* Then he saw The Hound in the reflection, and moved out of sight.

The Hound moved, then decided to go deeper into the upper level, and when he thought it was safe turned his back to do just that. *Mistake!*

Llan nailed him from ahead . . . in that short time the elf had moved through the entire back of the level and ambushed him.

If he was breaking the rules by running, The Hound didn't hear it, and he had long ago quit making an issue about other players breaking the rules. Turning in cheaters did not add to his score, and burned up precious time.

Somewhere back there, Llan was waiting.

The gloves are coming off. One on one. The way Father wanted it.

His pack up, The Hound went directly to where Llan had been, and found him, moving behind a wall; the elf was not moving fast enough, The Hound tagged him, and stood his ground, counting the seconds before his opponent's pack returned.

The score was too close for comfort. *Thumping time.*

A short span of maze, Llan at one end, The Hound at the other. While Llan's pack was down The Hound moved around to the other side, thumped the valuable back target, turned around and repeated the cycle four times. The elf must have caught on: when The Hound went around to thump him again, he wasn't there. The Hound had lost his momentum. *Where is he?*

He listened for Llan's pack; apparently he'd learned the speaker covering trick. *No sound, no elf. But he's back there somewhere.*

✧ ✧ ✧

The urge to use magic was strong; forfeiting the game if he did so kept Llan from it. Once the game began and he knew where his opponent was, Llan went after him bravely, using the warrior tactics common to his folk. But it was like walking into an army; Dobie was just too good.

Llan backed out of the minimaze the way he had come, and found the ramp completely open. Knowing there was a fair amount of distance between them now, he let his presence be known by "accidentally" hitting one of the walls, and then walking loudly down the ramp.

From a hole in the wall poured mist, and Llan thought for a moment that this was Mort's treacherous attempt to cheat. But the fog was part of the arena, he remembered. It pooled on the floor, and fogged up the entire area.

Let's use it for cover. . . .

Llan waited for The Hound to come down the ramp, but was met instead by his opponent's laser beam striking his shoulder target. He looked up and saw The Hound looking down through a grate from the second level.

Llan dashed out of the way, aware of Dobie following him on the second level, catching occasional glimpses of him through more grates. The human must have the place memorized! By the time his pack was up, though, no Dobie was to be found. Llan saw *another* second level, across from this one. *If I get up there I can hit him from across the arena,* he reasoned.

Indeed, it seemed to be what the builders of this place expected. Once he got over there Llan discovered a useful parapet, which legally concealed his shoulder targets. And he had perfect shot of the other level.

The Hound walked into view.

Llan tagged him, and ducked back. *Let him wonder where it came from.* On impulse he moved to another part of the level, and looked out. Nothing at first . . . then came the cautious appearance of the gun barrel target creeping up over the edge of a wall; Llan fired, burning up two of his rapid fire bursts to tag him.

Moments later, The Hound returned fire to precisely where he had been—but now Llan was at the other end, where he'd begun. The Hound must have seen what he was doing. As soon as Llan presented himself The Hound tagged him again.

The strategy worked, but not as well as he would have liked.

His gun told him he was still in second place, with eight hundred points. He moved to the back of the level, where he discovered a useful view of the ramp leading up to where he was. Llan positioned himself there, and waited.

The Hound took the bait. A minute later, walked up the ramp, passing directly under him. Llan let loose his beam and nailed the back target. The Hound shrugged it off and proceeded up the ramp, and Llan looked for better cover.

The Hound reached the second level and looked around for Llan; the elf had hidden himself again.

He prepared to go after him when he became aware of a presence behind him . . . and it wasn't Llan.

In a shadow, two red eyes peered at him.

Its voice blasted through his head like a blast of lightning.

You are a child, warrior. Without me, you are nothing. I said that you would one day pay for insulting me . . . today is the day!

From the shadows a black wolf leaped at him; The Hound held his right arm up instinctively, dropping the gun. The wolf's teeth sank into his flesh, clamped down like a vise, and held. The Hound let out a scream as he fell back. Although he was a mighty warrior in the past, in this life he was still, physically, a skinny teenager . . . and the wolf felt like it was as big as a bear.

The Hound hit the floor in a fury of growls, fur, and the unmistakable tang of blood . . . *his* blood.

Mort's equipment tracked the game through the monitors, and Aedham watched with one eye on the screen, one on Mort. The Foevor sat back vainly, watching the game with his hands clasped behind his neck and his knobby elbows jutting out, a singularly haughty pose.

At first The Hound seemed to be toying with Llan, then when the elf followed him up to the second level, the fireworks began. Llan got a few good hits in, Aedham noted with satisfaction, but when The Hound went into what had to be his fighting fury, hitting Llan repeatedly, not giving him much of a chance to fire back, it was clear who was going to stay in the lead. Llan had 810 points, The Hound, 1002.

"Why doesn't your champion just stay in one place and fight?" Mort said. "He looks like he's afraid to stand his ground."

Aedham let the comment pass. The monitors switched views, and now it was Llan tagging The Hound as he was coming up a ramp. Mort growled in response.

"Why doesn't your champion know he's been led to a trap?"

Then the weirdness began. As the camera tracked The Hound, a dark thing lunged from the shadows and attacked him. The two shadows wrestled back and forth in the shadow, The Hound's target lights clearly visible.

Mort stared at the screen, then checked something on the console. "You champion isn't playing by the rules," Mort said, with a mixture of triumph and anger. "Do you care to concede defeat now, or must I make it a larger issue?"

Aedham was unmoved. "Llan isn't attacking, Mort. Look, on that monitor. He's over there." He pointed to the monitor on the end. "I don't know *what* that thing is."

Evidently unconvinced, Mort leaped to his feet. "Seleighe treachery!" the Foevor shouted, pointing a long accusing finger at Aedham. "You break the rules, you forfeit!"

The King reached for the node power on impulse, but did not seize it. Instead he waited to see what the Foevor would do. But beyond the walls, Aedham felt a Gate powering up. *Somewhere on this floor something is getting ready to arrive from Underhill.* He remembered the single-legged Clapper with the enormous Long levin rifle on its shoulder, and didn't like the idea of facing one without a weapon. All the electronic gear made the task difficult, but not impossible: despite the interference he had the power lined up for a levin bolt, just in case.

"You foolish *sidhe*," Mort said, with a smirk. The Foevor's image flickered, as if he was some sort of a projection.

That can't be. The image was shielded!

Mort had become a mannequin, standing in a conceited pose, with his hands on his hips. Aedham reached out and pushed the statue. It fell backwards, smashing on the floor as if it were made of black porcelain.

A simulacrum! Mort must have been operating it from somewhere nearby.

The sickening understanding landed on him like a bucket of ice water. *The Gate wasn't for something arriving . . . it was for someone to leave! And I'll be damned if I'm gonna let him go again!*

Aedham ran out of the control room, down the flight of stairs into the lobby, where Sammi was waiting.

"What's happened?" Sammi asked.

"Something attacked Dobie, and it wasn't Llan. He

might be hurt. There's a Gate somewhere around here. Where is—"

Of course, I know where it is. In the arena. I've gone through it before!

"Follow me!" Aedham said, running into the weapons room, then the arena; he spied a yellow glow over to the arena's left side, past the center section of the maze. "There. Against the wall."

"He's not bothering to hide it this time," Sammi said, close on his heels. They zigged and zagged, took a wrong turn, then found the passage leading to it.

Mort was standing in front of the Gate, poised to leap through it. He looked back and howled at the *sidhe* with a long, angry wail, before jumping into the glimmering circle of light.

Aedham turned to Sammi. "Go back to Petrus. Tell him to put the army on full alert and be ready to fight. And wait for a Gate. I'm going after Mort. *And don't follow me.*"

"Don't *follow*?" Sammi said, looking like she wanted to argue the point. The King plunged into the Gate.

"Shit!" Sammi screamed at the Gate in frustration, fighting an overwhelming urge to follow the King in despite his command. But orders were orders. Llan and Dobie were somewhere in the arena, and Dobie was hurt.

"There have to be some goddamned cleanup lights in this place!" she muttered at nothing, then started back towards the weapons room.

She met Llan there.

"Where's Dobie?"

"He *was* upstairs," Llan said, visibly frightened. "Something attacked him. When I got to him, he was gone." The elf was shaking. "Where's the King?" he asked.

"Gone back through the Gate," Sammi said. "Told us to get back to the army!"

"But we must go after the King! It might have been a trap!"

"If it was a trap, then we'll *all* be trapped if we follow, and not much help to rest of Avalon," Sammi replied harshly. "We have to notify Petrus. It looks like there's going to be a war after all."

They turned to go into the arena to see if they could find some clue about Dobie's fate.

As soon as the beast attacked, it was over. The wolf thing that was Morrigan released his ruined arm and vanished. Dobie flung off the Lazerwarz vest and sat up, feeling the sticky mess of his blood.

An intense yellow light caught his attention. He stood shakily, and peered down at the first level. Below and against the main wall a yellow circle of light big enough to walk through appeared. Then Mort walked into view; he acted like something was after him. Dobie tried to call out, but only a whisper came from his lips. He was going into shock, quick. But he could still walk.

The Foevor vanished into the circle; that must be the exit. Dobie made his way down from the second level and, without hesitation, strode into the light.

Chapter Thirteen

Had he stopped to think, he might have seen the act of rushing blindly into the enemy's territory, unarmed, as strategically unsound. Aedham didn't stop to think. As usual, gating disoriented his sense of balance; Aedham stumbled as he hit the pavement on the other side, landing on his hands and knees. The hard surface told him where *down* was, and that's where he reached for node energy.

His new surroundings came into focus around him. This was one of the unfinished warehouse-sized passages of Mort's palace, branching off in three different directions. Torches glowed dully on the wall, casting murky, wavering light. Before him, at the far end of the passage, stood Mort with a Clapperleg towering behind him.

"How nice of you to join us," Mort said. "It will save me the trouble of tracking you down." He said something to the Clapperleg. "Looks like your army is going to have to do without you this round."

Then the King saw the long levin rifle perched on the Clapperleg's shoulder, aimed directly at him and building up node power.

As the Clapper fired, Aedham crawled backwards like a crab, rolling under the Gate and leaping to his feet on the other side. Before him was another passageway, big enough to drive a semi through. As he ran for it, the node blast struck, knocking him off his feet. His body running on autopilot, he scrambled to his feet and staggered forward.

The Gate must have taken the brunt of the blast, he noted as he looked behind him through hovering fragments of light, jagged like broken glass. The Gate healed itself quickly, reforming into a solid yellow portal. Beyond this he saw the Foevor hopping, determinedly, towards him.

At a dead run he fled down the passage, his only tools for self preservation now being his feet. The image of the moving Clapper stayed in his mind. He heard the Clapper's rifle building up for another blast.

As he ran he started feeding node power to a shield between it and him, skimming the energy from everything he could. The shield sputtered, collapsed, then slammed into place; this was something he normally did while standing still, with no outside distractions. And a rather fierce distraction was trying to kill him.

Still he felt a big red cross hair on his back, intersecting right over his kidneys. With luck the bigger rifle would take longer than thirty seconds to charge up.

On his left, a side passage popped into view; it had the immediate benefit of getting him out of the line of fire, and the more long-term one of being a bit small for a Clapper.

The moment he was around the corner the Clapper fired again. A ball of node energy flashed by harmlessly, its draft blowing out all the torches, then struck a wall somewhere, causing a brief, minor earthquake, with no apparent collateral damage. Aedham stood, catching his breath, in near darkness. The only light was from up ahead.

The Clapper's foot stomps drew nearer.

Running at top speed towards the light, he burst through an opening and entered a yard, finding himself in the middle of a drill. Standing at attention on either side of him were Mort's human army of rubyheads, rank upon rank of them, looking straight ahead at full attention. A few seemed to notice him; most resembled zombies, as usual.

But the most disturbing feature of the assemblage of youths was that twenty of the roughly three hundred of them possessed powered up levin rifles, lights blinking and ready to go. Above the packs hovered pockets of node energy, waiting to be released.

Mort must have made more, Aedham thought. *Maybe if I can get the ones with the rifles to surround me, we can call it even.*

Such tactics did not seem to be viable, however.

The rubyheads' stiff obedience dissolved some as a few turned to regard the elf who had run headlong into their drill. The apparent drill instructor—a tall, translucent creature, a form of wraith-like Foevor Aedham hadn't seen before—regarded Aedham uncertainly, as if trying to determine if he was one of their troops, out for a romp.

It won't take long to figure out I'm not a human, Aedham knew. He spotted another opening on the other side of the grounds, and made a run for it.

The wraith-like Foevor evidently decided then that he was an intruder, and barked an order. Aedham heard a chilling roar cry erupt from the entire army, followed by a pounding of many feet as they mobilized to pursue him.

The exit was the top of a long set of stairs which ran down the side of a wall; the grounds were actually on the roof of what looked like an even larger palace. *How big does this place need to be anyway?* he thought, before he had the chilling realization that Mort probably intended to populate the kingdom with many more Foevors, including the Clappers. Everything he'd seen here was in proportion to them. *Open for business.*

Aedham was halfway down the long expanse of stairs when he saw the teenaged horde skid round the corner and come down after him. Not much discipline here; perhaps they were unable to take independent action. They certainly seemed to be moving as one: after him. At least they weren't shooting levin bolts. Yet.

At the base of the stairs he found himself at the edge of a vast commons, across which he saw what had to be the main gatehouse entrance. Over the exit leading out of the palace a vast portcullis was poised like a guillotine. Two Clapperlegs guards peered over the ramparts, saw what was coming, and disappeared. A moment later the portcullis began to lower.

The prospect of being trapped in the monstrous palace with three hundred crazed teenaged humans, some armed with levin rifles, gave him another boost of energy. This was *not* how elves were supposed to die.

The portcullis was halfway closed.

From behind him, he felt a levin rifle power up.

He dodged left, still running towards the gate. A node blast rocketed over him and hit the gatehouse over the portcullis. Rock and dust rained down, but the structure remained standing, and the grate continued to close. Now the portcullis was two thirds closed; he heard the new wood creaking in the grooves.

Elves aren't supposed to be skewered on the end of a palace gate, either! he thought, flinging himself into a dive. He hit the ground just under the pointed ends of the portcullis, and rolled out from under them as it closed. He got up to flee, and found his T-shirt pinned under one of the timbers. Through the portcullis he saw the mob drawing closer. Two were aiming levin rifles at him as they ran.

He ripped the T-shirt away from the timber and ducked as two node blasts pummeled the gate. The walls bowed out over the portcullis from the impact, followed by what had to be the portcullis gears, creaking and groaning in protest. The node blasts must have damaged the workings.

You guys need to work on that, Aedham thought as he set about to put more distance between him and the palace. The palace's outer fortification looked like the Great Wall of China; he couldn't see where it ended, it just dissolved into the horizon.

The mist surrounding the palace thickened to a soupy mix; confident he was far enough away, Aedham reached for the power to conjure a Gate.

Dobie walked into the circle of yellow light, feeling some warm, tingling power move through him. His pain diminished, and he was able to see ahead of him another circle, darker than its surroundings.

He fell through to the other side on a hard, cold surface, and rolled over on his back. *I'll stay here a second,* he thought. He was getting weak, and all this moving around wasn't doing his still bleeding wound any good.

Somewhere nearby a horrible ruckus was taking place.

The flash of an explosion briefly lit the place, which was something between a cave and a cathedral. Something huge and lumbering like an elephant was moving around down there. He felt the vibration through the pavement, and he thought that maybe it might be a good idea to go somewhere else, at least until he determined *what* the big thing was, and what it was trying to do.

With difficulty, he sat up. When the stars cleared from his vision, he saw another creature, several paces away, studying him rather intensely. It was tall like the elves, yet looked nothing like them. As it approached, Dobie saw that it had no eyes, only a mouth, a slit for a nose, and two small conical ears that looked like funnels. A dark green reptilian skin covered it from head to toe, and it appeared to be naked, though he saw nothing that resembled genitalia of either sex.

Despite its strangeness, the creature did not feel threatening. In the mists of Cu Chulainn's memory Dobie dredged up the fact that Foevors took many shapes. Perhaps this was one of them.

Now to convince it who I am, Dobie thought, doubting his abilities to do so.

"I'm one of you," Dobie said, and the Foevor tilted its head quizzically at him. "I'm a Foevor."

Still, uttering the words sounded strange, and a part of him didn't want to believe them, not yet. "I need some help here," Dobie said.

The creature said nothing, but seemed to understand. It extended a hand, which Dobie took and pulled himself to his feet. A wave of dizziness threatened to put him back on the ground; the creature grabbed him, and draped Dobie's arm over his neck, and started walking him to an archway leading to another passage.

Aedham had to refortify the Gate after half the Seleighe army had moved through it. There was a power drain on the nodes; something was going on over in the palace that would require more energy and he didn't want to speculate on what that might be. In twos and threes, the Avalon cavalry passed into the Unformed realm, the outer wall of Mort's palace a towering behemoth on the horizon. With each new soldier, he felt the scale tip, slowly, in his favor.

But his mood turned dour as he considered the human puppets on the other side of the Gate, and what options he had in dealing with them.

We will not fight them. They probably think this is a big game of Lazerwarz, and in some way it is. What they don't know is that this game is for real, it's for keeps, and the weapons kill.

Then what to do? Mort was well aware that the Seleighe would hesitate before attacking human kids; in fact, he was probably counting on that. He'd send the kids on ahead of the Clappers to cover for them.

And with that hesitation . . . the Clappers will have moved into position. Not such a bad plan. But a plan completely without honor. The rubies controlled his unwilling draftees.

The rubies. Aedham reached in his pocket for the stone he removed from Joystik's head, and examined it. It was still dark and inert, but the path of matrices encoded within were still readable. *These are all synthetic stones,* the Mage remembered, *kenned from one original. The patterns of power are exactly the same! And I've already reversed Joystik's stone.*

Knowing that, the King knew he had the way to defeat Mort.

The King found the weapons master, who had what he needed: two levin rifles and a roll of duct tape. Non-Underhill gear, to be sure, but Aedham had learned the usefulness of duct tape while growing up in Dallas.

While his army set up camp around him under Petrus' watchful eye, King Aedham went to work on one of the rifles. He popped open the back, revealing the disc on which the diaspar stone spun. The panel he removed contained amene crystal, and under the disc was the topolomite. Aedham replaced the diaspar stone with the ruby, which was larger and didn't fit in the hole. A small patch of duct tape compensated for that. He snapped the panel back, turned the gun on, and looked for someplace to try it.

He moved to the edge of the camp to try out the new device. The mist was thick here, and he thought this might prove an impediment. The wheel was spinning, but he felt no node energy building behind it. This was good; he wasn't after node energy.

Aiming the gun into the mist, he fired. The mist reflected a large red spot, which he explored with his Mage sight. It did indeed contain the matrix code within its light. But would it disrupt the rubyhead spell? Without node power behind it, the gun was just a fancy projector.

I am, of course, a Mage, Aedham reminded himself. *I can feed it all the node power I want.* He explored this possibility, examining the code lurking in the light, then siphoned a bit of power from the nodes. The result was a tightly focused beam; he shone it on the ground before him, then into the mist. The beam spread with distance, he noted. Did that mean it weakened, too? His Mage sense told him it did.

At a distance . . . I have to feed just enough to boost it. And not so much that I inadvertently turn a kid's brains into tapioca with a levin bolt.

With the beam on the ground, he noticed something amiss in the patterns. *If I'm trying to reverse the spell . . . shouldn't the matrix pattern be reversed too?*

He removed the panel and turned the ruby around, taping it back into place, then projected a beam into the mist again.

There's the pattern, again . . . in reverse! That's what I will need. That should—I hope—cancel the rubyhead spell. But will it be enough for everyone? Or does Mort have some other protection on the rubyheads to prevent what I'm trying to do? Won't know till I try it.

Such is life with on-the-fly technology.

Dobie lay on a hay mattress, in a large room that reminded him of a barn. Other people apparently lived here, too. All around were more than a hundred hay mattresses, strewn with signs from the Overworld: a NIN T-shirt, a pair of jeans, a pack of Marlboros. He vaguely recalled the creature that brought him here, the lizard thing that tried to talk, but couldn't quite form the words.

Pain shot through his mauled arm when he moved it. It was definitely getting worse; the wounds were swollen and bright red. He knew an infection when he saw one. Perhaps he should have tended to this before coming here.

Then, at the end of the huge room, a light.

Father?

The light drew closer, a ball of light growing to a long oval which flickered with an image inside.

Yes, it was Father. Lugh was coming towards him, accompanied by the peculiar creature who had found him.

"I wasn't expecting you to come join me down here," Lugh said conversationally. The light folded into an envelope around him, and dimmed.

Was that anger, or displeasure, lurking somewhere behind those words?

"I followed Mort," Dobie said, then realizing how feverish he was. "The light brought me here." His words were a mere whisper. "You told me . . . you told me to report to him. To answer to him. I thought it was the way to find you."

"It was, as you can see," Lugh said as he came up beside him, holding the transparent staff which had the miniature thunderstorm churning inside. "So you have. *Now.* You've come to join the army."

"I've come for help," Dobie said, not believing Lugh didn't notice how injured he was. With a grimace he held the ruined arm up, biting his lip to keep from screaming. "Morrigan appeared in Lazerwarz in the form of a wolf. She attacked me and ripped my arm up," He lay the arm back down, not able to hold back an audible moan. The entire limb throbbed with his rapid heart beat. "It's making me very sick, father."

Lugh nodded thoughtfully. "I suppose that means

I'll need to get medical supplies for humans. You are half human, after all."

What? "You can't heal me? You healed me before."

"That was a long time ago," Lugh said. "Are you sure you can't fight? Be all you can be?"

"Can hardly get up. I'm running a fever."

Lugh continued his pep talk, "But it's not just a job. It's an adventure!"

Dobie stared at him. *This doesn't sound right. At all. Is he really Lugh? Was he . . . ever?*

"The Few. The Proud. The Foevorians!"

Dobie close his eyes, surrendering to the chill that had come over him.

"I'll return later," Lugh said shortly. "Try to get your strength back up. We have a war to fight."

Dobie watched their backs as they walked away. *Is this really my father? This isn't the one I remember.*

Dubh followed his leader out of the barracks into the grounds. Mort marveled at the creature's stupidity. *He sees a human, The Hound, and assumes he's one of the grunts. Never mind that he's half god. At least he had the presence of mind to tell me about it!*

Unfortunately, The Hound was practically useless for battle. Morrigan had made sure of that. His mood was such that he would have liked to divert all his resources in making sure she was destroyed, but with a Seleighe army camped outside the front gate he had a few other priorities to contend with.

The moment Mort had thrown off his Lugh glamorie, another crisis landed in his lap. Cikal Clapperleg, the commander of his army, was waiting for Mort outside the barracks.

"We have a Seleighe army at our doorstep," Cikal commented. "Any thoughts?"

Mort turned angrily on his commander, but the effect was not to his liking; it was difficult to stare down someone three times your height.

"I'm aware of the situation," Mort said. "I had not anticipated a confrontation so soon."

"*That* much is clear," the Clapper snorted. "We were promised a *legion* to fight the Seleighe, and were also promised seasoned mercenaries to lead us," Cikal continued. "What have we? Three hundred children who think they're playing a game. And not enough weapons for all of them." The Clapper paused, a full pace in front of Mort; he turned his long, hairy face with the single eye.

"*What say you?*" the Clapper hissed.

The barrel of the Long turned with him, but Mort noticed with some relief that the weapon was turned off.

Still, the meaning is clear, Mort thought. *Now, let's remind him why I'm the leader.*

"If you are displeased with my leadership, you may resign as commander, and as a Foevorian soldier, if you are of a mind to," Mort spat. "I am displeased that a few setbacks have demoralized you so."

The Clapper's look wavered, then turned away.

"Perhaps I have made a mistake in trying to bring my people the glory they deserve," the Foevor said, walking on without Cikal. "Perhaps I should rule the gargoyles. Or create my own race. I created all this," Mort said, gesturing over the entire grounds, the palace, the gatehouse in the distance. "I can create a race to inhabit it." Mort smiled pleasantly.

The Clapper followed, awkwardly. "You wish to rule all of Underhill. The elves must be exterminated, like vermin. But why are they such a threat?"

"They have always been a threat," Mort replied simply. He found it difficult to put into words the justification for the hate he felt; these Foevors had not experienced the humiliation at their hands as he had. "And they always will be."

The Clapper glared at him with his one eye, and Mort didn't like what he saw there. Raising his voice, he walked towards the Clapper and stared directly at him from his inferior height. "And if you think you can take me on you are welcome to try!"

The Clapper backed off a pace.

Mort continued, "Let me remind you that *I* have not been in Dreaming these aeons, I have been living in Underhill in various guises, gaining knowledge, gaining strength." Then he drove the knife in. "I may have assumed too much when I chose to wake *you* from dreaming."

"I do not . . . I do not question your command," the Clapper stammered, a gratifyingly bizarre sight. "We have had setbacks, to be sure . . ."

"Then quit grumbling about the elves and get back to your men. If there is a Seleighe army out there, why don't you start the attack now?"

"But there are over three hundred of them—"

"From the walls, you fool! Those weapons have a greater range than the Short rifles. Soften up their position and then send the grunts in to wear them down. The Seleighe won't fire on the children, I told you. Do you not believe me?"

"Yes, sire," Cikal placated, and bowed. The effect, however, was to look directly down at Mort. "We will begin the bombardment immediately."

"I don't like the looks of this," Petrus said, putting down the binoculars. The Bausch and Lombs were a cherished human-made tool, second only to the razor-sharp ceramic hunting knife he kept in his belt. They had set up an observation post at the edge of the mist; the army set up camp a bit deeper into the gloom.

He turned to Aedham, "The Clappers are on the walls. They're armed with the levin rifles."

"Spread your men out," Aedham said. "*Now.*" Petrus went into action, shouting orders along the line. "I think they're—"

The King never finished the sentence. The first

blast hit, some distance ahead of them, plowing a large crater into the unformed soil. The impact still threw the King backwards, and robbed him of his hearing for a few moments.

The King realized he may have misjudged the range of these weapons; he had thought they would be well out of reach of the rifles. As his hearing returned he became aware of his men making tracks further into the mist.

Time for a shield, Aedham thought, and reached for the power he would need. The air sparked with the energy; the enemy was preparing to fire again.

Node power . . . Now.

Another node blast struck the ground, closer this time, sending a shower of dirt over them. Aedham's concentration shattered. The node power slipped away.

The King rejoined his army, which had mobilized further back into the mist.

He caught up with Petrus, "Space your men out, Petrus. One blast from that weapon and we lose a third of our army!"

Petrus rode forward, leading the line of Seleighe parallel to the palace. Aedham caught a ride on a wagon, which followed the troops in a broad circle around Mort's palace. Another blast pulverized the ground again, throwing Aedham off the wagon; he got back on his feet and surveyed the damage.

They're shooting in the dark, he saw with satisfaction. *They can't see so few men in mist this thick!*

He opened up his Mage sight and surveyed the situation, seeing roughly fifteen Clappers with Long levin rifles, lined up along the top of an outer wall.

"Give me one of those!" he shouted at the weapons master, who handed him a levin rifle.

"But sire, you'll give away our position!"

"Keep moving!" Aedham shouted, and moved ahead, towards the palace.

Levin blasts continued to pound the earth around them randomly; Aedham advanced towards the palace and took refuge in one of the craters; he was now well within range of the Longs. He took aim at the Clappers on the wall. As the weapon spun up to full power, he reached again for the nodes, and focused it on his target. The rifle's aim was no good at this distance; perhaps augmenting the blast's trajectory might make it more accurate.

He pulled the trigger to find out.

The rifle spat a ball of light at the wall; the shot arced slightly before homing in on the target, a lone Clapper positioned over the gatehouse, then drove home. A direct hit; the parapet disintegrated, and the blast vaporized the Clapper.

Aedham's assault had given away his position, and he scrambled out of the hole, zigzagging back to his men. A node blast hit his position moments later.

Their range is just too great! he thought, going over his options. Either nullify the blasts . . . or divert them. It was a technique his father had shown him, and which had to some effect been used in the defense of the original Avalon palace.

Time now to put it to practice. Seize the power, he told himself, drawing again from the pools of energy. From this he made the strongest shield he could, then pulled it between the palace and his men. It was like pulling loose fabric, separating the weave; the shield became a net, spread along the front.

It wouldn't stop a blast. It could redirect it. Good enough for talking purposes.

The next blast struck the net, then went up and over, bouncing harmlessly away. A cheer rose from the Seleighe army, now scattered thinly across the perimeter. The Clappers fired again. The projectile made a sharp detour into the ground.

Their levin rifles are useless now, the Mage thought, his feelings mixed. It would force the Foevor's next hand: sending the kids in. From the wagon he retrieved his special ruby rifle and powered it up.

I just hope this thing works, Aedham thought frantically, aware now that all their options were expended.

"What do you mean, the aim is off?" Mort screeched at Cikal, just outside the gatehouse. "We tested these things."

"Not against a Mage," Cikal pointed out. "The King of Avalon has constructed something. I cannot see it in its entirety."

"He's thrown up a shield," Mort replied, impatiently. His neck was getting sore from looking up at the Clapper. *Increase my size so that I can communicate with my own men?* It seemed like a waste of node power, all of which he needed for his Lugh impersonation for The Hound.

The lad might yet come around.

"I can see the shield from my chambers," Mort pointed out. *A thin, wispy shield that couldn't protect the Seleighe from harsh language, much less a levin hit.* "It's not enough to stop *anything*!"

"I tell you, it's *diverting* the blasts. Not stopping them."

"Then tell your men to cease fire until further notice," Mort said with a frustrated snarl. *These Clapperlegs have no backbone whatsoever. And to think they were once warriors!*

Mort was still tempted to wait until The Hound could lead their unit of human soldiers into the fray. The situation had become a standoff—they had all the time they needed.

Or maybe not. While they delayed sending in the ground troops the Seleighe army was digging in. The humans were expendable, always had been. *Why not send them in now when they can exact the most damage?*

"I'm sending in the human infantry," Mort said. In

a way, he was relieved. Keeping the kids under the ruby spell had taken its toll on his power supply; without them, he might be able to construct an effective countermeasure to Aedham's net.

"They're going in *now*."

Dobie no longer felt his arm. At some point during his delirium he decided that the wolf had poisoned fangs, and had injected his arm with venom, and the worst of the effects were still to come.

He had fallen off the hay mattress and was on the cold, hard floor, which felt good with his fever. That he might die here was not much of a concern.

When his father appeared above him again, he thought it was over. Lugh's ability to heal seemed to have gone by the wayside, so the only reason his father would be here would be to claim him for the land of the dead. It made sense. Nothing else really did.

Death did not seem to be in the cards, though; Lugh held a hand over the swollen arm, and from his palm a rich blue light flowed, bathing the nasty wound with warmth.

Pain ended, and sleep came.

"There, by the gatehouse," Petrus pointed out. "They're shooting at their own fortress?"

"The portcullis is damaged," Aedham explained, feeling the node blasts chip away at the palace entrance. "They're just clearing the way." He rechecked the charge of the ruby based levin rifle he was wearing; it looked good. "They're sending the kids in, I bet. *Go.* Tell your men to hold their fire."

Aedham thumbed the rifle on, and looked up. The portcullis was clear now, and humans in black pajamas were scampering over terrain made rough by node blasts.

Here goes, Aedham thought, aiming at the youths. So far Mort had only sent out ten, but they all had levin rifles. The Mage pulled the trigger and held it down. The rifle spat a red beam at the human squad, pinning them in the light. With an extra push of node power, Aedham felt the rubyhead spell shatter.

The ten warriors looked confused.

"Hold your fire!" Petrus shouted, but the Seleighe army was already standing down. "Sire, we should go get them!"

"Yes, but get those packs away from them as soon as you can. They look like toys!" Aedham replied. *Gods help us if they decided to start playing with them!* Petrus and a handful of men moved forward, without packs or drawn swords, waving at the humans as they approached.

What must this look like to them? Aedham wondered, as he watched his men approach the humans. Without much discussion the elves carefully took the packs from them and led them over the churned-up ground to safety behind Seleighe lines. It didn't look so much like the taking of war prisoners as it did a Boy Scout outing. Apparently the kids were too stunned and confused to react to the weirdness of the situation.

Which is how it should be. They don't know what's going on. And it's our duty to keep it that way.

On the wall over the gatehouse, a Clapper leveled a Long rifle at Petrus, his men and the kids, and fired.

From the gatehouse rampart Mort stared in disbelief as the ten human foot soldiers shook free of his spell. The rubies fell from their heads, then they *dropped* their weapons like they didn't know what they were anymore. Whatever illusion Mort's magics had created were gone now.

Aedham did this . . . but how? This was not something a Mage could do, so quickly . . . and with all the node power flying around, the interference alone should have made the task impossible. Yet there they were, free of their spells. And the Seleighe were leading them back to *their* lines.

"Take them out!" Mort shouted to the nearest Clapper, who aimed and fired a Long; the node blast made a direct path for the Seleighe and the humans, but at the end made a sharp turn into the sky, bounced off into the unformed mist, and left the target unscathed.

"These weapons are useless!" Cikal moaned, from Mort's left. "The shield is deflecting our weapons, I tell you! We must take out that Mage."

If such were possible, Mort thought. *I would take the Mage out myself.*

But was it impossible? Aedham was behind his lines, somewhere back there, well hidden in the mist. The Seleighe had taken to guerrilla tactics this round, hiding behind the mounds his Longs had dug in the ground. The only thing able to penetrate the Seleighe's lines were the damned children and they weren't staying bespelled.

Children . . .

Mort had an idea.

Dobie sat up from dreamless sleep, bathed in sweat; the fever that had wracked his body with chills was gone now. At least he was alive.

"It seems the Morrigan has bested you once again," said a familiar voice; Dobie turned to see his father with his green cloak, sitting on a bench, a pace or two away. "I've seen to your wounds. How does your arm feel?"

Arm? He'd forgotten all about the attack. His right arm, though covered with fresh, pink scar tissue from elbow to wrist, was completely healed. He flexed his hand stiffly, but it worked, and obeyed.

"Why didn't you heal me before?" Dobie asked, remembering the encounter. "All you wanted me to do was fight."

"You have been tricked yet again," Lugh said gently. "It was not I, but someone, a Foevor shape shifter, pretending to be me."

The news came as a relief. "We are not Foevors? You didn't save me from the hotel room, from Morgan . . ."

"You saved yourself," Lugh informed him.

"Then who is—"

"Think for yourself," Lugh said. "Who would stand to gain the most from denying the Seleighe their champion?"

The answer is quite simple, Dobie had to admit. "None other than the Foevors. Their leader. *Mort.*" He got to his feet, shaking off the last of the malaise. The healing his father had performed was absolute; he felt not just good, but *terrific.* He took off the gold ring "Lugh" had given him and flung it across the barracks. It exploded against the wall in a tiny flash of fire and smoke.

It occurred to Dobie that he might have slept through the fight. "What has gone on? Has the war begun?"

"Indeed it has," Lugh assured him, sitting back on the bench and regarding his son with an appraising look. "It has certainly begun. In fact it is a bit of stalemate right now."

"You must take me to it!" Dobie demanded. "If there is still time—"

"Be patient," Lugh said calmly. "The fight will be in your court soon enough."

On the bench next to Lugh was a levin rifle vest. The Lord of Light glanced down at the weapon, then addressed his son. "I will broker one more fight. Prepare yourself for it."

"Looks like he's sending out the rest of them," Petrus said dismally, pointing towards the gatehouse. "*All* of them."

"Indeed he is," Aedham said, taking up his ruby rifle again. As the small army of human infantry scrambled to take up positions just outside the wall, the Mage reinforced the safety net, and moved it a little further out, to include this next wave. There were a few hundred, swarming like ants. Aedham's blood boiled; it was a senseless sacrifice. "Okay, you know the drill. I'll knock out the spell and you go gather them up. Get them back here as soon as you can."

Aedham had established a refugee camp some distance into the mist, and had put several of his men on it, to make sure no one bolted. The tranquility spell Aedham had put on the first ten seemed to work well, but with node power flying everywhere he didn't trust his ability to maintain it. In case the spell slipped, he didn't want to have to go look for lost youths in the fog.

When it appeared the last of the kids had moved within range of the ruby rifle, Aedham hosed them all down with the liberating red light. Through Petrus' binoculars he saw the rubies dropping from their temples, followed by the expected baffled stares. When the entire line appeared to have been despelled, Petrus led his soldiers out to gather them up. The Foevors opened fire from the gatehouse parapets, but their Mage blasts were going everywhere but into the Seleighe line, deflecting off Aedham's net like stones skipping across a pond.

It didn't take long to herd the kids back behind their lines, although the node blasts were a bit of a distraction. The kids didn't seem to know the blasts were intended for them, which was fortunate. That might have caused a panic, which they didn't have the numbers to handle. Instead there was an orderly escort of the two hundred or so kids filing past Aedham. Petrus walked along side the assembly, and Aedham spread a blanket of tranquility over them as they filed past. It taxed every thing he had, but the spell seemed to be working. The humans were as docile as cattle.

The King spotted one kid who still had a vest, and it appeared to be operational.

"Petrus, seize that weapon!" Aedham called, but his commander was already on the job, weaving through the crowd of humans who were not much smaller than he was. The crowd parted around a scuffle, and two more of Petrus' soldiers stepped in and separated the kid from the levin rifle vest.

"He's delirious," Petrus called back. "I think he needs healing."

After what they've been through, they all probably need healing, Aedham thought. He kept an eye on the boy, who bore a striking resemblance to his friend from Dallas, Daryl Bendis, before rehab: pale and pasty white skin, with black, stringy hair. With pointed ears he would have looked like an Unseleighe.

The boy turned, glared at Aedham, then moved on with the rest of the refugees. The hostile look sent shivers through Aedham, who had no doubts the kid would have taken him out with a levin rifle if given the chance.

"Sire! Another messenger!" Petrus called out, and Aedham looked up to see another Foevor on a black horse riding towards them.

I hope it's not another challenge. I am weary of this game. I want to be done with it!

The rider pulled up and delivered another note to Aedham. Petrus and a large contingent of his officers looked on as the King read.

Aedham looked up, smiling from ear to elven ear. "It's a surrender," he said, not quite believing the words. "We've won."

The acting commander of the Foevor forces, Cikal Clapperleg, seemed sincere in his desire to make peace. His forces, including the race of reptilian

Greens and the wraiths, had all lined up outside the gatehouse and had laid down their weapons before them. As a peace offering, the Greens had also turned over the youths imprisoned in the dungeon, and Petrus had them escorted to the camp. A fair number of gargoyles also had enlisted as mercenaries, but they seemed to have sensed the changing winds and had left shortly after the Unseleighe did. The Foevor army, standing proudly at attention, had cooperated fully in all aspects, except one.

They didn't know where Mort was.

"He deserted us," Cikal complained. "In our hour of need, he left us when we needed him the most."

"Let me guess," Aedham said, pacing before him. Standing still in front of the giant made him feel vulnerable; moving around somehow gave him the psychological feeling of safety. "You realized how he misled you, made you promises he never kept."

The one-eyed giant nodded. "And I couldn't remember why we were fighting."

"Aie, indeed," Aedham said, not fully convinced of the story. The situation stank. It smelled of a trap. But the Clappers had no weapons. The Seleighe were fully armed. Where was the catch?

A commotion from his army drew his attention from the Foevors. From the unformed mist a horse and rider appeared, and were heading toward the Foevor gatehouse. Aedham took a closer look and saw that it was the kid who hadn't wanted to give up the levin rifle. *He's flipped completely out! Why does he want . . . ?*

"Excuse me," he said to Cikal, and went over to one of the officers in charge of the refugee camp. "What happened with that kid who just took off?"

"What happened?" the officer replied, wild-eyed. "He kept sneaking out of the camp looking for a weapon. The levin rifles, in particular."

And the spell of tranquility had no effect on him.

"We were bringing him back when he made a dash for an elvensteed," the officer said. "And it . . . obeyed him. An elvensteed would *never* let a human ride him."

Perhaps he wasn't a human, Aedham thought. *I knew there had to be a reason why he looked like Daryl Bendis.*

"Who was that?" Petrus said, riding up to Aedham on Moonremere. "I looked up, and that human kid had already made it back to the gatehouse. On an *elvensteed.*"

"That was Mort," Aedham explained. "Good glamorie, too. Even though he copied someone I knew, I didn't detect it."

"Should we gather up a unit and go after him?"

"Not yet," Aedham ordered. "It could be a trap. He's on his home territory. I want to find out more about the layout before we go in."

Something above them caught his attention; looked up at an eagle circling over them. "I think we have another visitor."

The eagle kited over them, then dove down to land; as the bird touched the ground, it transformed into a robed man with a green cloak. The god stood calmly, unmoved by the anxious army surrounding him.

Lugh stepped forward and bowed, respectfully, before Aedham. The action surprised him. *With a god, isn't it supposed to be the other way around?*

"Well done, Seleighe King," Lugh said. "You have successfully conquered the enemy, and have liberated a large number of young beings who do not belong to this realm." Lugh paused, and smiled congenially, putting the King at ease. "I trust you will see that they are returned to their homes?"

"Indeed, I will," Aedham replied. "But is the battle really over?"

"*Your* battle is," Lugh said, with a slight edge to his voice. "As you may have guessed, you had Mort in your midst, and didn't even realize it. He has returned to his palace."

"He's going to escape," Aedham said. "Again. This is not the first time."

"He won't escape," Lugh said. "He will be . . . challenged."

Aedham raised an eyebrow. "By whom?"

Lugh winked at him. "My son. The Hound of Culann."

Dobie?

Lugh continued, "I would not normally meddle in elven affairs, but your actions have displeased me. Since the realms split with the Tuatha's defeat, the various clans have lived in balance." Lugh pointed to a levin rifle held by one of Aedham's men. "The balance has been upset by your invention. As you said shortly after slaughtering the Unseleighe army, this is no honorable way to fight."

In the presence of Lugh, Aedham had difficulty arguing his defense. "So you have intervened."

"As gods have been known to do."

"For what purpose? What do you intend to accomplish?"

"To even the playing field," Lugh said. "Two warriors. Two levin rifles. One large arena. Mort's palace."

"A duel?"

Lugh shook his head slowly. "Single combat. Your people are familiar with this concept, I trust."

"Mort is no warrior!" Aedham objected. "He will win any way he can."

"I have made the contest equal in every way," Lugh countered.

Aedham believed him. "What will the outcome determine?"

"The winner, of course," Lugh replied. "One will die. One will live."

"And if Mort lives?"

"He will remain the leader of the Foevors. That

is," Lugh said, glancing at the giant Clapperlegs, "if they will have him."

At this point it doesn't look like Mort is the leader of anything, Aedham thought. *His men have surrendered, and they believe Mort has deserted them.* Yet the King didn't like the possibilities. *He would escape. He would be out there, consolidating another empire, perhaps even by someday convincing the Foevors again he was worthy of their loyalty.*

Yet it was clear to Aedham that Lugh's mind was made up, that no amount of gentle persuasion would change matters.

"Then may the best warrior win," Aedham said, forcing a smile.

Laura said, glancing at the plant Gharghax. "If they will have him."

At this point it doesn't look like Mort is too [illegible] of anything, Andlan thought. He may have surrendered, and [illegible] Mort has deserted them. Yet the King didn't like the possibilities. He could accept [illegible] would be our [illegible] contemplating another campaign [illegible] by [illegible] he was worthy of their loyalty.

Yet it was clear to Andlan that Laura's mind was made up; that no amount of gentle persuasion would change matters.

"Then may the best warrior win," Andlan said, forcing a smile.

Chapter Fourteen

Sammi was sleeping in her car when she felt the power reach through the realms; she sat up groggily, sensing the Gate's point of entry somewhere inside the arena. Her clock read 4:00 A.M. Monday morning.

The media covering the megaliths had long since packed up and gone on to less stale news. The lone cop at the megaliths looked up as she got out of the car, then returned to his newspaper, disinterested. Sammi had introduced herself to him earlier that night after sending Llan to notify Petrus of the change in war plans. Creating the Gate, even with Llan's help, was exhausting. Sitting watching unmoving rocks was all she was up to, afterwards. So far as the locals were concerned, she was a new FBI recruit given the tedious task of a round-the-clock watch on a business. Dull work for any cop.

All that was about to change.

In the arena she saw the Gate form in its usual spot against the wall. Once it was up a familiar face came through it.

"Are you ready for your new arrivals?" Petrus asked. He was dirty and bruised from battle, but grinning from ear to ear.

"Yes, send them through," Sammi said. "So what's going on down there?"

"Oh, we won. Sort of," Petrus said. "The Hound and Mort are having it out in single combat."

That didn't sound like the Seleighe had won just yet, she thought, before returning her concentration to the problem at hand. "How many are there?"

Petrus looked exhausted; it took a moment for him to respond. "All of them."

"Even the ones in the dungeon?"

"Them, too." He looked around the darkened arena. "No witnesses?"

"None. It's early morning here. What do they think happened?"

"A UFO cult kidnapped them from the arenas. The story is rather detailed; they should be able to tell you all about it."

UFO cult? Sammi groaned. *What better way to stir up an already psychotic situation.* "Send them through."

Petrus went back into the Gate, and a moment later a small army of human kids started filing through. Strangely enough, they were all wearing loose black clothing. *Something Mort cooked up, I guess.*

She punched in Hawk's number on the Nokia, roused him from a sound sleep, and told him to get his tail down to the arena. While she waited for him to show up, she needed to come up with an explanation that would correspond with the kid's implanted memories.

Meanwhile, as the former hostages arrived, congestion developed around the Gate, and Sammi had to usher them away to let the rest come through. Soon the arrivals started to come out of their stupor, and started babbling. Sammi took a few aside and questioned them on what had happened.

"Nothing really," one kid said, a tall blond boy who still looked half asleep. "Oh, now I remember. It was these UFO crazy people. They thought aliens was going to take them away, and they kidnapped us to diversify their DNA pool or some weird shit like that . . ."

That was the story she was waiting to hear. *Aedham's cover story will work quite well, I think. Especially with those black clothes . . .* She remembered a case of mass suicide in California that had similar trappings. Fortunately, this story had a happier ending.

As soon as they were all through, the Gate blipped out of existence. She hoped there would never be another one there again.

"Time to call in the cavalry," she said to herself as she dialed the FBI office to report the discovery of a few hundred kidnapped youths in the Lazerwarz arena. The FBI promptly contacted local law enforcement, who summoned an entire squad of crisis counselors. Moments later fifteen police cars pulled up in the Lazerwarz parking lot, lights spinning. The media wasn't far behind.

A happy ending, she thought, trying to focus on what was happening here, instead of the war in Underhill. *I like happy endings. Maybe Avalon will soon have one too.*

It was all over. The kingdom he had carefully crafted from the leftovers of their former glory had collapsed; his people were cowards, all of them.

They don't deserve me, Mort fumed as he dismounted the elvensteed, flung off the disgusting human glamorie, and rushed into the palace. *They never did. At the first sign of trouble they give up. How dare they, after all I have done for them: roused them from long-term Dreaming, gave them the most powerful weapons ever to exist in Underhill, and returned them, however briefly, to their former glory.*

And they repay me with surrender!

Mort took the massive set of stairs to the upper levels, where his chambers lay. He was *not* fleeing unarmed. There was one levin rifle left, stashed behind his throne, the one he used to blast Morrigan. For that reason alone it had substantial sentimental value.

The rifle was where he had left it behind the throne. Mort took a long look at his chambers, and was seized with a sudden grief which turned quickly to anger.

I will return. And I will not be denied again.

The King of the Foevors reached for the node power needed for a Gate . . . and frowned. *It's there,* he thought. *The node power is there. Why can't I reach it?*

There was a barrier around the nodes. Subtle, nearly imperceptible, but there, and in the way. *Did Aedham construct a shield around the nodes?* Mort wondered, but whatever the reason he had nothing with which to make a Gate.

In his haste he hadn't noticed the note tacked onto the back of his throne. Now he pulled the piece of parchment down and read.

> To His Majesty, King Mort, ruler of the Foevors,
>
> You have been hereby challenged to a contest of single combat, to be carried out in this palace and its grounds, starting immediately, under the stipulation that no magic be used except the node power generated by the levin rifles. There will be no points. Physical contact is encouraged.
>
> Have a nice day,
> Lugh, Lord of Light
>
> P.S. Perhaps this will teach you to not toy with the son of a god, you buffoon.

After reading the note he calmly wadded it up, dropped it on the floor, then switched on the levin rifle.

Curiously, the screen on the gun came to life. The

levin versions didn't use the screens, they were only an interface for the game arenas—but there it was. *Lugh must be manipulating it.* The color Lazerwarz logo and timer popped up.

The countdown began at thirty seconds.

Who could be my opponent? he wondered, before the sickening realization of who that would be took hold.

The Hound of Culann stayed close to the wall as he surveyed the great arch leading out of the sector. He had made good use of his time exploring the palace, and he was beginning to understand the enormity of it; the place was made up of sectors, each the size of a large enclosed shopping mall, with empty rooms of different sizes. Some had two or three levels, with catwalks and ramps connecting the floors. In the first sector he explored, light didn't seem to come from any one source; it was everywhere at once, and nowhere was it completely dark. The Hound had no shadow in this place.

Evidently "lighting" hadn't been installed in the second sector yet; wooden torches lined the halls and primary passages, but not the small rooms. He took one of the torches down and explored a few small rooms. They were the same as the others, empty, with a homogeneous surface that looked like spray-on granite.

Dobie nearly jumped out of his skin when his levin rifle's screen came to life, and started beeping a countdown. With sweaty palms he pulled it out of the holster. The game had begun.

As the prospect of battle neared, The Hound felt his senses sharpen, and his vision narrowed just the slightest bit. *Something out here is trying to kill me,* his body told him. *I'd better kill* it *first.*

He peered around the arch, to the enormous courtyard beyond. He'd seen pictures of Tianamen Square;

this looked like about five of them, laid end to end. The great outer wall rose up on the left, extending into the horizon, and on the right, the palace. The Hound was tempted to explore the gatehouse, off in the distance, but that was where the game boundary ended, his father had said. Besides, there was no cover. Anyone from the palace could take him out.

Where to go from here? Before him was a wide expanse of wall, then a wide stairwell going up about five stories, to the top of the wall.

"Nowhere to go but up," The Hound muttered, and started for the stairs.

This sucks, Mort thought as he traversed the long hall to the armory. While his gun was up and running, he still didn't like the thirty second downtime between blasts, and was seeking to compensate for this by finding a second rig. Whether that would work as he hoped was still in doubt, but at least it would give him an edge. He might know the palace inside and out, but his soul raged for more advantage; he didn't like the equality of the game. It made the outcome too iffy.

Alas, the armory had been cleaned out by Aedham, damn him. *Why isn't he my opponent!* Mort's mind screamed. *I wasn't trying to kill your son, Lugh. I was trying to make him a champion!* My *champion!* He thought that maybe the cowardly Clappers might have stashed a bazooka-sized Long here—wouldn't *that* have made things interesting—but no, the place was empty. *Shit.*

Not knowing where The Hound was bothered him. He needed a vantage point, but no one place gave him a view of everything.

Think think think! Where was he? In the barracks, of course! Which would mean . . .

Mort had no reason to think that was where The Hound had begun the game, but it was a start. He rushed back out into the hall, which led to a walkway overlooking the courtyard.

Nothing, at first. Across the way, at a bit of an angle, was the part of the palace that would have become the peasant's village, which adjoined the barracks. A large arch opened to it, and a broad stairwell from the second major level led down to it.

Where is . . . he wondered, then saw *movement.*

The Hound of Culann had emerged from the arch, regarded the area cautiously, the approached the stairs.

"I don't believe this," Mort said to his weapon. Lugh had said it would be fair, and until now Mort didn't believe him. But here was a perfect shot, all lined up for him.

He's going up the stairs . . . even better! At the top of the stairs was the drill yard, yet another area with very little cover.

The Hound hesitated; Mort poised the gun on the parapet, and aimed. Then his target started up the expansive stairs.

Mort tracked his opponent with the gun's sight, waiting for him to reach the midpoint on the stairs. It seemed to take forever, but Mort forced himself to be patient. At the midpoint it would take him longer to find cover, if he missed.

I'm not going to miss, Mort assured himself, and pulled the trigger.

The Hound started up the stairs, knowing something was wrong, not knowing quite what it was. Perhaps it was being in the open. It made him feel vulnerable. He moved faster up the stairs, eager to get someplace with cover.

From the palace, up and to the left of his vision, he saw a flash of light, followed by the hum of what had to be a levin blast.

Hate it when I'm right! He turned and dashed down the stairs, three at a time. A split second later the blast pulverized the wall where he had stood, and the concussion threw him forward. As he landed on his side, debris from the blast showered down on him. Knowing he was still a target, he scrambled to his feet and ducked back in through the arch.

Thirty second downtime, thirty second downtime, The Hound chanted the mantra. He checked his weapon, which seemed to be undamaged from the fall.

If he had thought faster, he would have returned fire immediately, but his reflex had been to get his ass out of danger first. Now he contemplated a disturbing fact: Mort knew where he was.

I'd better fix that, The Hound thought, moving back into the sectors he'd just covered. *There must be another way into the upper levels . . .*

Mort tore himself away from the parapet and started running. He knew a way down through the palace that would take him to the barracks, which was where the little shit was probably holed up. He tested his abilities for other magical ways of moving faster, such as teleporting, or floating, but nothing was available.

He ran past his chambers, down a stairwell, into a service tunnel—that was a wrong turn—backed out of that and took another tunnel. *This is the one.* His pace slowed to a walk, and he held the gun up, probing the way for him.

Mort held still, and listened. Nothing.

The door to the barracks was down the tunnel on the right. He eased toward it and slowly looked around the corner. The barracks were empty save for several hundred hay mattresses, and the human soldiers' former clothing that was strewn everywhere.

Looking deeper into the barracks to the door on the other side, he caught sight of a figure, just inside the sector. It was dim in there, but the shape . . . it had to be him.

Mort aimed and fired at the figure; the node blast took out the doorway and everything beyond it. Dust and debris showered the barracks; beyond the door, a cloud of dust concealed everything.

That had to be him, Mort thought, but decided to wait anyway. Once the dust had cleared, he moved towards the pummeled doorway, and looked. Beyond was another, larger area, leading to the series of sectors.

Off in the corner, he saw a still shape. No sign of the levin rifle. But it *was* a body.

Mort decided to check it out.

On returning to the barracks, The Hound discovered the other passageway, which from its direction and increasing size, appeared to lead to the portion of the palace where the blast had originated. He considered ways of ambushing the tunnel, but the tight quarters and his weapon's potency made the strategy untenable.

Trap. Must lay a trap, The Hound thought frantically, looking around the barracks, the hay mattresses, the clothes.

Of course. He picked up a pair of Levis and a black sweatshirt, and started stuffing some of the mattress hay into it. From a few pairs of shoes, he pulled out the laces and tied the pieces together, then suspended it just outside the door from a torch holder. He examined it from different angles. It looked good. *But would it be good enough?*

The Hound moved back into the sector and, against a wall looking towards the barracks, lay down in a sniper position. And waited.

It seemed to take forever; he had nothing to measure time with. The dummy hung limply from the holder, like an executed cattle rustler.

Without warning or preamble, a node blast roared through the door, taking out part of the wall. For a brief moment The Hound wondered if the whole place was going to come down.

He waited, and waited. The dust cleared, and a black, spindly form appeared in the doorway, holding a levin rifle. He seemed uncertain of his quarry's destruction, looking over the area before apparently seeing something of interest.

The Hound kept his target lined up on the sight as Mort walked over the debris.

Now.

The Hound pulled the trigger. An instant before the fireball hit his opponent, Mort looked up and saw the destruction flying his way. There was no time for him to do anything else.

The node blast caught Mort and slammed him into the opposite wall, carving a massive hole; he lay crumpled on the floor before it.

The Hound stared at his work a good long time before moving. Another wave of falling rock and debris passed. Finally, when his gun was back up, he decided to get up and verify the kill. He walked carefully around the rocks and pebbles that littered the floor, keeping his gun up and on the still form on the floor.

As he stood regarding his fallen opponent, Mort's body lit up from inside with brilliant, white light; The Hound jumped back. Light pierced through Mort's every orifice—eyes, nose and mouth, which was locked in a silent grimace. The light turned from white to blue and spun a dense net around Mort which picked him up and lifted him towards the high ceiling.

Mystified, The Hound watched as the body disappeared into the ceiling.

He looked down at the screen on his gun.

Game Over, it said.

The Hound made the long walk to the gatehouse with a spring in his step, thinking nothing in particular, and feeling a bit drained from the ordeal. At the gatehouse he waded through still more destruction, until he stepped past the ruined portcullis, and looked out over the assembled Seleighe army.

"There! It's The Hound!" someone shouted, and a hundred elven warriors turned to him, and erupted in a spontaneous, deafening cheer.

Chapter Fifteen

Avalon was celebrating.

At the conclusion of the Foevorian War, as it had come to be called, King Aedham arranged a massive feast for the entire army. The banquet overflowed the dining room and great hall and spilled out onto the courtyard, a long, joyous ribbon of food, feasting and music. Throughout the meal the Outremer warriors burst into spontaneous song, and the Avalon warriors, not to be outdone, began their own chorus. The contest flowed up and down the tables, raucous battle songs sung out of key which soon degenerated into X-rated limericks.

Aedham cupped his hands over Dobie's ears. "You're not old enough to hear *these*."

"Like hell," Dobie countered, around a mouthful of mutton, and playfully batted the King's hands away. "If I'm old enough to fight for my country, I can sing my *own* dirty limericks!"

"Your country?" Aedham asked. "Avalon?"

"No," Dobie said, clearly pleased he had gotten the undivided attention of everyone around him. "The United States. I'm going to join the Marines."

Applause erupted around the table. "Gods help your enemies," Aedham said.

Perhaps the strangest turn of the afternoon was the

arrival of the Foevors. Aedham had extended an invitation to Mort's former minions to join them in a festival of peace and, perhaps not so surprising, they had all accepted. The Clappers brought entire cows to contribute to the banquet, and the Greens buzzed about nervously, as if unsure of their welcome; soon it became clear that the conflict between them had been set aside. The King made it known to everyone that the battle was over, once and for all, and that Underhill's future lay in cooperation, not war.

"Is Niamh drunk?" Ethlinn asked, sitting beside the King. "I believe he is." With a noticeable flush of intoxication, the Engineer was entertaining the guests at his end of the table by hanging a dozen silver spoons off his face. Llan was assisting, and the two occasionally whispered secretly between them, while casting furtive glances towards the King and Queen.

"Those two are up to something," Ethlinn said, with a suspicious smile. "That's trouble waiting to happen."

After the meal Aedham, Ethlinn, and Dobie, and as many of his officers as could fit comfortably in the small area, retired to the modern drawing room. CNN was on the big screen, and the King watched attentively as the results of their handiwork broadcast across the globe.

"In other news," newscaster Bernard Shaw began, "the FBI continues to investigate the so-called UFO cult that abducted two hundred eighty-seven young men from laser tag arenas around the world. Special Agent Samantha McDaris, who was in charge of the investigation, is still looking into how all the hostages were hidden in the Lazerwarz arena located in Tulsa, Oklahoma."

"Look. It's Sammi," Ethlinn said. Footage of Samantha supervising the roundup of hostages as they filed out of the arena, all still wearing the black pajama uniforms.

"And what might be related news," the newscaster

said, with a sly grin, "the return of the Stonehenge megaliths to their original location in England has all officials scratching their heads."

The camera switched to Alfred Mackie, standing in front of Stonehenge on the Salisbury plain. "We have no bloody idea how it happened," he said to the camera, looking and sounding utterly exhausted. "If anyone has any information we would love to hear it."

Aedham and Ethlinn burst out laughing. "Dear Morrigan," Aedham said, at last. "She certainly was eager to make good on her promise to make peace." After the war the goddess had approached Avalon, humbled and embarrassed, wishing to make amends. She had apparently put all her eggs into Mort's basket and in so doing had alienated herself from the realm of the gods. With Mort's betrayal, she had nowhere to go. Lugh had seen to that. "Return Stonehenge to its rightful place," Aedham had instructed. "Then we'll think about it."

"Well?" Ethlinn asked the King.

"I'm still thinking about it," Aedham replied.

Then the screen suddenly went blank for a moment, then returned with a familiar face.

The room fell silent.

Aedham stared at the screen. *Mort?*

"We interrupt your regular programming to bring you this news flash," Mort said; he sat at a news desk, with a suit and a loosened tie. "Four giant UFOs piloted by what appears to be *elves* have been spotted hovering over Washington D.C."

Mort's alive?

Aedham leaped to his feat. "What the *hell*?" he shouted.

"You are evil evil *evil*," Llan said, setting his stein down on the table next to the monitor. "He'll kill you, you know."

In the engineer's workshop Niamh, Llanmorgan and

Petrus sat around their war spoils from the Lazerwarz arena: a high end file server and monitor.

"No, he won't, he won't," Niamh said as he drank directly from a carafe, dribbling burgundy all over himself. "The King has a sense of humor."

"What did you call this again?" Petrus asked.

"Computer graphics," Niamh said proudly. "There was plenty of security footage of Mort stored in the file server. I just pasted his face over an off-the-shelf animation, patched into the palace's cable feed, and *voila*!, Mort's back delivering the evening news on CNN, he is!"

After a somber, contemplative pause, all three exploded in laughter.

"Should we tell him now?" Llan suggested.

"Naw," Petrus said. "Let's wait a while."

THE END